To Doris, Morgan, and Jack

Prologue

I was only ten years old in 1929, not old enough to understand the unsalved and visceral fear that was the Great Depression. I was, however, old enough to be in the swamp with my father, hip deep in mud and water moccasins, when Spence's daddy was killed. Or murdered.

I see it, I assure you, vividly in the mind behind my eyes. I see the Clyde skidders at work, some Yankee's invention from hell, a wood-fired, steam-powered winch mounted on a chassis so massive it had to be towed by rail. I see a sawmill large as a city erected in a Florida quagmire. And for what purpose? To turn cypress and pine grown before the birth of Christ into boards for houses and hotels.

I see, as well, the slight perspiration of oil on the quarter mile of steel cable that cut Spence's daddy in two. I remember the moss that morning, how it hung sparsely from the yellow-heart pine and massive cypress that late that night a black man from my father's camp would fashion into a coffin. Spence held a lamp for that labor, a kerosene lamp, the coffinmaker's handheld saw following by that wavering illumination a line marked with the stub of a pencil.

I see Spence's daddy, one blue eye and one brown one in a black face, floundering awkwardly, arms extended as if in supplication. And I can see my own father reaching out to take the black man's arms, to pull Saint MacGrue from that waste of fetid muck.

It was not until Tink took hold and heaved on those arms and Saint jerked too easily from the mud that he knew his best man was cut in two. There is my father, Tink Buchanan, a hard man standing hipdeep and horrified in an awful embrace with the torso of Saint MacGrue's corpse, the severed body twitching in his arms like a snake with a broken back. He let his man go, Tink did. Just let him go.

The body slopped back into the sammy earth and so once more Washington Saint MacGrue was baptized in a muddy Jordan, those mismatched eyes rolling as if seeking his missing brogans. That's when Spence, my childhood friend, maybe my only true friend, came screaming from the skidder.

Calling for his papa.

Chapter one

Innocence,
Hedyotis procumbers

I t's impossible to describe the joy I used to take in simply running beside Spence MacGrue. Running is something best done when you are joy-filled and young, I think. People run nowadays for reasons related to cholesterol, or stress, or as a compensation for diminishing sexual prowess. Sometimes for money. That is not the fleet-limbed release of childhood, something you experience only briefly, when you are very young.

There was nothing hidden, nothing ulterior to spoil the footraces Spence and I ran through the Sand Pond.

There was just the sheer joy of the thing.

The Sand Pond, I should explain, is a sort of geographic anomaly that borders the more ordinary land my father's father owned and lost and my own father fought to regain. It was the front line in a war that raged between the Buchanans and the Ogilvies, between my father and Julia's father, an internecine war of whose origin, cause, or consequence I was, while running through the Sand Pond with Spence, blissfully unaware.

I was raised with a sure notion of property lines, of course. As a boy of ten I knew where our four hundred fifty acres of land ended and where the Ogilvies' property began. But not because of fence lines. There was little fence about in the old days, those days of running unfettered. It had not been so many years before that the whole of Florida was virtually an open range. After the Civil War there were drives of cattle and even pigs across our state to match the better-known cattle drives of Texas. Tens of thousands of beasts were driven by horseback to markets in Georgia or farther without a yard of fence anywhere to present an obstacle.

But by the late 1920s, when Spence and I were running, there were tracts of farmland east of the timberlands that had long been fenced in. Those people made their claim of property explicit with split rails or, if very prosperous, with barbed wire.

You couldn't fence in the Sand Pond, though. Well, you *could,* but it would be a waste of time. The Sand Pond was really a series of three ponds arranged in an enormous dogleg like sand traps on a giant's golf course. Each spring they filled with rainwater backed up from the flatwoods—that country of cattle and timber stretching west of our property more than thirty miles to the Gulf of Mexico.

It was a poor region before the time of the timber barons, a region unpopulated but for a handful of Indians and a scattering of local crackers in stump-mounted shacks. Men who stubbornly resisted the habit of steady employment.

But there were trees.

Tidewater cypress and longleaf yellow pine towered untouched in the flatwoods. There was a fortune to be made from this antediluvian timber, so in the early '20s a giant industry was engaged to cut them. Railroads drove steel lines deep into the flatwoods. Cities sprouted overnight on the peripheries of swamps. Cash and credit took fishermen and hunters off their self-reliant islands and hammocks and made them dependent on company salaries and company stores. Most of these men did not look past their week's pay and hunting season.

My father did.

It was Tink Buchanan's ambition to become the largest private landowner in Lafayette County. Toward that end every nickel he earned and every hog, cow, and chicken he owned contributed. "God quit making land a long time ago," Tink offered as if the quotation were his own. "But He never quit making people."

Tink would buy land anywhere under virtually any circumstance. He would trade hogs or cattle or sometimes whiskey for a piece of dirt everybody else thought worthless. But the land Daddy wanted most was the land *his* father lost to Old Man Ogilvie. That property being one hundred forty acres of good ground, plus a frame house, taken under hard circumstances.

Tink was just a boy when it happened. I was almost grown before I heard him bitterly recall that first winter, being turned out of the only home he'd ever known to live with his mother and father in a tent in the swamps. Living on deer meat and squirrels. Shitting off a stump. It was the loss of pride, I am certain, as much as the loss of land that left a taste in Tink's mouth that became no less rancid over the years.

But in the running years I was insulated from that history. I never thought twice about who owned the land and who didn't. Sometimes when my father went to survey company land he'd take me along. Those were long, tiring expeditions deep into the flatwoods. We'd ride our mules, usually, though by 1930 there were a few roads, sandy, rutted ribbons that pierced the damp interior.

Tink rode with his rifle, always hoping to kill himself a deer or turkey or gator. Maybe even a panther if he got lucky. That was my father's idea of a sporting time. But for me, a boy of ten still unblooded, unsure if he wanted to be blooded, running close to home on sand so white it hurts your eyes was sport aplenty. Any land beyond was merely a place too far to run to.

Not that I could ever outrun Spence. People said it was stubbornness that kept me trying. Me, a white boy, they would say, trying to outrun a nigger. Others said it was just plain stupidity that kept me gasping at Spence's flank.

It was neither.

Spence was simply a joy to run with. A thing of beauty, barefoot and black, Saint's son had in his own ten years already the confirmation of a seasoned athlete. He paced himself on our longer jaunts, taught me to talk or sing when I ran. "Keeps yo' lungs in line wit yo' heart," Spence would tell me as I labored alongside. And so in meters measured by our youthful endurance we would sing. Black spirituals mostly, since that was what Spence knew how to sing, and I, never seeing a church house, had no substitute to offer.

Was it a trial? Put it this way—try running four miles on rough ground to "Have a Little Talk with Jesus," and you may just *have* one. But there were days when it seemed effortless. Imagine gliding on chaste sand beneath a virtually unbroken canopy of shade, a long glissade beneath a parasol of oak trees with limbs spread so long and low that on occasion squirrels would parallel our path on mossy avenues overhead, chattering in angry competition.

And the smells! Sight and sound seem somehow thin beside smell's conjured image. Odor. Of hay drying on a new-cut field. Of rainwater. Of smokehouses or tobacco curing in wood-fired barns. Even now I recall the thick fecundity that spiced the air of the Sand Pond, the competing aromas of decomposition and new life. Of rotting hickory and the smell of hyacinth.

It was a garden rioting persimmon and cypress and crepe myrtle, bursting with water lilies and black-eyed susans. Live oaks and pecan trees carpeted the loess with their hard-shelled fruits, and berries! We'd scoop huckleberries and blackberries and wild grapes off their vines at a dead run and never break pace.

I remember, in particular, a mayhaw grove set just about midway on the second pond. The mayhaw was a curious berry, pink, smaller than a crabapple and unique to our region. We'd come each year when the water was still high beneath the thorny mayhaw trees, climb up into those razor-sharp branches, and shake the ripe red spheres into the water, where my mother would scoop them with tea strainers or sieves into a rowboat. Then she would clean those berries and crush out the juice and brew it into a jelly that she swore prevented colds and influenza.

Sometimes on long runs we'd bring victuals, a burlapped sack of hoe-cakes, or maybe biscuits smothered in mayhaw jelly. Sometimes a length of sugarcane. And something with salt. Bacon, usually, or sausage from our own hogs. We'd need something to wash down a feast like that. Generally if the creeks that fed the ponds were running we'd dip right in and quench a righteous thirst on the spot. If the water was still we'd detour off the pond a quarter of a mile to raid Old Man Henderson's well, a shaft barely thirty feet deep that pulled up the coldest water in the county.

We'd latch onto that pump handle and go to town, splash our faces, splash water generously onto our nearly naked bodies, and drink deeply.

Then we'd return to the Sand Pond and build ourselves a fort. Fort building gave purpose to our boyhood expeditions, and play for our imaginations. We'd keep at it until darkness or chores called us home.

Spence ran home to a sharecropper shack about a half mile from what his people called the Big House. Tink himself built the dwelling where I was born and raised. It was a large shotgun house with a wraparound porch, shaded generously by pecan and mimosa trees and mounted, as all houses were in those days, on stumps of pine.

Saint bartered rent on the Little House from my father in return for unspecified terms of labor. There wasn't a sprig of grass on the yard around that shack. Spence's mother had a deathly fear of snakes, so each morning she swept the yard from the house to the fence with a broom made of palmetto stalks. It left lines in the sand, her sweeping, as if a schoolyard full of children had dragged lines across the loam with the nails of their fingers.

From that spotless yard to the back end of the Sand Pond was a little over a mile. A mile and one-sixteenth, to be exact (my father, being a surveyor, was very exact in these matters). Our running campaigns took us farther and farther from home until we had fashioned dozens of forts from the flora available beneath the Sand Pond's bounteous and completely shaded canopy.

Dog fennel made an acceptable stockade, but you could make sturdier structures from palmetto. Spence showed me how to weave palmetto into a roof, rainproofing our boyhood citadels from anything except a hurricane. Being lazy, I preferred the easier construction of dog fennel. Spence lectured me often on this demonstrated sloth.

"You know about what happened to dat pig?"

"What pig?"

"The one made his house outta straw, Carter! Wolf come along. Blow it down!"

"It's just a story, Spence."

"I know it's a story. What—kin pigs build houses?"

We ran a bit farther before Spence completed his chastisement.

"You gots to see the *point*, Carter. 'Bout the pig."

"Uh … ! Huh … !" I'd reply in rhythm to the labor of my lungs.

"An' the *point* is—you wanna have anything, youngun, you gonna hafta learn to *work!*"

In addition to giving me my first lessons in physical education, I freely admit that Spence was my first and best tutor in matters of faith, morals, and literature.

It was glorious, running along those scented paths, scaring up a redbird or a covey of quail, occasionally a rattler or moccasin, our heartbeats racing, then, till that minor danger was far behind. Far behind! And then breathless falling into a bed of Spanish moss with a thatch of palmetto and blue sky overhead. To gnaw on a length of sugarcane, wolf down hoe-cakes soaked in mayhaw jelly. To rest, to sing, to sleep.

And then to run again. To a well-fixed home.

We had just made our longest foray, I seem to remember, had run for miles and built forts all day. It was only days later that Spence's daddy was killed in the woods.

Chapter two

Crow Poison,
Zigadenus densus

Spence was with his daddy the day it all happened. Saint MacGrue had already been in the woods with my father for weeks; it wasn't unusual during one of these long absences for Spence or me to take a mule or hitch a ride out to where our fathers worked. Shamrock was a thriving town in those days. A company town. It was the jumping-off place to the slews and flatwoods and swamps where Spence's daddy and mine made their living. Spence and I would get employment ourselves, stocking dry goods at the store, say, or sweeping the barbershop. Sometimes we'd work in the woods, fetching water for the men.

Tink was gang boss over Saint and perhaps a dozen other men responsible for getting felled trees from the rough ground or swamp where they were cut to a railroad track. There the trees were cherrypicked or craned onto cars pulled by wood-burning jennies to Putnam Lumber's massive mill.

It was never easy to keep men in line in the woods. My father managed it through example, an innate sense of fairness, and through a demonstrated capacity for violence.

By present-day standards, Tink was not a big man. He stood well under six feet. He was strong, though; his shoulders and arms looked to be attached to his chest with cable. But his hands were the thing. Gnarled, callused, and large to the point of being misshapen.

Tink would crack hickory nuts in a single hand with the ease the rest of us managed peanuts. A crushing, Neanderthal vise of a hand.

He carried a short-handled axe and a saddle carbine everywhere he went. I still have the Winchester, an octagonal-barreled 30-30. Tink also handled a .38-caliber revolver and a pair of brass knuckles that looked to be pretty well nicked up. With those tools and a frank, open gaze peering from beneath his Stetson hat, he either won your heart or he beat the hell out of you.

Or, in the worst cases, he'd kill you.

He was an impressive man physically, but it was what was inside that made Tink exceptional. And terrible.

My mother told me this story: my father's first job with Putnam was to survey the three hundred thousand acres that the company had bought from the state of Florida. Tink'd be gone for weeks at a time at that job, just him and his mule, his sextant, and weapons of choice. He was working a region known as "the Trough." The flatwoods do not run level to the Gulf. The land dips below sea level one or two miles inland to form a long, low gutter that runs for forty miles parallel to the coast. On the occasion of this story, Tink was in that trough, not far from Dead Man's Bay, when he got caught in some weather. Hurricanes were not referred to by locals as *hurricanes* in those years simply as *big blows* or *storms*. This particular storm hit at full tide, pulling up a swell of saltwater that flooded into the depression where my father was surveying. The Trough where Tink was trapped filled up like a kitchen sink. He could not outrun the water, no time to reach higher ground.

But there were palm trees.

In a remarkable refusal to panic, Tink packed his instruments and weapons securely onto his mule, tethered himself and his animal to a tall palm tree, and then simply waited. Within minutes the water began inching up the tree. Within an hour the Gulf of Mexico was coursing through the Trough. My father then shot his mule and floated with its carcass on the rising brine to the very top of the palm to which he'd tethered himself.

Tink clung to those fronds for three days and for three days and nights beat off snakes and gators until the water, receding after the hurricane, lowered him and his bloated mule back to terra firma. Then Tink unpacked his slaughtered beast, cleaned his instruments, revolver, and rifle, and for two more weeks worked alone in the Trough before trekking back to Shamrock.

My mother would report, smiling, that Daddy never told her anything about the incident. She only learned about it years later at Land's Hardware Store when Taff Calhoun reminisced about "that big blow when we all heared Tink got hisself kilt."

Tink knew how to handle himself, and he knew the topography of northwestern Florida from Pensacola to Oldtown. It was no trouble getting hired on as a foreman for the gangs who would bring timber to the Shamrock mill. The only inconvenience, and Tink viewed it as no more than that, was that he would be gone from home for weeks at a time.

Transportation was too primitive and the mill too distant to allow any sort of regular commute. Most employees lived with their families on the site. To accommodate that necessity, Putnam's Yankee owners borrowed Northern money to build a city more modern than anything we locals had ever seen. The residents at Shamrock enjoyed indoor plumbing and electricity twenty years before my house ever saw a water closet or a light switch. The company had its own school, a post office, and an infirmary. And, of course, there was the company store.

Employees were paid in cash, sometimes weekly, more commonly twice a month. Fifteen dollars per month was considered a good wage. Black laborers were required to turn over their already unequal salaries for store-issued coupons, which soon put them hopelessly in debt. It was a form of indenturement that, for lack of other opportunities, was endured.

Shamrock's operation was massive and efficient. At its peak the mill cut a hundred and forty million board feet of original-growth cypress and pine per year. The mill's planer could handle three hundred thousand feet of pine and cypress in a single day. A tree that took centuries to mature could within minutes be fully dressed and loaded and stacked like sticks to become a bungalow in the West Indies or a town house in Philadelphia.

I loved to watch the old Ross carriers hauling wood to and from the mill's wide variety of sorters and yards. And I was mesmerized by the sight of trains loading lumber and lath thirty cars at a time from immense sheds that sheltered Putnam's product alongside company-owned tracks.

A sawmill of such size and complexity was a dangerous place to work. But the most hazardous labor at Shamrock was in the woods. The climate was brutal. Temperatures in the summer ran higher than a hundred in the shade with humidity to match. The infirmary saw heatstroke, severed limbs, and rattlesnake bites on a regular basis. Men died. Six workers met their Maker in the year before Saint met his.

The first challenge was simply to fell the trees. The cypress were so large they'd normally be girdled at the trunk for a year or more before any attempt was made to actually cut them down. I can remember Tink working a crosscut saw on a tidewater cypress so massive it occupied an entire railroad car. Cutting that kind of timber was risky work. Getting it to the mill was equally perilous. Someone had to drag the felled logs of cypress and pine out of the swamp and up to the railway so they could be craned onto a railroad car and pulled to the mill.

That's what Saint MacGrue was doing the morning he "got hisself kilt."

I can see the early swelter of heat and humidity. I can hear the curses of men and the rumble of the wood-fired steam engine that powered the distant Clyde skidder.

A skidder looked something like a dragline on rails. Its engine drove a kind of winch. On the capstan of that winch a thousand yards of steel cable coiled like a snake. Harold Boatwright manned the skidder. The sheen of oil I remember clinging to that long cable was picked up off the skidder's roller, the detritus of lubricant that Harold squirted onto its shaft.

Tink and his gang were a quarter of a mile away from Harold and the skidder that morning. They were hauling in a big one, a tide-water cypress fifty feet in circumference at the base. A log of any size could rarely be pulled in a straight line to the skidder; some obstacle or another was bound to get in the way. Finding the most direct route to bring a log to the skidder was called "snaking a path." Tink and Saint were snaking a path that morning, leaving the remainder of the crew to pull the cable behind.

Cable looks flexible when rolled onto a capstan, but that is an illusion. In practice the stuff is very unwieldy, very stiff. Sometimes two or three men would be required to drag a cable over the course of an especially long pull, and I have seen mules recruited for the job.

Saint MacGrue had been known to manage the task by himself.

At six and a half feet tall and well over two hundred pounds, Saint was the largest and strongest man on my father's gang. Of the other lumberjacks, only Red Walker and Taff Calhoun are vivid in my memory. Red was a cracker, a native-born Florida white man with no formal education or professional skill. He was lean to the point of translucence, a reed of a man in overalls and brogans and a railroad brakeman's hat. He had very thin skin, constantly disrupted with lesions that he treated, or exacerbated, with a mixture of kerosene and pine tar. Blue eyes, watered down. A stubble of beard, a broken nose, and no sense of humor.

That was Red.

Taff Calhoun was a contrast in type. Loose fleshed, fun-loving, loquacious, and, except in my father's presence, almost always drunk, Taff was one of those rare characters who could make you laugh even dead tired. Or maybe you *had* to be dead tired to appreciate his humor.

Taff was half a hand shorter than my father, which meant he barely came up to Saint's chest. He crabbed along on short, fat legs made to look even shorter because they were so badly bowed. His arms bowed so badly that when he walked his elbows stuck out like chickens' wings, the result, my father said, of carrying whiskey jugs continually in each hand. He kept his round face low in a bib cap in the manner modern anthropologists depict for *Homo erectus,* an ancestor I am quite certain with whom Taff, apart from missing his alcohol, would have felt at home.

Taff Calhoun was the laziest human being who ever lived. Taff was so lazy, my father used to say, that he'd piss in his pants rather than take two steps to a privy.

I asked my father about that one time. Why he put up with such a slothful excuse for a worker when there were so many eager men wanting.

"Always need one lazy man on a job," Tink assured me. "Because if there *is* an easy way to do anything he's the son of a bitch'll figure it out."

That morning there was no easy way out. I can see Saint now, hip deep in water. He's got the cable stretched out, lots of slack still in the line. It gleams like a python. Tink and Saint have already wrapped a choker chain around the base of that massive cypress. It's on that choker that Saint secures the cable's steel hook. Saint tests the hook. Holds fine. When he lets it go I can hear the rasping clink of chain falling on hardwood.

Then Tink and Saint follow the cable back along its watery path, pausing as they go to see that it's properly threaded through the snatchblock, a rugged pulley that, changing the cable's direction of pull, guides the log on its zigzag path to the skidder. Depending on the terrain, there might be a half-dozen such pulleys necessary for that task. This morning only a single snatchblock is required.

The Clyde's steam-powered drum will soon pull the cable to a tension of over twenty thousand pounds. The only things securing the snatchblock against that awful strain are a U-shaped shackle, a clevis pin, and a cotter key. If shackle, pin, or key fail—the cable will cut like a steel whip through whatever or whoever stands inside the bow of its path.

The snatchblock this particular morning is rigged by Red Walker's crew.

"You checked on this yourself, Red?" Tink inquires mildly.

"My boys know what they doin'."

"Not asking the boys, Red. Asking you."

"She'll pull."

Tink ignores Red's assessment. Walker remains sullenly silent as Tink inspects the equipment himself. Then Saint double checks. Red doesn't like having a nigger looking over his boys' work. Tink waits patiently for Saint's assessment.

"She'll pull."

"Right, then," Tink says and takes a position maybe ten yards up the line toward the skidder.

Tink is careful to remain outside the line of the cable's pull. It's the cardinal rule of logging—when you bring in a log you *never* wander inside the line because if you do, and if something causes a cable under tension to break free—

Just imagine a quarter mile of razor blade snapped like a bowstring through flesh and bone and gut.

Saint MacGrue knew what a cable could do, knew it better than anybody in the woods. So I did not know, and nobody knew for certain, what it was that made Saint step inside the pull of that cable. Maybe he saw something fouling the cable. A snag, maybe. Something. Maybe he was getting away from a moccasin.

Nobody knew.

All Tink ever said was that he'd sent the signal up the line to reel in the cable. Taff relayed Tink's command to the skidder. I can just see Harold Boatwright idling atop that machine. He sees Taff's dirty white flag; he engages the skidder's driveshaft to the capstan and begins to wind up a quarter mile of steel cable on the skidder's drum. In no time that cable's stretched tighter than Dick's hatband. So tight it sings in a slight, muggy breeze.

The timber groans from its seat in the ooze. Tink turns away from the log and away from Saint, walking back toward the skidder.

Said he hadn't taken more than twenty steps when he heard something explode. Like a shotgun.

That was the sound of the snatchblock bursting from its anchor. The snatchblock blew, the cable sang like a bowstring, and in an instant, less time than it took my father to jerk his head around—

There was Saint. Inside the line. Floundering in a pool of water and blood. Tink staggered back to his man. He plunged into that water and reached for the two black arms which spread widely, now, as if to embrace an angel.

My father pulled Saint MacGrue up from that terrible place. Pulled up half of him, anyway. And saw. And was terrified. And let him go.

Spence came running up then. Dropped his water bucket and came running like I'd never seen toward his father, his boy's feet barely touching the soft earth.

"PAPA? PAPA?" He seemed an animal in flight as he ran. Wild. Frightened.

Like a fawn running from a fire.

"PAAAAA!"

~

They found the snatchblock. Part of the shackle, too. Appeared to be broken in two, the shackle. Did a steel pin take Saint MacGrue's life?

Company investigators weren't concerned with those questions. He was inside the line, they said. Inside the line.

That's how Saint got hisself kilt.

The Company's response didn't satisfy my father. Didn't satisfy Saint's wife, either, not Eida Mae nor her son. They wanted to know what it was made that shackle break in two. Was it the cable's twenty-odd thousand pounds of tension that snapped that horseshoe of iron? Did the clevis fail?

Or was there something else? Someone else?

Did Red Walker standing nearby and seeing Tink's best and black man inside that deadly steel bowstring realize that he held Saint's life in his hand? Did he then, seeing his own opportunity, lean over the shackle and with a tap of his own axe pop its clevis free? A six ounce tap would have done the job. Less than half a pound of force to trigger twenty thousand.

It wasn't something Tink talked about at the time, mind you. Wasn't something anybody talked about. Not until much later, when my father—for reasons unrelated to Saint's death—tracked Red to Leb Folsom's lean-to shanty did anyone speak of this final and vile possibility.

They took Saint's body back to the mill on a speeder. That little cart usually ran the rails like a taxi. Today it would be a hearse. My father insisted on working the seesaw arms by himself, leaving room for Spence to squat stunned beside the oilskin that covered his daddy's amputated corpse.

Chapter three

Stinging Nettle, *Urtica chamaedryoides*

When a man was killed in the woods he normally got buried on the spot, there being no easy way to preserve corpses. But Tink was determined to get Saint back to Eida Mae. He had the doc at the mill's infirmary do as much as he could. It must have been a macabre undertaking. But Saint was reassembled roughly, the surgeon's indignities a slight thing compared to what he had already suffered. As soon as his coffin was made and Saint in it, Tink loaded the lot into Mac Morgan's Model-T truck and rolled out of Shamrock. It was by then close to sunup on Sunday and was raining.

I can imagine that Sabbath journey, Mac driving, a dirt road rising beneath his truck, its twin ruts gleaming in the hours after dawn like a snake's upturned belly. The silver water on either side captures the makeshift hearse in its smooth, unblemished mirror until a heron or some other waterfowl heaves into flight, disturbed by the Model-T's incessant rattle. A gator bellows somewhere along that winding trip home. Spence bounces in the back with his father's coffin.

It is a matter of record that Tink and Mack got to town around noon, only a few minutes after the doors opened on Laureate's First Baptist Church. The church was newly raised, a fancy thing all white-washed with double doors and a regular steeple. Its congregation loitered outside beneath a spread of pecan trees. Nobody left right away. You didn't just leave church in those days. Neighbors didn't get to see each other all that often, so, after the Lord was satisfied, you satisfied yourself. It was a time for children to play and for grownups to relax in secular conversation, the claims of gossip and crops and politics being a necessary emollient for previous admonitions regarding hellfire and damnation. Dave Ogilvie was there, as he always was, a deacon in this church, tall and straight in a white starched shirt and store-bought suit. This Sunday the talk would have run pretty much as usual, with less successful farmers and businessmen coming to Dave on any excuse, this one seeking advice regarding his tobacco, that one concerning his corn or sugarcane or livestock.

It was the preacher, I later learned, who first saw Mac's Model-T coughing and rattling up the town's only asphalted surface in front of his newly limed church, Saint's coffin nosing out the tailgate.

"Dave?"

"Yes, Preacher."

"That Mac's truck? Mac Morgan's?"

"I believe it is."

It was about that time Ed Land's twin girls decided they'd gambol across the street, obliging Mac to stop his vehicle while their mother waddled in pursuit. Preacher O'Steen then left his shade to stroll over, nodding once to Mac before inspecting the sad burden in the truck's wooden bed. Spence turned away, spreading his thin black arms over his daddy's box. O'Steen shaded his eyes with his hands.

"Who is it?" he asked Mac.

"Tink's man," Mac replied, and the preacher for the first time noticed my father propped rigidly in the cab's shotgun seat.

"I'm sorry." The Reverend's condolences were directed to my father, interestingly, not to the poor child draped over his father's coffin.

"Let's move on," Tink muttered to Mac. But a tall man stood now at Tink's window to belay that order.

"Tink. I understand this is your man?"

There stood Dave Ogilvie, clean-shaved in a freshly ironed suit. And there sat my father in the baking cab of a Model-T truck, unshaved, unwashed and in the same bloody khakis he had worn while pulling Saint MacGrue from the slough.

"Your man?" Dave inquired again.

"Was," Tink nodded.

"How'd it happen?" Dave offered a pleasant smile.

"Got hisself kilt," my father replied grimly.

"Needs a Christian burial," the preacher intoned.

"Where I'm takin' him," Tink responded curtly.

"Anything we can do?" Dave offered.

That's when my father turned to Dave Ogilvie and with a voice clear and calm enough you'd have heard it in the choir loft said, "You don't give a good shit about my nigger, Dave. And you don't give a shit about me. Now, get out of the goddamn way and let me get my man home."

Dave's pleasant smile went rigid in his face.

"You waitin' for, Mac?" Tink growled.

The poor man stripped gears, leaving Preacher O'Steen and Dave Ogilvie stranded on the street. The blistering sun pooled tar at the leather soles of their Sears-bought shoes.

※

I knew for a long time that my father and Dave Ogilvie were enemies. But I didn't know more than that. Dave Ogilvie was universally held to be an honest man, if hard with his family, a man fair to his neighbors and generous. Tink did not go out of his way to discredit that assessment, and so I understood my father's enmity toward Mr. Ogilvie to derive solely from the fact that *he* had *our* land. Nothing more would be required to make him Tink's antagonist forever.

But I respected Dave Ogilvie. Besides his position in the

church he was admired for his success in financial affairs. He was an innovator in all things. Take tobacco, for instance; Olgivie was one of the first men in the county to cultivate that plant and make it pay. And Dave was sophisticated in matters far beyond agriculture. The stock market and Wall Street were mere abstractions for most citizens of our region. But Dave understood where the directors of Lafayette County Bank put bank money. He began pledging a tithe for investment as he did for his church, putting cash earned from tobacco acreage into pork bellies and commodities and stocks. He even had a broker, right there in Jacksonville.

By the late '20s Dave Ogilvie had garnered a considerable portfolio that, taken with his land, tobacco, and livestock, made him the wealthiest man in the county. Envious Lombards dubbed ol' Dave the J. P. Morgan of Lafayette County.

Except Dave knew when to quit. In fact, Dave Ogilvie was one of the very few investors anywhere in the country who foresaw the consequences of Wall Street's reckless speculation. He sold his stocks in time to beat the October crash. The nation's disaster left Laureate's favorite deacon cash rich at a time when banks were broke. Only weeks before Saint's death Dave had bailed out the county's only bank, paying fifty cents on the dollar to farmers afraid of losing everything and underwriting the directors' promise to make good for the rest. Cost him somewhere around twenty thousand dollars and made Dave Ogilvie savior to his whitewashed community, second only to Jesus himself.

It seemed natural that folks deferred to such a man, on the church lawn, at the hardware store, but I never saw Dave Ogilvie court that attention or take advantage of it.

Nor did he display his success too openly. A Sunday suit was fine; he allowed himself that minor ostentation, and a Packard automobile, but everything else in Dave's life was a study in frugality. He was known to be considerate in all matters, patient, dispensing counsel and encouragement to whomever sought it each Sunday beneath the gentle shade outside Laureate's First Baptist Church.

The one thing Dave didn't have, and couldn't, was a big family.

And that, people clucked sympathetically, was because of Sarah. A truly modest woman, Sarah Ogilvie shared the Sunday shade with her husband, quiet in a simple gingham dress. She was a small woman. Bones like a bird. People trusted Sarah with their secrets. She was a woman people instinctively sought out for counsel or comfort. A selfless woman. But she couldn't have the six or eight or ten children common to well-off families of that time.

Not that she hadn't tried. In fact, Sarah had nearly killed herself laboring to bring Dave a family. Only three children survived birth. Caleb was just a toddler then, but active as a tadpole even with that withered leg. Wyatt was a couple of years older than I, twelve or maybe thirteen, and already growing to his father's tall stature. A quiet, almost hostilely reserved boy. I didn't know him well.

And there was Julia. I seldom ran into Julia in those days. We would occasionally cross paths while visiting the feed store, say, or maybe over to Dr. West's Pharmacy. I recognized her, certainly. But it wasn't until later, when we were coming into our years of sap, that I really *saw* her.

It was at Ray Henderson's tobacco field. We were by then fourteen or fifteen years old. I was a newly hired field hand, a cropper. It was the croppers' job to harvest the ripened leaves. The flue-cured tobacco grown in our region made leaves big as a hat that started near the sand and spiraled up the plant's primitive stalk. The stalks in those years were planted twenty-four inches in the drill. Rows could be a half mile long.

So you'd go down a row, stack as much plant as you could carry from your ankle to your armpit, and then rack that load onto a sled. A mule pulled the sled to a barn where the tobacco was unloaded onto a waist-high table. Women, and children, frequently black, whipped the tobacco off the table into "hands" of two or three leaves, then fed those hands nonstop to the stringers.

Julia was a stringer. It was her job to tie each hand of tobacco securely onto a curing stick. Good stringers were highly prized. I never could get behind a stringhorse; the job requires too much speed and dexterity. Julia, on the other hand, had the fastest fingers in the county. She was working that day with three other girls, whipping the hands of tobacco onto alternate sides of a five-foot stick, fingers and string moving in a blur. Like a hummingbird's wings. Once strung, the sticks of green tobacco would be hung inside Ray's barn. It took a thousand sticks to fill that barn.

I was riding in from the field one noonday, draped over a sled filled with tobacco. You could feel the sun beating like a furnace off that mattress of nicotine and poison.

"It's hotter than a fresh-fucked fox in a forest fire."

It was Tommy Spikes I believe who offered that assessment. I could think of nothing at that moment but how pleasant it would be to drown in a lake of ice water.

"Git the sled on the table, boys," Ray called out when we arrived at the barn.

Tommy and I grabbed an armful each and got to work.

The handers started feeding Julia as fast as they could. She was a tall drink of water, was my Julia. And slender. A compromise between her mother's bones and her father's regal stature. And her face was not, truthfully, what held me. She was plain in the face. But she had a gorevan fall of hair. And eyes! Good Lord. They were green, those eyes, virid, in fact, and brilliant. When she returned your gaze, which she did not do with everyone, you could not escape their clear, unstartled inspection. But it was not her hair or her eyes, even, that got my attention. No. It took a ball of twine to do that.

You see, stringers tied tobacco onto the curing sticks with ordinary cotton string. Julia was in racing form that morning, snatching the heavy green leaves from four handers at a time, looping them with a twirl of string onto the stick stretched across her horse. Slap-slap-slap, each hand snapped into a tight knot of string, four leaves to a hand, fifty hands to a stick, a thousand sticks to a barn. Slap-slap-slap, I swear Julia was stringing that sled by herself. A marvel of coordination, the tying twine singing through her taped fingers, her blouse damp with sweat and unbuttoned at the middle so the slender cord could feed to a ball of twine that danced unseen, normally, beneath.

I was following her hands at first, the hand, the loop, the tie onto the stick. Almost lulled to sleep by the easy rhythm of her work. Her auburn hair swaying over her shoulder, the sway from hand to hip to stick. And then I saw the button loose or maybe torn at her middle, and I followed the dancing white strand to its source.

I saw a ball of twine unraveling cotton white inside her blouse. It tumbled back and forth, back and forth, tossing in time with Julia's labor. And then I saw her breasts. Still nascent. Small and firm as pears. Wet as if with a heavy dew. When I looked up, Julia was gazing straight into me. I blushed beet red. But those eyes, clear and cool as emerald, held no censure. She smiled once, briefly, and I knew.

I often ask myself, if I had known at that moment what would follow, what would come to be, would I have turned away? Would I have chosen differently?

I do not know. I *do* know that at the time Saint MacGrue was killed I had not yet seen Julia Ogilvie in any important way. I had not seen her family in any serious way either. Not her mother. Not her father. I was still a boy, after all. Innocent.

Chapter four

Rattle Box,
Crotolaria spectabilis

I will never forget the sight of my friend Spence draped over his father's coffin in the open bed of Mac Morgan's truck. Spence saw me, I am sure. But he never spoke, never even acknowledged my presence.

My chief recollection of Saint MacGrue's funeral is of the bleach bottles Eida Mae broke at the neck and strung by wire around her cypress shack. There were dozens of those bottles, splintering the sunshine on white sand in a kaleidoscope of colors that shifted in the breeze.

The yard was scraped clean, as usual, as if by a single hand, perhaps Eida's hand, the widow's nails carving furrows across her yard without aid of rake or palmetto.

You hear that a tragedy brings friends together. That was not the case with Spence and me. Spence became distant from me almost from the moment of his father's death. I can't reconstruct all the signs. But I recall that when my father rode up with Mac, and Eida

Mae saw the box in back, saw her son stricken, prostrate on the oil-cloth, not even my father—the man who owned the shack she lived in, owned the land and the well and everything else—presumed to enter Spence's mama's yard.

And so I did not walk my friend to the door with his grief. Saint's people carried his coffin inside. Spence turned to them for comfort. He would not look at me, did not respond when I spoke. The black men enveloped my running friend into their bosom like a great, dark blanket and bore him silently away. I remained with my father outside. Shut out by a sand yard, a stretch of fence, and a jangle of shattered amber glass.

The bleach bottles bothered me. Irritated me for some reason I could not name. What on earth were they for? I asked my mother.

"They're to keep out bad spirits," Mother replied.

"What spirits?" I felt vaguely unsettled at the notion of a bogey-man a quarter mile from our larger house.

"Their spirits, Carter. Their stories. It's how they make sense of things. Same as my people."

I was astonished that my mother accepted such superstition so equably, she the most devoted woman I had ever known to her Savior, her Lord Jesus. Mother's tolerance seemed out of step with her faith. Shows how little I knew of either tolerance or faith.

Martha Oglethorpe Buchanan was daughter to Old Man Oglethorpe, a polygamist. One of whose wives, Martha's mother, my maternal grandmother, was a Creek Indian. Now, it should be granted straightaway that virtually everyone in Lafayette County liked to claim some Native American blood. Interestingly, too, that red blood was always claimed through the maternal line. Tink once said that if everybody in the county who claimed to have Indian in him *had* it, there'd 've had to've been a dozen Creek squaws waiting for every convict, deserter, and debtor who originally came to occupy, if not pass through, Lafayette County.

Creeks and Seminoles were nearly absent from our county by 1929. Most natives had moved with their tribes, either north to Alabama or south to the Everglades. By the time I was grown their legacy survived only in whispered stories, tall tales, or myth.

But only a single generation spanned the claims of a pagan past and a Christian present in my mother's heart. She had heard her mother relate stories of the Creek ways, of spirits dwelling untamed in turtles, in panthers, in alligators.

I still have daguerreotype, the old tintype photographs people used to take before the Civil War, of my mother and her people. You can see my grandmother in those pictures, a young woman squatting with her mother and father, attired half in gingham and half in Creek regalia. The women with hair braided long and dark, the men displaying a necklace of gator's teeth below a starched, white collar and stovepipe hat.

You didn't need a picture to see my mother's heritage. High cheekbones and smooth, burnished skin. Jet-black hair and eyes like almonds. She was tall, a good three inches over six feet, Brobdingnagian for a woman (or man, for that matter) of her place and time. And her hair accentuated her height, falling as it did straight as a curtain and black as a raven to a place well below her waist.

She loved our house, our garden. She didn't like to go into town much; I doubt Mother went into Laureate a dozen times a year. But her presence, so striking, so tall, inevitably provoked comment.

I was at Punk McCray's barbershop on one occasion when Alton Buchanan, a distant cousin my father disowned, speculated what it was like for Tink, being married to a woman half a head taller than himself.

Taff Calhoun, predictably, had an answer.

"Wouldn't be so hard," Taff declared. "When you're nose to nose, your toes is in. And when you're toes to toes, your nose is in."

The men often spoke this way, in conversations either salacious or violent, with no regard for me or any other youngster who might be sitting there beneath Punk's clippers.

But no one, not any man, ever ventured any comment regarding my mother in Tink's presence. He was too unpredictable when it came to Mother.

I remember one Christmas some gentleman, a widower, bought my mother a comb. Gave it to her right there at the hardware store.

She politely refused the gift.

"But why, Martha? It's just five cents."

"Tink wouldn't like it."

Mother never got a Christmas gift after that. Not from anyone.

My mother's relationship with my father would not meet the standards of equality expected in present-day arrangements, I'm sure. However, their marriage lasted longer and overcame more than most unions today could even contemplate. And I know that my father never raised his voice, much less his hand, against my mother. He cared for her, was considerate of her needs. They were intimate, surprisingly and openly so by the standards of their place and time.

But Tink did not share his wife with anyone, even me. He didn't share much of himself either. We were all of us—I and my mother, Saint, Spence and his mother—bound to my father in an almost feudal hierarchy. There were duties and obligations on both sides of that equation that had to be kept in balance. With outsiders Tink was invariably harsh when enforcing his view of that balance. With his family his measure could be very tender.

For instance, it was Mother's duty to raise and tend our vegetable garden. One scorching July afternoon Mother had cut okra, a hot, stinging business even in the shade. She had gotten into the garden much later than normal and had been exposed to the worst of the day's heat. But the okra had to be cut—that was Mother's obligation. Tink was waiting for her on the porch.

"Mother, what are you doing in the sun?"

"Cutting okra."

"What for?"

"Supper."

"You can't cut your okra before the heat, we can do without."

A few days later my mother found a hat waiting on her bedside. A hat, homemade, woven from pine straw, with a single scarlet

ribbon crudely fastened about the crown and a brim so wide it had
to be pinned up to keep from flopping in her face.

Mother wore that hat till the day she died.

Tink took care of Mother. Took care of me. And while most
white men of that time would simply have left Eida Mae and Spence
to fend for themselves, Tink determined to take care of them too.

My father fulfilled his obligations. Always. He would do his
duty. But if you were the beneficiary of Tink's concern or conscience
it's also fair to say that there would always be a price.

Saint MacGrue had not been buried a day before Tink told
Eida Mae that her boy would be quitting the colored's one-room
school that Spence attended. And why was that? the widow inquired as
obliquely as she could. "Because come January," Tink replied directly,
"your boy won't be workin' for Putnam. He'll be workin' for me."

≈

Tink had already told Saint of his plans to go into business for himself. Tink knew twenty-four cents an hour wouldn't get you a land
baron's domain, so the December after Saint's burial Tink quit Putnam Lumber Company and started the first business of his own, a
sawmill. Big companies left a lot of timber unhauled from the flatwoods, timber too small to be efficiently processed by their massive
machinery. Tink knew where all this timber was, so months before
giving his notice to Putnam & Co., he began to quietly acquire
stumpage under terms that allowed him to retrieve timber and cut
secondary growth.

You couldn't make any money selling logs rough, so sometime
early in '29 Tink put together the makings of a mobile sawmill, a
pepperbox. Didn't take much to start. Daddy got himself a circular
blade, a six-footer, as I recall. He needed a means to drive the blade;
he swapped hogs for a rebuilt donkey engine. And Tink needed an
index to regulate the blade for cutting logs to size. Had to buy that
item for cash, which he hated.

Once he acquired those three basic elements, Tink began spreading the word that by year's end he'd be in the business of salvaging, cutting, and processing timber. If you wanted to build a house, a tobacco barn, *anything,* Tink promised to sell you two-by-fours, six-by-eights, any standard dimension, much more cheaply than you could get it from Putnam. And Tink would haul your lumber to site. No extra charge.

For labor Tink recruited the same men he'd crewed with over the years. They weren't the best, but he knew them, and, jobs being so scarce, the threat of firing kept even the laziest of them in line. Even Taff.

Tink could get lumberjacks and yard help any time he wanted. There was one crucial hire, however, that gave Tink trouble—the position of sawyer.

No one is more important to the success of a sawmill than its sawyer. A good sawyer will look at a rough log, figure to the inch the timber in it, and then have the genius to know just how to cut the timber to minimize waste. The sawyer was also the accountant, the man who knew to a dime how much the mill turned and where the money came from—a kind of Johnny Inkslinger who could also use a peavey or an axe.

Saint MacGrue was to have sawyered my father's mill. Tink made no bones about hiring Spence's father, an intention that didn't sit well in the community. White men everywhere were outraged by Tink's announcement and by the fact that Tink intended to pay Saint a white man's wage.

Red Walker was especially galled. From the moment Tink told his crew of his plan to build a mill, Red expected to be hired as sawyer. Red was the only man in Tink's crew, after all, with any sawyering experience. He had even inked three years for Putnam until, according to Walker, the mill's foreman took the job from Red so he could give it to a relative. That was bad enough, losing a good job to another white man. And now here was Tink giving away a white man's job to a *nigger*!

This all started percolating around midsummer. Just about the time people were in their second or third croppings of tobacco. You began to hear little things, second-, third-hand. Always behind Daddy's back. It wasn't that people cared about Red Walker, understand; it was that a black man was slated to get a job meant for a white.

My father didn't care a June bug about anyone's opinion, white or black; in that sense he was truly without prejudice. Tink would be paying blacks and whites an equal wage; in that sense he was unusual. But it wasn't a high, moral purpose that drove my father's decision to choose Saint over Red. It was simply that Tink saw two qualities in Saint that he considered invaluable.

First, Saint MacGrue was a natural sawyer. Tink had many times seen Saint take the measure of a log in his eye and estimate its yield in any dimension—two-by-fours, six-by-twos—including the waste left over by the one-eighth inch of timber taken out by the saw's blade. Red Walker used to pair off with Saint, scribbling on the backs of boxes or reckoning in the sand to compare estimates. When they'd get back to the mill the whole crew would check to see which man came closest to the finished mark. Saint's eyeballed estimate would invariably beat Red's labored attempt. That stuck in Red's craw.

The second quality my father valued was the black man's unquestioned loyalty. Custom and obligation bound Spence's father to my father in bands of iron. Tink Buchanan trusted Saint MacGrue, an asset beyond price.

Red Walker was naturally furious when Tink told him that Saint would be sawyering his mill. But Red's fury seemed unimportant at the time, certainly insignificant compared to a deeper, darker, better-organized hatred that emerged.

The Klan was a powerful force during the Depression. Easy to forget now that in 1929 the Ku Klux Klan was a legitimate political party with over twenty *million* members, most of whom resided outside the South. The headquarters for the Klan in North Florida was established near the Gulf coast in a town called Perry. Its Grand Wizard, a well-known businessman and deacon in his hardshell church, enjoyed a minor fiefdom in that region.

His name was Tarrant Sullivan. He had an older brother,

Stanton Lee, a backshooter and true bully, the most dangerous of men. Stanton Lee regularly terrorized weaker men, or women, and had been accused, if not convicted, of a half-dozen homicides. Tarrant circulated word that if Tink hired Saint MacGrue over Red Walker or any other white man, Stanton Lee would be looking into his business.

Taff Calhoun, faithful as a lapdog, brought the word. Taff found my father one summer night cutting slices of pear with a Barlow knife on our porch swing.

"Klan's got it in for you, Tink."

"That's just talk, Taff."

"Reckon not. Tarrant's done put out the word. Stanton Lee."

"Well. We'll see."

A week later we saw from the bib of our veranda a cross draped with burlap, soaked in kerosene and blazing. It lit up the sky on the pine ridge behind the Sand Pond. I never will forget the chill that gripped me that night, watching those flames rise ghostly and pale above that perverted crucifix. A cold, wet hand seemed to run down my gullet and into my bowels. I wanted to pee.

Tink looked on for a minute or two, employed absently as was his custom of an evening with his slice of pear. He looked on and then, suddenly, stretched his back as if with some minor irritation.

"Martha."

"Yes, Tink."

"Have Eida Mae and Spence over here for the night."

Spence's pa was nowhere near home that evening. A revival had kicked off at Saint's small, and distant church; he left early to be on time for the Lord's holy work and would not be back until very late.

"I'll make 'em a pallet in the kitchen."

"Son, run over and get 'em. Take your shotgun."

My father then tossed the remains of his pear into the yard, closed the blade to his Barlow knife, and pocketed it in his khaki trousers. Then he took a step back from the porch, inside the house. The Winchester was always loaded and racked above the front door.

Tink took it down, reached deeply into his trouser pocket. I could hear the soft clink of metal and metal.

"I'll be taking the truck," he said, pulling his hand from his pocket, and without further preamble left Mother with me on the porch.

I have endured several vigils in my life. Nights filled with fear. But this first was made worse because I wouldn't know what happened that night, what my father actually did, until years later.

My uncle told me, Uncle Ernest. He was dying of tuberculosis when I asked him about that night.

"Well, he knew it was the Klan," Ernest wheezed. "And the Klan never did a damn thing without Tarrant Sullivan. You know Tarrant?"

I did. So then, in measured breaths squeezed out from the last hours of his life, my uncle told me what happened while my mother was making a pallet on the floor of our kitchen and while I was running faster than I would ever run again to my friend's house.

When I got there, Spence's mother was rigid on the porch, looking east to the false dawn that the terrible cross had brought to our horizon. Her eyes were wide and fixed and distant. Her hand dropped limply, as if on its own, and then snapped up again as if jerking a trotline, or maybe a yo-yo. The drop and jerk of that dead hand over and over, over and over. As if her unfeeling hand were retrieving nothing more than a child's toy.

"Miss Eida."

She didn't turn to my voice, and I knew that the cold fist in my gut must be a flimsy thing compared to the terror now being visited on Spence's mother. Spence and I had to lead Eida Mae by the hand to our house.

What I didn't know at the time, what Uncle Ernest told me later, was that my father wasn't taking the truck across our property to douse that burning perversion. No. In fact, Tink let it burn. Wanted it to burn. Because all that night as that cross consumed itself in fire and men in white sheets drank whiskey and fired rifles, talked big, and defiled our property, my father was on his way to Tarrant Sullivan's tin-roofed house outside Perry.

It was a twenty-mile drive. Tink got there just about sunup. He parked his truck outside Tarrant's gate. Two big dogs guarded that gate, a mongrel and a bulldog.

Tink didn't bother with the animals, just shot them both. Tarrant scrambled out of bed after those explosions from Daddy's carbine, must have scrambled for his own weapon. But he was way too late.

Daddy smashed through Tarrant's porch-side window, came into the house through his bedroom. He caught Sullivan in the hall shoving buckshot into his double-barreled shotgun.

According to my uncle, Tink spun Tarrant around, slammed the butt of his carbine into the man's kidneys, and, as the wife and children ran screaming from his house, beat the holy living shit out of that Grand Wizard with the brass knuckles Tink always carried in his pocket. Beat him to a fare-thee-well.

Once he'd pretty much mauled Tarrant past recognition, Tink hauled Mr. Sullivan out to the yard and tied the Klan's most feared enforcer in the posture of Our Lord on a crucifix of field fence and cypress.

Then he took out his Barlow, the same knife he used to slice his pears, and he cut Tarrant's ear off. Cut it off with the wizard screaming for mercy, bawling beside his two dead dogs and spilling urine onto the dirt.

"I'm leaving you with one ear, Tarrant," Tink told Sullivan before he passed out. "Tell Stanton Lee if I see him, you'll be missing two."

Then Daddy drove home. By the time the sheriff got there it was all over. No charges were filed. Taylor County's sheriff knew this was a Klan matter, and if the Klan wasn't strong enough to protect its wizard from that nigger-loving axeman out of Lafayette County, well, goddamn, *he* surely wasn't going to risk *his* hearing tryin' to do better.

That was midsummer of '29. Come November, Saint got himself killed. Unlike others, my father could not believe that Red

Walker was capable of such audacity. Would any man kill Tink's best man with Tink himself not fifty yards away? Would *any* man do that? And, ever the pragmatist, Tink was concerned first to take care of his business. He had already given Putnam & Co. notice and was committed to starting a mill of his own.

Didn't take Red long to come around.

"Figure you're gonna need a sawyer, Tink."

"That's true." Daddy was back to slicing pears with his knife. Same knife.

"I know Saint was a good man ..." Red began.

"That's white of you, Red."

"Sure he was," Red acknowledged, missing the irony. "But Saint's gone. I'm here. And you know I kin do the job."

"Maybe," Tink allowed. "We'll see."

That was how, in January of 1930, Red Walker came to be sawyer at my father's donkey-run mill. But there was a shadow at Red's shoulder, a child just turned ten, a child making twenty-four cents an hour. Daddy took Spence out of school, made him a gopher at the mill, working the yard, doing all but the heaviest work.

I wonder if it made Red nervous, seeing the son of Saint MacGrue so near? Seeing Saint's eyes in Spence's? Seeing that quick, eager intelligence in a body growing daily to be as powerful as his father's?

Probably not. Red had no conscience to bother him, and a tar-baby boy, why—he would be beneath a sawyer's notice. If I had to guess, Spence's apprenticeship held no significance to Red at all.

Chapter five

Paintbrush,
Carphephorous corymbosus

I saw less and less of Spence, bound to apprentice with my father, turned from child to man. Spence was nearly always with my father at the mill, and I, almost always separated from my father, had changed schools. In 1931 Tink took me out of Laureate's four-room schoolhouse for matriculation at the grander, better-equipped school in Cross City.

Hoover was still president when I left Lafayette County's all-white institution. FDR would be elected two years later, and in that short span I lost virtually all contact with my old school friends. Aside from that memorable occasion in Ray Henderson's tobacco field, I even lost contact with Julia.

I cannot honestly say that I missed Julia. I didn't know her well enough then *to* miss her. And I didn't really miss my schoolmates, never having been close to anyone at Laureate my age. But I did miss Spence. A hollow began in my heart the day my father took my boyhood companion to the forest.

Gone were the days of dog-fennel forts and mayhaw jelly. Gone were the long runs in the Sand Pond. Spence was a wage earner now, supporting an invalid mother, fixing breakfast and supper. Cutting the firewood. Raking the yard. Eida Mae wasted away like an old crow, her hair coming out in patches to bare the vacant skull beneath, her hand twitching as it had when the Klan came, twitching to catch the yo-yo that was not there.

At first I felt that hollow place all the time, carried it in me consciously as a great weight. But then the unfilled space, though always present, began to be muted by the most unexpected of events.

We were making money. Preachers nowadays say in one way or another that if the things of the soul are squared away, money does not make a difference. But money, whether gained or lost, earned or never attained, always makes a tangible difference to human beings, wealthy or poor, sinners or saints. The question for an ethical man, especially one claiming to be Christian, is not whether money makes a difference but rather how to behave in light of the difference that money makes.

As a teenager during the Depression, I have to confess I was not terribly concerned with the answer to this question. All I knew was that in an era of nationwide poverty and failed enterprises my father's fortunes bloomed. He went from one mill to two, then three. I found myself driving to Gainesville to shop for school clothes. A real store, not a Sears catalog. What a thrill to buy a jacket in summer, just because you liked it, even though winter was months away! To have more than one nice shirt. School shoes separate from brogans. I even bought a pair of loafers.

By the time I was a senior in high school, I had an automobile of my own, a Ford coupe, unheard of for a youngster of that period. I abjured the tobacco field for the dance hall, playing trombone for a swing band of North Florida crackers imitating Benny Goodman in Elks clubs and dance halls all over Dixie County. I wore a derby hat, donned a scarf when the least bit chilly, and smoked cigars.

I had five dollars in my pocket to throw away when men could feed their families, but often failed to, on five dollars a week.

And as for Spence, why—a black making close to forty dollars every month was not much short of fantastic. Why should I worry about Spence?

Only a couple of years earlier, when I first started school in Dixie County and when Spence started working for my father, I still saw my old friend, if less frequently. Then our passings became both infrequent and irregular. By the time we were fifteen it was catch-as-catch-can. The vivid memories of our younger years blurred, our unfocused camaraderie diffused now, Spence with work, me with high school and dance bands and hangers-on happy to receive the largesse of my new money.

I can't recall the slow slip of those days with any detail. There was no great argument to mark the shift between Spence and me. No great conflict. I can remember, however, the afternoon that I realized things had changed between us.

Arriving home after school I saw Spence in shirtsleeves mending the fence that guarded my mother's garden.

"Spence!" I called out, unbuttoning my coat as I strolled over. "What has Tink got you doing now?"

"Mr. Carter." He smiled politely. He paused with his posthole diggers buried halfway up the handles in the sandy loam.

Mister Carter? I hadn't expected that, although I suppose I should have. Anyone competent in Southern mores ought to have taken Spence's response for granted. I was now seventeen, a young white man with privileges and son to the boss of this Negro in front of me. But still—

"What's ruining the garden? Hogs?"

"Deer."

"Be easier just to shoot 'em."

His laugh aped mine.

"Why don't we go hunting sometime, Spence? Just go out and get us a buck?"

"Aw, I ain't much for hunting n'more."

"Sure you are!"

"Never thought *you* was."

Well, I wasn't. Spence knew I didn't like to hunt. That wasn't the point. Then Saint MacGrue's son wiped his brow with an arm grown powerful, and I noticed the veins swelled up.

A silence fell that I did not know how to breach.

"Well," Spence squinted into a sun hidden behind lead clouds, "I 'spect I better finish up."

"'Spect you had."

I turned away.

"Gonna be a nice day." Spence spoke to my back, seeming to invite conversation at the exact moment that I knew he had severed it.

"Regards to Eida Mae." I pumped my head. And then, searching for the familiar, "You take care of yourself, you hear?"

"Yes, sah."

The handles of the posthole diggers came together with a sharp report. Spence pulled a cylinder of soil effortlessly from the ground. Dropped a cedar post into the new hole. That was all.

I walked away angry. "Mister"! Seemed like an insult. I might expect that kind of attitude from a field hand. If there was something on his goddamn mind, why didn't he just come out and say it?

Kierkegaard, I later learned, wrote that the chief characteristic of despair is this: one is unaware of being in despair. As parents living daily with their children never see them grow, so I living a bare quarter mile from my boyhood friend never saw us grow apart. I had become warm, whereas Spence, even during the most prosperous of summers, had steadily become colder.

I was preoccupied. Busy during the school year with dances and bands and friends bought easily with pocket money and a Ford. I was as isolated from the plight of my local community as the people of Lafayette and Dixie County were from the larger affairs brewing in Europe. Affairs that would greatly affect us all in a whisk of time.

I lived the life of a playboy. I'm sure people speculated behind my back as to why I was not fully about my father's business. Why was Carter not in the woods with Tink? Why wasn't he wrestling the peavey and cant and axe, learning what he'd have to know to take over those sawmills?

The answer was simple. Tink's ambition to become a land baron had not changed, and the sawmills were simply a means to that end. But that was not Tink's ambition for me. Tink wanted to see his son become an educated man. A doctor.

It was my duty to fulfill that ambition. To that end I was given every resource, every aid to education that was within my father's capacity. Tink bought me books and hired tutors. And most importantly, my father gave me Time.

It takes time to become educated, to read, to cipher, and to study. Tink knew that. Hours at the mill were hours that could not be spent on school. Tink put me on a different path. I could make money here and there so long as it didn't affect my school. But my job was bookwork.

Fortunately, I was passionately curious about everything in every book I saw. I was quick and eager to ferret out the secrets of mathematics and chemistry. I took Latin and algebra and absorbed as much literature as I could find.

There were forty-seven students in my class, most of them sons and daughters of sharecroppers or day laborers. It was not hard to graduate at the top of that congregation, but could I get into a good university from the swamps of northern Florida? I was largely self-taught. Could an autodidact from Dixie County compete with students graduating from preparatory schools in the larger cities or out East? I wasn't sure.

The University of Florida had no medical school back then. In fact, the Sunshine State would not graduate doctors from her own medical schools until sometime around 1960. Says something about priorities. But I applied to Gainesville anyway, thinking that chemistry or biology might be good preparation for medical school. I applied to the Universities of Tennessee and Alabama too and, on a whim, to Emory-at-Oxford, Emory University's original campus at Oxford, Georgia.

My principal at Dixie County High assured me that Emory

was *the* Harvard of the South. I thought I had as much chance of getting into Emory from my rural secondary school as a frog had of wearing a saddle. But I read widely and well, had much encouragement and tutoring from a variety of teachers. I had my father to support me, and I had time.

In the spring of '36 I took the placement exams that determined my fate. I did well. In June I received the letter informing me that I had been accepted into Emory-at-Oxford, Class of Nineteen Hundred and Forty.

I didn't know whether to shit or go blind.

Once I allowed myself to believe that I had been accepted to Emory's Oxford campus, I had to figure out how to pay for it. The tuition in 1936 for one quarter at Emory-at-Oxford was, I'll never forget, fifty-five dollars. Room, board, and tuition together ran around a hundred forty-five per quarter. Taking laundry, travel, and other expenses into account, I could manage three quarters a year for something like six hundred Uncle Sams. Daddy sold twenty hogs at ten dollars apiece to cover part of that expense. The rest was up to me. I thought I had a fortune, one hundred and fifty-five dollars of trombone money in the bank, but even with that money and the hog money I was a hundred and forty dollars short of making the bare necessaries for my first year of school.

Tink took my car, sold it, and put the proceeds in the bank to only partially cover my *second* year of college. He told me flatly that was all the help I'd be getting. My playboy days were over. I'd be living on a shoestring at Emory, working more hours there by far than I ever had to work at home.

Time came to leave. You had to take everything you needed to college in those days, travel being expensive and breaks far apart. We sent a couple of trunks on ahead. Night before I left Mother packed me a bag. Tink drove me to the train station in Live Oak.

I had never ridden on a train. Had never seen a passenger train except from a distance. I checked my tickets at least a dozen times while waiting with my father at the Live Oak station. Perched on a rude bench in a stiff new suit beside my khaki-clad, lumberjack father, I felt like a hayseed.

"What if I'm not good enough?"

The question came out almost against my will. As if somebody else were asking it.

That's the only time I can ever remember my father touching me in a tender way. He laid his massive, gnarled hand gently as a feather on my knee.

"There's not a blue blood in the world can hold a candle to a boy spawned from Creek Indians and convicts."

I smiled. Tink smiled too, holding my entire knee as if it were a walnut.

He seemed to gather himself a moment before he went on. "They'll have some manners that ain't familiar. They'll have ways of talkin'. Prolly they'll make fun. Just stick with your books, Carter. You get the grades, they'll respect you. And if they don't—"

"Yes, sir?"

"Just tell 'em to kiss your ass."

I laughed out loud. Tink laughed too. We were still laughing when the whistle blew, far up the track. Is there any summons more lonely than a train's?

Tink turned to me. "Your mother told me to tell you something. Didn't make much sense. But she made me promise."

I waited.

"Something 'bout bottles."

"Bottles?"

"Bleach bottles. Said where you're going, to the university—?"

"Yes, sir?"

"Said you wouldn't see any."

I didn't offer an interpretation. Tink didn't seem to expect one. He just let go my knee, stood up from the bench, and straightened his hat. The locomotive pulled into the station, nothing larger than I'd seen at Shamrock. That was a comfort. But the sound took me unawares. The whistle's blast came with a physical concussion. And then brakes screamed. Cars crashed steel-on-steel in a maelstrom of steam and confusion. My insides shook.

"Go on, now," my father bellowed before the din was yet settled. "Catch your ride."

Chapter six

Black Medic,
Medicago lupulina

I traveled from Live Oak to Tallahassee, changed trains there to catch an express to Atlanta, where, changing again, I journeyed forty miles east on the Georgia Railroad to Covington, a small town about a mile south of Emory's rural campus. Biggest thing I remember about that trip was my discovery of the coach's toilet. The Pullman's loo was, to my mind, a mechanism of advanced civilization.

I was seventeen years old. Had never been away from home. I don't know what I expected of Emory: ivory towers, I suppose. Dons dressed in robes. My first view of the campus fell something short of that vision. I hitched a ride on a horse-drawn wagon to the Harvard of the South. There were cars, of course, but not a single paved road. The campus itself was no more than a squirrel of buildings set on flat land amidst a spire of hardwood trees.

There was no landscaping to speak of on Emory-at-Oxford's frugal grounds. The handful of buildings were set on a carpet of clay soil that trees pierced like spears. The lawn, so well tended now, was then only hardpan broken in patches by desperados of bermuda.

I was assigned a dorm room in Haygood Hall, named, I was told, after Atticus Greene Haygood, a former Emory president and Methodist bishop. The notion of a bishop on campus rekindled possibilities for the exotic—bishops for me being long-dead creatures, similar to vampires, their influence confined in about equal parts to fairy tales and European history. There was no running hot water in Haywood Hall, which disconcerted some of the students, though not me. I was used to pumping a handle even for cold water.

My class was male, only a single young lady attending in '36. Many of the men came from true Southern aristocracy, only a couple of generations removed from the plantations and gray uniforms of the Old Confederacy. But there were a fair number of Yankees too. Mostly old families from the East. And there were foreign students, Orientals mostly, products of Methodist missionaries working in that region.

My horizons were considerably broadened that first term away from home. I roomed with a Chinese student from Shanghai, the son of medical missionaries. He too was expected to become a physician. It was my job to tutor the young man in English. We were administered by quarters in those years. I tutored my young mandarin for a winter and spring. In the course of that experience he naturally tried to instruct me in his own language. I cannot remember my roommate's name or a scrap of mandarin.

I do recall my roommate asking me questions about Europe— Germany in particular. Questions about the aftermath of Versailles, about something called the National Socialist Party. I had no idea what he was talking about.

There were no robes at Emory-at-Oxford. The professors wore shirts and ties, frequently bow ties with summer slacks, it being hotter in Oxford, Georgia, than a June bride in a feather bed. There was no ivory tower on campus, though there were touches of architecture that now seem romantic. The arched doorway on Hopkins Hall, for instance, was designed in the late 1800s to allow carriages inside the building. By the time I arrived the interior had been given over to a swimming pool, the first I had ever seen.

As for academic life, Emory-at-Oxford provided a splendid and rigorous education, but there were no frills. The basics were excellent. The library, for instance, a place in which I spent countless hours, was considered a masterpiece of nineteenth-century design and well stocked. The laboratories, on the other hand, were fitted with hand-me-down equipment that encouraged constant efforts at improvement.

If we needed something in a biology class or a physics class we first tried to make it ourselves. The faculty led the way in this sort of improvisation, always on the lookout for ways to improve Emory's assets on the cheap. A dray horse killed on the road, for instance, was got for two dollars from its owner, skinned, the bones boiled and reassembled to provide a life-sized skeleton of a large mammal. Today a professor would hire a consultant to write a grant to apply to the government for funds to serve a similar purpose.

It was a place where a faculty limited in resources was unlimited in passion and imagination. I have visited a fair number of institutions since my days at Emory-at-Oxford, but I have never been on any campus where a student might hear his professor discuss the motion of molecules one afternoon and the next morning (after mandatory chapel) dismantle a still.

The classroom provided a place of respite for me—money or caste did not count in calculus class. But outside the lecture hall there were some for whom social position did matter. And so did money.

There was no GI Bill or Pell Grant in those days; if you needed money you had to earn it. I worked everywhere from the cafeteria to the hogpen, a fact that provoked derision from upperclassmen I was too unsophisticated or insecure to ignore. I frequently felt myself an outsider, my rural background betraying itself in any number of ways—my accent, my ignorance of social graces or sports. There is always a cadre of snobs who notice such deficiencies, and Emory-at-Oxford was no exception.

I was the butt of more than practical jokes. We boxed at Little

Emory in those years, that activity still being regarded as the manly art of self-defense. A young blue blood challenged me, Fenton McKalb, a well-heeled upperclassman from Virginia. Fenton was on the boxing team. He had been trained from an early age as a pugilist. But here was Mr. McKalb challenging the cracker from Florida. I couldn't refuse and live with myself. So I met Fenton in the ring, and for three rounds he cut me up pretty badly.

It was great sport for the upperclassmen. My foreign roommate was the only student I can remember offering serious expressions of encouragement or, afterward, of sympathy.

Luckily, I had my trombone. Weekends I'd take my instrument to the only night spot in Newton County, the Alcove, where for tips I'd slip 'n' slide with local bands beside the Alcovy River. I got to know a number of locals in that setting, most of them musicians and farmers.

I also got to know my professors. Didn't have any choice, really. Professors at Emory-at-Oxford knew you by name. Their wives knew your name. Their *children* knew your name. Students and faculty frequently lived in the same building. Four professors lived with their families in my dormitory. It was common for faculty, on campus and off, to invite students into their homes.

A trip to a professor's residence usually meant a good feed. Sometimes the meal would be informal, an outdoor barbecue or fish fry, say. But there were other invitations, formal affairs, that had the authority of pronouncements ex cathedra. Those summonses could come, as you might expect, printed on an elegant card. But the word might also be delivered just as surely and authoritatively in passing, "Mr. Buchanan, we're having some people over Friday evening. Seven. Wear a tie."

You simply could not duck an invitation. Believe me, I tried. I was petrified at the notion of enduring anything involving a knowledge of etiquette. I'll never forget those first sit-downs, where I was regularly embarrassed with instructions regarding the proper use of utensils.

"You needn't cut your bread, Carter," my literature professor mildly instructed me over a plate of biscuits. "Just break it with your hands."

I dreaded these occasions, but eventually I learned and then, hallelujah! I never had to fear being embarrassed anywhere, ever again.

There was a great deal to learn here. Whether conversing at a dining table or debating in a classroom, I was required to integrate and relate *facts*. "Process" was not a word that had, in Emory's pedagogy, destroyed the notion that critical thought could not take place without something to critically think *about*.

We memorized poems that still give me joy and solace. We memorized passages from the *Iliad* that still exalt and compel and challenge. And in the sciences we had a mnemonic for almost everything. Kingdom, phylum, class, order, family, genus, species—? King Philip Chewed on Fresh Green Strawberries. How about the cranial nerves? On Old Olympus's Towering Top a Finn and German Viewed Some Hops.

History and philosophy were closely integrated in the Oxford curriculum, and the past was constantly related to events of the present. European machinations, so distant in Lafayette County, were the stuff of evening smokers on campus. We even had a professor in our dorm, Dr. Keaton, who predicted that Germany would once more take France and England to war. He predicted too that the United States would eventually be forced, along with the other democracies, to join that conflict.

My more sophisticated classmates thought Dr. Keaton was simply crazy. A hundred thousand casualties "over there" had been enough to generate in the United States an isolationist fervor that had not come anywhere close to dissipation. France and Britain, having lost millions in the first world war, were even less inclined than we Yanks to engage the Germans in a second.

The evening smokers ridiculed the Old Confederate, albeit gently. "He just needs a windmill to tilt against," they said, and I smiled to express appreciation for an allusion that in truth I did not understand.

History and philosophy were slippery things for me. I had come to Emory, after all, to be a doctor. I expected the hard, even edges of biochemistry and anatomy to be my chief interest; Dr. Aenid's botany class changed that supposition in a single quarter. The physiology of plant life amazed me. But there was a history here too, a different sort of history that I had never conceived. "Imagine a time," Dr. Aenid began his first lecture, "when there was no such thing as a flower."

He charted the history of everything from sunflowers to bacteria and would take us a hundred miles to see clues of that evolution locked in stone. Soon you had a dozen Sherlock Holmes deducing how the fern gave way to deciduous vegetation, or why the pine survived from its ancient race of conifers. How spores and seeds might have competed—on and on.

It was Dr. Aenid who taught me the joy to be had in the placing of names, Latin names and Greek for the common things I used to love in my Sand Pond. From him I learned that the common red oak is in reality *Quarcus falcata,* a delineation that combines the old Latin name for oak with "falcata," or sickle-shaped, to describe the leaf of the species.

Newly named, the flora I had before taken for granted seemed fresh and vital and interesting. I had no idea, for instance, that there are nearly a dozen species of azalea, the botanical name for the species most familiar to me being *Rhododendron canescena.* I had no idea that our Florida maple *(Acer barbatum)* was different than maple trees found anywhere else. Even my humble mayhaw had a distinctive pedigree, *Crataegus,* meaning "strong," establishing the berry's niche in the hawthorn genus, and *aestivalis,* meaning "of summer," completing the picture of a hardy, hawthornlike fruit of summer. Sounded grand to me.

God told Adam to name the things of His garden. It seemed to me there in Dr. Aenid's class that we were most purely and truly advancing the Creator's work.

I ignored my classmates. I completed my first quarter sleepless from exams. We were allowed two weeks for Christmas. I was eager to be home for the holidays, looking forward to the prospect of a late morning's sleep and the gifts of the season.

Chapter seven

Tread Softly,
Cnidoscolus stimulosus

I journeyed home expecting to find my father waiting for me at the Live Oak station. But it was Taff Calhoun who was there, stamping his feet in a December chill, arms bowed out like penguin's wings.

"Merry Christmas, Taff." I offered the greeting as I dropped off my train to the dock.

"Colder'n a well-digger's ass." Taff hit a spittoon with a wad of Red Man so hard it rang like a bell.

"Good to see you too."

"Yer drivin.'"

It was a long haul home. The sky pressed a table of lead lower and lower until I felt its weight on my chest. Winter rains come often to lands near the Gulf and had come this season. The ditches gleamed full and silver. The roads weren't much more than muddy ruts.

Taff finally offered some relief.

"Yerself a drink?" He produced a pint of Jack Daniels.

I took a cautious sip. The liquor coursed like fire down my gullet, lit a furnace below my cowhide belt.

"There ye go." Taff took his sour mash back.

"Give me the news," I said.

"Well, your daddy's got himself into another business."

"And what would that be?"

"Turpentine," Taff belched.

I should not have been surprised. Once Tink acquired the stumpage to cut timber it only made sense to tap the land's uncut loblolly and yellow pine for its amber resin. And it was profitable. It's hard in an age of synthetics to appreciate how ubiquitous was once the need for turpentine. A universal solvent, turpentine was found in everything from common paint to naval stores. But one of its most interesting applications had to do with something called tung oil.

For a long time the preferred finishing agent for exposed lumber was an oil extracted from *Aleurites fordii,* the tung oil tree. The tree derives its common name from the Mandarin, *yu-t'ung,* and had been used by the Chinese for centuries. But even though tung oil is an excellent preservative, it is too thick by itself to penetrate hardwood.

Turpentine solves that problem. Found to be a natural carrier for tung oil, turpentine mixes with the tree's natural oil, allowing it to seep deeply into the hardest oak or mahogany or maple. Once treated, a wooden surface, an aircraft carrier's deck, say, or a seaside dock, could be expected for months at a time to remain impervious to the challenge of water and wind.

A surge in ship building and railroads triggered an enormous appetite for turpentine and tung oil in the '30s and '40s, but it was hard, badly paid work. Turpentiners in particular had a reputation for being the lowest class of working men. Small wonder. Who could be persuaded to endure the hellish interiors of a Florida swamp, loading fifty-gallon turpentine barrels, three or four hundred pounds of awkward weight each, across swamps, sloughs, and snakes for free wages of forty cents a day?

And there were wars too, turpentine wars, they were called,

waged over disputes of territory. A turpentiner would tap his own trees dry, wander a hundred yards or half a mile onto another man's stumpage, and tap *his* trees. The transgression would be discovered and combat ensued.

Whole camps would go at each other, guns and knives and axes adding to the natural hazards of heat and snakes and quicksand. Lucky men died when shot outright. Others lingered while wounds from bullets or blades went to gangrene.

Was it any wonder turpentiners couldn't keep men hired to do the work? But when it came to finding labor, my father was the master of unconventional solutions.

"Who's Daddy got working the turpentine?" I asked Taff.

"Families, mostly," Taff replied.

"Are you serious, Taff?"

"As a heart attack."

"Where's he get a family to tap turpentine?"

Well, it turned out that Tink could get them pretty much anywhere. Many families in these years were split up, mothers and children separated from a man who rode the rails or hoboed to find work. Hobo camps weren't havens for bums only in those years. Most men on the road or in camps were simply desperate for work. They congregated around industrial towns or railheads and hired out for day labor.

Tink recruited these men, promising them work *and* giving them a way to stay close to their families. He brought them down, men, women, and children, to form communities of turpentiners in the flatwoods.

"Pays forty cents a day," Taff nodded. "Plus he gives what they need for housing. Single men bunk. Families go two to a house."

It was a mark of the times that I saw these arrangements as generous.

"Jesus. And who ramrods this operation?"

"Mac Morgan," Taff replied brightly. "And Joe Boatwright. Remember Joe? Harold's brother? Used to work the convicts when Putnam would lease 'em from the state."

I did remember Joe. Started out as a prison guard but quit the state after some thirst-crazed felon bit off his passion finger and started working for Putnam. Up until 1920 private concerns could lease convicts for a nickel a day for most any purpose. Story was that the same old boy who bit off Joe's finger in prison turned up in one of Putnam's gangs. Wasn't too long after the trustee got himself drowned.

"Yessir," Taff chuckled. "That Joe don't tolerate no nonsense."

We drove in silence a moment. The truck hit a pothole and flushed a confusion of mallards from the wetlands along the road. I watched their wings beat in flight.

"Taff."

"Ah-hah."

"If Daddy's running the turpentine, who takes care of the mills?"

"Red Walker." Taff took another swig from his Jack D.

"That working out?" I asked.

"Couldn't hold his ass with both hands."

"Doesn't sound like a vote of confidence."

"I warned your daddy. I told him, 'If you could put Red's brains on the edge of a razor blade, they'd roll around like a BB in a goddamn boxcar.'"

"What'd Daddy say?"

"Said he'd be there to check up. Then we got this damn turpentine. Your daddy got off with the gangs. Tell you what, if it watn't for Spence we wouldn't have those mills at all."

"Spence?"

"He already knows the cuttin' and yard work better than Red *ever* did. An' now he's got this thang with numbers. 'Rithmetic? Boy kin cipher his ass off."

"Spence didn't even finish the sixth grade."

"Just you give him a string of numbers. Many as you want. Then tell him whatever you want done whatever whichaways, and I guaran-goddamn-tee you that boy'll come up with the right cipher ever' time."

"Every time?"

"In his head. Never seen nuthin' like it. Not even from a white man."

"Sounds like Spence might make a good sawyer," I offered. "His daddy would've."

Taff rolled down a window to release a wad of snuff. A cold, cold wind sucked the heat out of the Ford's metal cabin, and I found myself wishing for a blanket to warm the sudden chill in my limbs.

"Don't miss yer turnoff," Taff spoke sharply.

I swapped one set of muddy ruts for another. We were close to home now. I could see beneath a pair of pecan trees the chimney and porch of my father's Big House.

"How is Mother?" I asked.

"That's Tink's business," Taff replied tersely.

I knew then that I was truly home.

❧

As soon as I was unloaded Taff took the truck straight back to my father and the flatwoods. But where was Mother? I had dropped my cardboard suitcase onto the porch when I noticed a gingham sheet spread on pine planks and I remembered it was a Monday. Wash Day.

I turned south from the bib of the porch, and sure enough, even against that leaden sky I could see the dark curl of smoke that would lead me to my mother.

She was down by the lake. Garner Lake was famous for its well-shaded shores, largemouth bass, and gators. It was distinguished too by the skirt of sawgrass that crowded the freshwater shore nearest our home. That's where Mother would be, I realized, amazed at how in the short span of months I could have so easily distanced myself from the routine of my former life. It was Monday, and so, naturally, my mother would be down by the lake doing her wash.

Today you can do a week's wash in four or five loads of your Maytag. It took my mother all day to clean a week's worth of laundry,

59

and it was arduous labor. The routine never varied. Mother did her laundry on the same day every week through summer or winters of the most bitter cold. It was a good hundred yards from our front porch to the lake. The smoke-blackened kettle remained beside the water, but everything else had to be hauled down. Those necessaries included four vat-sized washtubs, a scrub board, battling pins and sticks, an axe to cut the pine kindling (or lightard, as we called that wood), and soap Mother made herself at great expenditure of labor from ashes (or Red Devil lye) and cracklin'.

I could see her now, spearing clothing like flounder to the bottom of the pot. I used to love to do that, spear garments puffed with air to the bottom of that boiling kettle. A stiff, steady wind whistled from some arctic source, a wet, bone-chilling cold. Couldn't have been much above thirty degrees, and yet I noticed how careful my mother was to stay upwind of her wood-fired kettle. I knew why.

It happened when I was a boy, not yet seven. It was a wash day, sometime near Christmas. I accompanied my mother to the lake, complaining bitterly of the cold, shivering sullenly as Martha cut her wood and stoked her fire.

The fire caught quickly. Big. Bright. I leaped to the kettle.

"Careful, Carter," Mother cautioned.

But I was cold, and here was a fire. I shuffled in close.

"Careful, son."

I remained on the south side of that pot, luxuriating in a pleasant sting of flame. I never will forget the smells that day, of cold weather and lightard burning, homemade soap and dirty laundry. Of the inside of my shirt as I buried my nose away from a wind tasting of metal. And then I smelled something new—

"CARTER!"

I was on fire. My entire backside was on fire. Fire on flesh! And then I did the worst thing you could do.

I ran.

But if there's anyone who can run faster than an Indian, it's an Indian's mother. My mother tackled me and in two giant strides drove me headlong into the lake.

I couldn't swim. In seconds I went from burning to drowning! And then I was coughing, jerked up from the freezing cold water in my mother's arms. And now crying. Freezing all over again.

"I'm cooold!" I wailed. If I was expecting a show of sympathy I was disappointed.

"Don't you dare, Carter Buchanan." Mother's voice now had the edge of my father's. "Don't you complain a word or by heaven I'll have you sit in this lake all morning!"

She took me to the house and undressed me. I had received some serious burns, mostly along my legs.

"It won't hurt," she told me calmly, sterilizing a pair of scissors over a candle.

"Mama!"

"I'm only going to cut the dead flesh, Carter, not the live part."

It didn't hurt at all. Mother didn't use butter or clabber or any kind of oil to salve the remaining flesh. She didn't use bandages either. She simply cleaned my wounds with well water and left them open to the air. Had me sleep on my stomach for a while. I couldn't wear pants and had to go barelegged that entire Christmas. Made for a cold winter, I can tell you, but the only thing I have to show for the experience is a long patch of only slightly paler skin that runs up my calves.

When Mother was finished with me she brought me a jelly sandwich. Mayhaw jelly on hand-baked bread.

"I'm going to finish the wash," was all she said.

Saint Paul admonishes that when we are children we are allowed to think as a child and regard the world as a child, but when we are grown we must put childish things away. Coming to my mother as a young man of eighteen, seeing her hair fall pewter and black over a thin jacket not overlarge on that remarkably tall frame, seeing her proud carriage bent with years of stick and axe and board, I felt ashamed. How could I ever have complained about something so trivial as a chill?

I will never be so selfish again, I said to myself. I shall put all things childish behind me.

That I am sure is what I intended.

"MOTHER." I was careful to hail from a distance, not wanting to startle.

She looked up then, saw me, and rewarded me with one of the longest sustained smiles I can ever remember.

"Welcome home, son." She dropped the stick long enough to give me a quick, fierce hug. "Why don't you cut me some lightard? I'll be filling the rinse tubs and we can talk."

So we began our coming-home conversation.

"Taff meet you?"

"Yes, he did. I expected Daddy."

"Taff told you about the turpentine?"

"Yes, ma'am."

"Well. That's where your daddy is."

We delayed the rest of our discussion until the clothes were rinsed, hauled wet and heavy back up behind the house, and hung out to dry. Then, with the sun low and the wind rising, thank the Lord, we went inside.

In the kitchen a wood-fired stove spat and hissed as the resins from its pine wood expanded and burst. A common sound at one time, that cheerful combustion. My mother had already scooped a lapful of acre peas into her apron. These were dried peas, saved from the summer's bounty for seed and also for winter nourishment. Martha was shelling a mess for supper, snapping the hulls open, casting the peas like pellets into a pan at the table. When I was a boy I imagined I heard in her lap volleys of rifle fire, the cracking shells cartridges fired by some Lilliputian regiment, the peas bullets reporting from the pan's metal tympanum.

Our talk was timed to her labor as surely as a metronome, the broken hull's sharp snap followed by the report of peas.

"Seems like Daddy's bit off more than he ought to be chewing," I said.

"Takes money to buy land, Carter."

"Whose land? Dave's? You don't mean Dave Ogilvie?"

"He's lost a couple of crops."

"Tobacco? He can afford it."

She rifled a volley of peas into her pan.

"This year it was blue mold got his beds. Last year worms. Two years before that nobody made anything what with the drought."

By drought my mother meant that rain had not come in time or quantity to water the fanners' tobacco in the field. There was actually plenty of water caught in the sloughs and lakes and hammocks. But irrigation was rare, the investment in pumps and pipe being prohibitive even for a man of Dave's means.

"Just because he's lost some crops doesn't mean he's near to losing his land, Mother."

"Your father seems to think different."

"Why can't he back off?"

"Who, your daddy?" Martha seemed never to have considered the possibility.

"Working himself to death just on the *chance* he can buy Dave Ogilvie's farm? It doesn't make sense."

"Dave's daddy took that place from Tink's," Mother said as if that was all there was to it. "Tink wants it back."

"Granddaddy lost a hundred and forty acres, Mother. Not a thousand!"

She sprayed peas into that pail rat-tat-tat.

"We don't need Dave Ogilvie's land," I persisted.

She leaned forward fiercely, color high in those high, high cheeks, taller, even seated, than her own son. The volley of peas stopped abruptly.

"See, Carter, for you that Ogilvie place, it's nothing but tobacco and livestock. You don't need that, do you, son? You don't see any need for that at all!"

She folded her apron.

"Truth is, Carter, you don't know what *need* is. You never missed a meal because of a failed crop, have you?"

"No."

"Your daddy has. You never known fever because medicine wasn't to be had. You never known cold for lack of underthings or covers or coats. You never known a thousand things your daddy has known, and every time Tink passes Dave's land he knows it all over again."

She paused, but only briefly.

"Your daddy had a sister."

Died when she was little, I knew that.

"A younger sister," Mother nodded. "Your grandmother was carrying when Old Man Ogilvie threw them out of their house. Same house the Ogilvies now call their own. Her name was Karen. Little Karen. She was born early in a tent near bad water in Cook's Hammock. Couldn't nurse her mother's milk. She needed goat's milk. They had it at the store, had plenty of it, but Old Man Ogilvie wouldn't give Tink's daddy credit even for groceries.

"She lived less than a year."

Mother went back to her peas. Rat-tat-tat.

"Tink didn't hunt for sport in those days, Carter. He hunted to eat."

I cleared my throat.

"He still does."

"Well." She smiled grimly. "Some things don't change."

We sat a while longer. I made up some kindling for the stove, placed it in a pail beside the oven.

"Where's Spence?" I asked. Mostly to mend fences.

"Working," Mother answered without rancor. "Just like his daddy. Lord. Talk about two peas in a pod—that's Spence and Saint."

"I should go over there," I said.

"You might catch him." Mother glanced for emphasis in the direction of the Little House. "Though sometimes he stays in the woods with Tink. Just like Saint used to."

❧

It was a short quarter mile to Spence's place. I got to the front porch near sundown. Eida Mae was there in her spindly rocker, looking west into the smoldering ball of fire that had briefly broken through the day's lead dome. Closing like an ogre's eye beneath a heavy gray lid.

"Eida Mae, how are you?"

All I got was the squeak of her rocker in reply. Her hands, I noted, were limp over the claw of the rocker's arms. Waiting, waiting, waiting for some return on that invisible string.

"Eida Mae, it's Carter." I stepped now onto the front steps.

No reply.

"SPENCE?" I called out. When no answer came I turned to leave. "Jesus!"

"Well, if it ain't the college boy."

He was standing not ten feet behind me.

"Spence! Damnation, you scared me to death!"

"Scared *me,* shoutin' like that."

"Haven't seen Tink, have you?"

"Comin' home I did. Said he'd be by directly."

"He in the truck?"

"Naw. Hoover."

Hoover was Tink's favorite mule. I took time now to give Spence a look. He had grown a foot and a half it seemed. I could see Saint in him everywhere.

"Mama," Spence said, "I'm home."

No reply except for the squeak of her chair.

"Brought some swamp cabbage," Spence went on anyway.

I hadn't even noticed the heavy cylinders of palm tucked like a pillow beneath Spence's arm. A favorite of mine, swamp cabbage. A species of palm, actually, *Sabal palmetto.*

"We'll have it t'morrah," Eida Mae smiled vacantly.

Spence turned then to me. "Why don't you come on back?"

I followed Spence around the house to a rear porch. A deer hide was tanning on the porch. A cutting board was rigged nearby next to a hand pump. Spence took out a long knife and began peeling his cabbage.

"I hear you're in the turpentine business," I began.

"Your daddy is," Spence nodded. "Keeps me pretty close to the mills."

"Red still sawyerin', I hear."

"Mmm hmmm." Spence cut off a tender shoot of cabbage and offered it to me.

"What's three-eighths times two-thirds divided by one-eighth, Spence?"

Spence smiled.

"You been talkin' to Taff."

"He tells some stories," I allowed.

"Equals two," Spence said and offered me some more cabbage.

I don't think I really expected an answer. When it came I realized I'd need a pencil and paper to check it out.

"Damnation, Spence, how long you been able to do that?"

"Well, Red got me started."

"Red?"

"Mmm hmm. We'd get in a forty-foot log, say, have an order to finish it off in two-by-fours. Red would figure the board feet and cost per foot to charge the customer." Spence peeled off some more cabbage. "I noticed every now and then he was overchargin'."

"You noticed?"

Spence shrugged, "Don't know how else to esplain it, I just noticed."

"You tell Red?"

"Hell, no, I look like a fool? I tole your daddy. Now, this is funny, got time fo'a story?"

It had been a long time since I had seen Spence so relaxed. Here was a confident young man, and as he spoke I could imagine that we were boys again, just two boys sharing victuals on Eida Mae's back porch.

"I always have time for a story," I said.

"It was of a Thursday," Spence began. "I had done tole your daddy Red was taking the extra money."

"Wait a minute; are you telling me Red was overcharging on purpose?"

"Well, he makes mistakes alla time, but yeah, when it's in his favor it's generally on purpose."

"Goddamn. What'd Tink do?"

"I give your daddy copies of a couple of receipts. Tole him what the rough lumber comin' in was, what was finished out, and what was charged. Tink came in like he found this out all by hisself!"

"Tink…" I'd never heard Spence use my father's given name. But if Spence noticed my surprise he didn't show it. Just chuckled as if my father's deception were the cleverest thing in the world.

"You daddy ripped Red Walker a new asshole. Time he left they was blood all over, I can tell you."

"But Red must have realized it came from you, Spence, I mean—if Taff knows how you can figure!"

"Oh, I 'spect by now Red knows," Spence nodded. "But they ain't a lot he can do."

I was astounded. There wasn't a lot *Red* could do? Red was the sawyer. A *white* man! What did Spence mean?

Then I saw Spence peel another sheet of cabbage away from its cylinder. Effortlessly. I saw him break off the pulp with his fingers. Just like snapping a pea hull.

"You need to be careful about Red, Spence," I said huskily.

"Red ain't gone be no problem fuh me," Spence wiped his knife on his trousers. "Not but once, anyway. Here, Carter—git some cabbage."

Chapter eight

Bloodleaf,
Iresine diffusa

By the time I walked back to the Big House it was dark. Things had changed since I'd left, but I didn't have time to dwell on it. I loped up the front porch to our door. The front door took you into a long hall, a dog run, with rooms coming off either side. I opened the screen door first, then the wide cypress door that led into our hall.

I pulled a croker sack up to the sill to dampen the draft. I could see the fireplace's glow from my parents' bedroom. It was the only room, apart from the kitchen, that had any source of heat at all.

"I'm home," I hung my coat on a peg beneath Tink's carbine.

When I turned around I saw my father, still dirty in his khakis, sitting with Mother by the fire.

"Hullo, son." He remained seated.

"Daddy! Didn't think you were going to be home."

He offered me a smile. His eyes were streaked red and I saw

something else, something also red that spread in a stain beneath his shoulder.

"Carter, you need to go into town." Mother was calmly taking a pair of scissors to his shirt. "Your daddy's been shot."

It took me just a moment to register what I'd been told. "Who—?"

"We don't know." Mother shook her head. "Now, go get Doc West."

"Better have Spence come over," Tink was telling Mother. "I doubt anyone would come here wantin' trouble, but if they did, I'm not able to do much about it."

Spence would be handier with a gun than I, no doubt about that.

"Can't leave Eida Mae alone." Mother was applying a towel directly to staunch the wound.

"Give her my room," I offered without thinking. "Spence and I can make do in the kitchen."

I thought I saw approval in my mother's eyes. Tink acknowledged the suggestion with a terse nod.

"Sorry to be a bother."

Mother looked me through the door. I didn't need her to tell me to hurry.

Hoover was waiting out back, his reins looped over a nail in the smokehouse wall. He backed up when I neared, and I wished to hell Tink had driven the truck in from the woods.

"Easy, son."

I had heard my father address our mule that way times beyond count. The animal settled immediately and let me on.

I urged Hoover into a trot, but not out the front way. The sandy road that led to our front porch ran due south before turning west to reach the hard road and Laureate. It would take me at least two hours to reach Doc's house following that route. It would be quicker to cut north across the Sand Pond. Even in the dead of night I knew the way. Crossing the ponds, even allowing for a ford or two, would take thirty minutes off my time.

And there was another, better reason to head for the Sand Pond. The Ogilvies' land bordered our Sand Pond to the north. Dave had a Packard that could get to Doc's house inside thirty minutes. The problem was, I knew my father would never let himself be carried to help in Dave's automobile, even if his life depended on it. However, Doc West also owned a car. If I could persuade Dave to take me to town in his Packard, Doc could drive me back. I could cut a three-hour trip in half.

I urged Hoover to a dangerous lope. Low-lying limbs of oak and hickory threatened to dismount me from my mule. I tucked my head next to Hoover's and dug my heels into his flank. We were galloping now, the sand unrolling in moonlit patches beneath the mule's blind hooves. Brambles and vines raked my body like a witch's comb. But it seemed as if I were ploughing in a wet field. I wondered if I would not be better off running; I was certain that Spence on foot could make it to Dave Ogilvie's porch quicker than my sorry charge.

We scraped beneath the limbs of oaks and pine, passed the mayhaw grove, took one quick, bone-chilling plunge across a neck of water. Hoover was ready to drop when I saw the dim outline of Dave's wide veranda.

The dogs bayed like mastiffs as I approached, fangs open and hair bristling along their backs. Couldn't have been more than a hundred of 'em. So now I'd broken faith with my wounded father to beg outside the gate of a man he despised only to be torn to pieces by the son of a bitch's dogs.

I stopped outside his gate and called, "MR. OGILVIE, IT'S CARTER BUCHANAN."

No reply.

"IT'S CARTER, SIR. CARTER BUCHANAN."

After what seemed an age the door opened. Dave stepped through the door. He stood tall as a tree, a shotgun cradled in the crook of his arm. He'd pulled on a pair of broadcloth trousers and an undershirt.

"It's me, Mr. Ogilvie."

"Let him in, boys."

The dogs lurched away as if jerked on leashes. I scrambled off my mule, threw open Dave's front gate.

"What can I do for you, son?"

"I need a ride, sir. Tink's been shot."

"I'll take him." Dave turned back inside for his coat.

"No, sir!" I stepped onto the porch. "I'm sorry, Mr. Ogilvie, but I'd be obliged if you could just take me into town. Dr. West can drive me back."

Dave frowned deeply. At that moment Julia stepped onto the porch. She was in a shift, ghostly pale and shivering in the cold.

"Papa, who is it?"

"It's me, Julia," I spoke up.

"Carter?" She shaded her eyes from her father's lantern. The shift fell from her shoulder when she raised her arm. I saw a tan of skin running to a firm shoulder.

Sarah came out next, small as a bird, coatless herself but carrying a jacket for her husband.

"Is that you, Carter?"

"Yes, ma'am."

"Tink's got himself shot," Dave said as he broke open his shotgun.

"Shot? How, Carter? Who?"

"We don't know who, ma'am. I haven't had time to find out about the rest."

"Turpentiners." Dave pronounced the word as if it were profane. "There's a war in those swamps, men killing and looting for a barrel of resin."

"Does your mother need help, Carter?"

"I believe we'll be fine, thank you, ma'am," I said. "Soon as we get Doc West to the house."

"Go, then, go!" She seemed suddenly to appreciate the necessity of swift action.

"Come on, son," Dave commanded me. "Car's around back."

I followed him but glanced back at Julia. Her face was cast as if in bronze—half in shadow, half in the lantern's unsteady light. She had taken a porch column into one hand, leaning out like a lover searching for a ship's mast on a distant horizon.

"We'll be all right!" I called back.

"Come see us when you are." A gust of frigid wind carried her words.

I hurried after Julia's father to the Packard—"the car that needs no nameplate!" I fumbled with the door latch.

Dave opened it from the inside.

It was an odd ride. I shivered in the front seat, half frozen from my dash across the Sand Pond. Wet to my shorts from fording its narrow neck. I pressed my hands to the seat beneath me.

"Sorry, sir," I mumbled.

"It'll dry," he replied calmly enough but quickly enough, too, to let me know he had noticed. "How bad's your daddy hit?"

"Looked like a shoulder."

"Not a gut shot or anything?"

"No, sir, not that I could see. But it looked to be some blood."

Dave settled back with that information as if calculating the futures on a very narrow market.

"Turpentine." He shook his head finally. "God-awful way for a man to make a living."

"Yes, sir."

"I'm surprised Tink got into the business. Aren't the mills doing well?"

"Yessir. Far as I know."

"Be better off investing than messing with turpentine. Who's he got working?"

"Men with families, mostly," I replied.

"I can remember when they used convicts," Dave said with just the ghost of a smile. "Leased 'em from the state like cattle. Five cents a day. Crime working a man for five cents a day."

"But they were convicts, weren't they, sir? I mean—in jail they wouldn't be earning anything."

Dave regarded me a moment. "You think paying a bad man a nickel a day makes you better than paying a good man a nickel an hour? That what they're teaching you in that college?"

I didn't know Dave knew I *was* in college. My whole body shivered once, violently. He reached for a knob on the dash.

"Heater," he explained. "Comes standard."

In less than thirty minutes we glided past Laureate's First Baptist Church. A minute later Dave flooded Doc West's porch with his lights.

Doc opened sleepily to our assault on his door.

"Dave," he said, blinking. And then, "Carter. Well, I'll be damned."

I blurted out a quick summary of Tink's situation.

"Wait here. I'll get my bag."

Couldn't have taken a minute to tell Doc what I needed, but when I turned around to thank Dave—

He was gone. I saw the Packard purring up the street, its headlamps pulling Dave into a pale tunnel with their great long arms.

"I'm ready." Doc broke my reverie.

It took just over an hour and fifteen minutes to get Dave, get to town, get Doc roused and back to the house. Spence and Eida Mae by now held vigil with Mother. They withdrew wordlessly as Doc rushed in, making room beside Tink at the fireplace.

His face was as gray as fine ash, all the ruddy exposure and complexion drained as if life itself were being sucked into the red stain that kept growing like a cancer beneath his shoulder.

"How bad is it?" I asked Doc.

"It's nicked an artery," he answered, not at all confidently. "I don't think direct pressure will staunch it. Can't tourniquet this high, and even if we could I'd be worried about gangrene."

Gangrene. Rotting flesh. Blood poisoning. Not until World War II would the world know about penicillin.

"What did you bring?" my mother asked.

Doc shrugged his shoulders.

"Some catgut. Instruments. Hydrogen peroxide and bandages, of course."

"Can you clamp the artery and stitch it?" Tink asked.

"I did once or twice during the war," Doc said grimly. "But I ain't a real doctor, Tink. You know that."

Doc West was our pharmacist. The nearest thing to a surgeon was more than a half day's drive away. My father's life lay in the hands of a man who ran the town's drugstore.

"It's a clean wound." My mother broke the silence.

"'Pears to be." Doc ran a rough tongue over his lips.

"You have any morphine in that bag? Or some laudanum?"

Doc looked at my mother in astonishment. "What do you have in mind, Martha?"

"We can cauterize the artery," my mother said.

"Oh, God," Doc paled. "I don't know."

"Don't seem to me we have a lot of choice." My father could have been speaking of someone else.

"Don't know I have anything in my bag that we can use to..."

"Rifle rod," Martha interrupted him. "Tink has one in his kit. Carter—"

"I'll get it."

By the time I came back with Tink's gun-cleaning kit, Doc had Daddy prone before the fire and was giving him a shot of morphine.

Martha had set up a pair of tubs and gathered every clean towel in the house. Water was already well heated from the kettle she always kept in the fireplace.

"Give me the rod, Carter."

It was a brass rod, shorter it seems now to me than a yardstick. There was a slot in one end of the rod, a notch to accommodate a piece of rag or silk used to clean the barrels of his weapons. Mother fished the rod into a bed of red-hot coals.

"How you doin', Tink?" Doc was washing his hands.

"Don't give a shit if syrup goes to a dollar a sop."

"That's good. You just relax. Martha?"

"Take a few minutes."

"Carter, wash your hands. Then have another syringe ready for me. Just in case we need it."

"I have a drink?"

This request from Tink.

"'Spose, if I was a doctor, I'd say not. But hell yes, drink one. Drink one for me while you're at it."

My mother poured a good shot of bourbon into a broken coffee mug and, as the brass rod heated in its bed of coals, cradled my father's head in her lap and nursed him, sip by sip, with a cup of whiskey.

It seemed to take forever for that rod to glow white enough for my mother to say, "we're ready."

"Don't take your time." Daddy offered it as a joke.

Martha smiled as if it *were* a joke. Just as if this were no more than a splinter she was taking from his hand.

Doc looked at her. "I've not done this before."

"I have."

She said it as if she had expected all along to be the one to bear this burden.

"Carter, you'll need to help Doc keep him still."

"Can I have another drink first?"

"Surely," mother replied and in the instant purchased with that promise pulled the rifle rod from its glowing bed and plunged it without pause swiftly, surely, through my father's shoulder, through his wound, and out the back.

He screamed once. A high, long scream of surprise and pain. He bucked like a madman in our arms. But only briefly.

"He's passed out," Doc croaked.

"Hold him still," Mother said in a voice belayed of pity. "He needs another."

Doc left us that night with supplies of dressing and laudanum, giving careful instructions on how to clean Tink's wound and detailing what signs of pus or inflammation ought to cause concern.

"What are his chances?" I asked Doc when we got out of ear-shot from my mother.

"Most men die," he answered simply. And then, offering grudging hope— "The bleeding's stopped. For now. And it is a clean wound."

I spent the rest of my Christmas vacation tending my father or spelling my mother, who was tending my father. The laudanum helped greatly. Spence was a help too, taking care of chores around the house that Mother was too distracted and I too clumsy to do.

Taff came by. Told Daddy everything was just fine, yessir, couldn't be better. Tink groaned from his bed when Taff was gone.

"Be a miracle anything's left of those mills time I get back. And speaking of miracles—" Tink turned abruptly to me. "That was a quick trip you made. Getting Doc out here."

"How would you know, you old coot?" Mother intervened smoothly.

"I had my Hamilton." Tink thumbed the stem of his jeweled timepiece in proof.

"Not a mule in the world can make a watch run fast, Tink," Mother said. "And you weren't in any kind of shape to be tellin' time, I can warrant you that."

"Well," Tink let it go. "I guess I wasn't altogether in my right mind. Maybe I'm still not—hiring the likes of Taff Calhoun."

"You've got Joe and Mac looking after him. Anyway, Taff can't ruin you in a single month." Mother's head almost brushed the ceiling as she rose from his bed. "And a month's all he's got 'cause after that I'm going to kick you out of the house. You old coot."

Tink turned to me with a slow wink.

"Don't never get on your back with a wife, Carter. You do, they'll take advantage ever' time."

It had been nearly a week since the shooting. By that time Mother and I had dragged every scrap of information we could get from my father. It wasn't much.

"I was riding home from the Rosewood mill," Tink told us. "I had to go around that slough there on the roadside—it was filled up with water. Next thing I know somethin' hits me in the shoulder like a baseball bat."

"Think it was a turpentiner?"

"Who told you that?"

I tried to shrug it off. "Been all this talk about the wars and all."

Tink looked at me a moment before he nodded.

"Been some up in Taylor County. Down south too, but not on my stumpage."

"Guess we'll never know." I was trying to get off the subject.

"Oh, we'll know." Tink grimaced with his own short laugh. "Man did this ain't gonna keep quiet," he went on. "Man did this is gonna brag."

"He does, I'll tell the sheriff," I declared.

"You won't have to." Tink shook his head. "I'll done have killed him."

Mother's hands fluttered in her lap. Here was her husband still bedridden, and already anticipating the braggart's crow that would send him straight into the iron sights of some backshooter's rifle.

"You want to get well before you go off man-huntin,'" Martha chided as gently as she could.

"I'm well enough," Tink replied roughly. "Goddamn, how much does it take to pull a trigger?"

I was reluctant to return to Emory-at-Oxford, leaving Tink's health uncertain. But mother insisted I leave and Tink demanded it.

"If you'd been a sawbones I'd already be up and about." Tink framed his ambition in an attempt at humor.

I could not then tell my father that my ambition was to name an unnamed flower.

"Yessir," I assented.

I had to run an errand before I left for the Live Oak station. A short trip into town for staples and medical necessaries from Doc's apothecary.

I was glad this time to have the truck. Forty minutes after leaving my front porch I pulled up to Doc West's Pharmacy. The drugstore was on Main Street, a block down from Land's Hardware, directly across the street from the courthouse.

Chapter nine

Rain-Lily,
Zephyranthes atamasco

Doc got a good bit of traffic from the courthouse. People would drop by after tending to their taxes or buying their hunting licenses. There was no fishing license required yet, as I recall. Surely none that was enforced.

This being a Saturday, I expected to find some customers at Doc's store. In fact, I hoped to see a sampling of my old schoolmates, maybe a girl now married, or pregnant—some boy now taking his daddy's farm or sharecropping a few acres of sandy loam set beside a shack.

"What you up to, Carter?" they would ask.

"Aw, just school," I'd reply with the affectation of modesty.

"Thought you was way out of school."

"Not high school. The university." I would supply that information hiding every hint of condescension. "Emory. Oxford campus."

Problem with my scenario was, first, no one would know

anything about Emory, or any other university for that matter, and second, there was not one customer inside Doc's store.

The place was empty as a poor man's purse. Except for Doc, of course. He was minding the pharmaceuticals, which ran the entire back length of the store, half hidden behind a barricade of pills and liquors that, catching the early morning sun, sprayed its fractured light in lacquers of red and green and amber across the polished pinewood floor.

I was reminded of bleach bottles, for some reason, broken at the neck, splintering an amber sun across white sand ruled like school paper.

"Carter. Morning." Doc's greeting interrupted that association. "Got your daddy's fixings all wrapped up."

"Mind if I work on a Coke first?"

"Hmm? Oh, no! No, set yourself at the counter. I'll be right over."

Doc's soda fountain had about every kind of ice cream and licorice and soda water you could want set up beside combs and brushes and mirrors, things of that nature. You could buy cigarettes, of course, Lucky Strikes and Chesterfields if you liked ready-made— Prince Albert and papers if you rolled your own. A potbellied stove heated the place in winter. An oscillating fan gathered dust in this season above a General Electric radio whose vacuum tubes glowed constantly to bring the latest music and news.

"Waltzing Matilda" gave way as I reached the fountain to yet another news story analyzing the man accused of kidnapping and murdering Charles Lindbergh's infant son. Folks who now wring their hands over our newly found national obsession with high-profile crimes and criminals clearly weren't around during the four *years* it took to find, try, and execute Bruno Hauptmann.

"Think I'll have a cherry with that Coke," I told Doc.

"Sounds nice." A voice behind me seconded the motion. "Think I'll have one too."

It was Julia.

"'Lo, Carter."

"Julia. Have a seat. Stool, rather."

She laughed at that and swung in beside me. Our thighs brushed through their winter protection. I was taken unawares. My last vision of Julia had her in a clinging shift on her veranda. She settled beside me now in a blouse too thin for winter that collared high above a narrow waist and long gray skirt. Russet hair tossed casually back over those wide shoulders.

Her eyes, wide as a deer's in that plain face, looked *down* to meet my own, and I realized that Julia had grown taller than I. Not so tall as my mother, no, but tall enough. How else had she grown? I reconnoitered the high-collared top as casually as I could. No buttons unfastened on this occasion, but yes, something more than a ball of twine now tightened the fabric above her small, firm waist.

"Make that two cherry Cokes," I told Doc.

"Coming up."

"How's your father?" She ran a hand through her hair, and I saw in that small moment something discolored on her skin. Deep and blue. The hair fell back. It was gone.

"Your father, Carter? How is he?"

"Hmm? Oh, fine, fine. Thanks again for your help."

"That was Papa."

"Thanks to him, then."

"You've thanked him aplenty, Carter. When are you going back to school?"

"Taking the train tomorrow," I replied, pleased that she knew I was attending the university.

"I am too," Julia replied modestly. "Leaving, that is, tomorrow. By car. Not the train."

"Leaving for where?" I ignored the carbonated drinks fizzing on the counter.

"Why—Florida State College for Women."

I didn't know Julia was attending college at all. "Majoring in education," Julia replied to my somewhat incoherent queries. "I'd like to finish all four years, but you can teach with two."

"You want to teach?"

"Oh, yes!" she said, and her eyes shone like jade.

"I've been out of touch," I apologized.

She greeted that observation with a peal of laughter. *"That's an understatement!"*

"Well, fill me in. Where's Harvey Buchanan?"

"Don't you know what's happened to your own cousin, Carter?"

"No idea."

"Harvey married. Some girl in Suwannee County."

"Pity her. How about Tommy Spikes?"

"He joined the army."

"The army? What for?"

"Used to be a Southern tradition, Carter. Joining the military."

"Still fighting the Civil War?" I grinned.

"Or making up for it." She winked. "If it wasn't for Deserters' Island, you and I and most of our kin would never have been conceived."

Probably true. A fair proportion of the county's orginal population did not share the usual Southern enthusiasm for horse and arms. Young men, or old men, for that matter, who didn't like the idea of being shredded by cannon, or dying of gangrene, or shitting themselves to death with dysentery found sanctuary on Deserters' Island, a place that was not an island, that was in reality no more than a mound of land not far from where my father encountered his hurricane near Dead Man's Bay.

Some of Laureate's most prosperous families could, had they wished (which they did not), trace their family line to Deserters' Island.

"And it didn't end with the Civil War," I pointed out. "You think Ed Land ever served a day in Flanders fields? Or Leroy Sessions?"

"Why get yourself killed when you can stay home and turn a profit?" Julia chuckled outrage over her cherry Coke.

We talked for an hour. Julia was animated and abandoned as I had never seen her, commenting on everything from politics to academic life, filling me in on local gossip, sketching for me the fates and aspirations of a dozen or so classmates with whom we had once parsed verbs and played kickball.

I listened, absolutely ambushed with enchantment, taken with her voice, her hair, the cadence of her movement. I was reminded again of stringhorses and one-room schools. Of a cloakroom where, Julia reminded me, I had once helped her off with her wrap. It was startling for me to realize how separated I had become from all that was once familiar.

"Don't you remember, *anything?*" she finally asked in mock exasperation.

"Oh, yes!" My first lie, like all others, was not intended to injure.

"No, you don't." She smiled sweetly. "But that's all right."

"Would you like another soda?" I asked, my own throat suddenly gone dry.

"Sweet o' you to ask. B'lieve I will."

It was not Julia's voice that answered my timid proposal. This was a gruff voice. A grown, callous, too-much used voice.

I turned around.

"Well, what about it, boy? You buyin' or aren't ya?"

A large man filled up Doc's door frame. I could not make out his face at first, buried as it was beneath the wide brim of a filthy hat. He wore dungarees over long Johns. Some kind of ratted wool coat that dragged the floor next to scuffed, square-toed boots. He was loose-boned. Had a bloated face with patches of beard. A straight white corridor ran underneath that beard, like a road beneath a power line.

"What's the matter, boy?" Stanton Lee Sullivan smiled, and I could see the rot of his teeth. "Cat got your tongue?"

I'd never seen Stanton Lee in my life. He was, for me, a kind of bogeyman. A myth. But I knew for certain that this man was Tarrant Sullivan's brother.

"Have a seat if you're going to, Stanton Lee," Doc said sternly. "I'll hold you good for a drink."

"That's the spirit, Doc. Christmas spirit, even if it is a tad late."

He settled over a stool, legs bowed out. The coat spread wide to display the bowie knife and pistol protruding defiantly from a cowhide belt.

"Heard your daddy had hisself an accident," Stanton Lee chortled without preamble.

I was slow to find his meaning.

"He's going to be fine," Doc said quietly, pushing a cola in the big man's direction.

"Heard he was shot." Stanton Lee slurped his drink.

"Shot," I finally managed to say. "But he's getting better."

"Shit," Stanton Lee's reply seemed at first perfectly ambiguous. He drained the Coke at a gulp, and then—"Serves him right. Messin' with other people's business."

"What business?" I asked. "You mean the turpentine?"

"Turpentine?"

Sullivan rotated slowly on the stool to face me squarely. A grin spread to split his face like a jack-o'-lantern.

"Turpentine—is that whut he tole you? Some crazy, coon-ass turpentiner got the drop on Mister Tink Buck-an-an?"

"Nobody's said anything," I noticed Doc West's jaw was rigid as iron. "Not till now, anyway."

Stanton Lee turned with a snarl to the Doc. "You don' want to get in the middle o' this."

"Not in the middle of anything, Stanton Lee. Man gets hurt I try to help him. Might be you one day."

The snarl turned into something I'd have to describe as a laugh. It started in Sullivan's loose gut, made its way at leisure up his broad chest and out his fetid mouth.

"Ain't nobody gonna get the drop on Stanton Lee. I got two good eyes. And *two* good ears."

He swept the glass that held his Coke onto the floor. Tiny glass crystals now shattered the morning light. Stanton Lee rose from his stool and headed for me.

I still don't know how I got to my feet.

"You tell your daddy," his breath stank, "that it watn't no goddamn turpentiner shot his sorry ass."

I wanted to say something brave. I wanted to say, "Fuck you!" or at least, "Tell him yourself."

But I didn't say anything.

I was a rabbit charmed before a rattlesnake. Waiting for Stanton Lee to do ... whatever he wanted to do.

"I don't think you ought to be bragging, Mr. Sullivan."

It was Julia who stood up to the bastard.

Stanton Lee turned amazed to this source of challenge.

"Papa said if Mr. Buchanan can be shot by a coward, anybody can." Julia was sheetrock white, but her voice was steady. "He said the county should think about putting out a bounty."

That brought a gleam of enthusiasm to Stanton Lee's wide-set eyes.

"Bounty? A bounty! You mean to tell me Stanton Lee's gonna have a price on his head!" He hooted delight and derision. "Goddamn, a reg'lar Bonnie and Clyde!"

"You finished, Stanton Lee?" Doc kept his hands on top of the counter.

"You'll be the first t' know," Sullivan growled. Then he heaved off his stool, turned back to me.

"Tell your daddy I'll be seein' him."

He pirouetted slowly toward the door, his full-length coat spreading wide at the bottom like a tepee, and sauntered out onto the street. For a while I remained frozen at my stool. I was no longer the confident student from Emory-at-Oxford. I was just a boy, barely eighteen, scared to death and not thinking straight. Not thinking at all.

"I better go tell Daddy," I stammered.

"No, you hadn't." Doc West spoke with authority.

"Sir?"

"Carter, if you go tell your daddy it was Stanton Lee shot him, what do you think Tink is going to do? Or—*try* to do?"

I knew, of course. Tink would gather his revolver and his carbine, pocket his well-used brass knuckles, and then go hunting.

"We're the only ones who know," Doc said. "For now let's just keep it that way."

"Yes, sir." I nodded vigorously.

"Are you going to be all right?" Julia reached out to me.

"I'm fine," I said as I pulled away.

"Carter—?"

I staggered to the door, my legs like lead beneath me. Tears came unbidden as I stumbled down the street. I was embarrassed. Frightened. But most of all ashamed. I left behind the cache of medicals that was to have been my reason for stopping by the drugstore.

Later that day Doc would bring them out to the house.

Chapter ten

Bog Bachelor's Button,
Polygala lutea

W hen I returned to Emory-at-Oxford in the winter quarter of 1937 it was not obvious to anyone except to Dr. Keaton that the world was drifting to war. The big news in '37 revolved around another flyer, a woman: Amelia Earhart seeking to round the globe in her silver aeroplane was lost at sea. Only slightly less spectacular was the explosion of the *Hindenburg* over New Jersey. Aside from those sensational stories people scanned the paper, as they do now, mostly for sports and entertainment.

The Washington Redskins and the New York Yankees dominated their professional arenas in 1937. Clinton Frank, the rugged footballer from Yale, won the Heisman. Walter Young won the Boston Marathon in the still respectable time of two hours, thirty-three minutes, and twenty seconds. Walt Disney released *Snow White and the Seven Dwarfs,* and Spencer Tracy won an Academy Award for best actor in *Captains Courageous.*

There were rumblings of things more ominous, of course, some of them quite recent. Even the year before, when my classmates and I cheered the newsreels documenting Jesse Owens's Olympic triumph over Hitler's Aryan pride, we should have seen that gold medals and world records were not the only things at stake in that contest of ancients. When we now read in our newspapers that Italy had invaded Ethiopia, or that Britain had announced the production of gas masks for every single one of her citizens, we young scholars would have been wise to pay more serious attention.

And as for those disturbing reports concerning the treatment of European Jewry—well, Lord, that had been going on forever, hadn't it?

"Over there's them, over here's us." My father's crude summary of his interest in foreign intrigue was not substantially different from my classmates', or the nation's. We had problems enough at home. All through 1937 and then 1938 and '39 we gathered round our radios to hear FDR's soothing reassurance that America would prosper, that America would remain at peace, that the only thing Americans need fear was fear itself.

The wireless had replaced the fireplace as the hearth about which Americans took such comfort. And after our president's nasal, aristocratic encouragement we'd remain beside our Philcos or West-inghouses to sing along with tunes such as "Jeepers Creepers," or "Flat Foot Floogie with a Floy Floy." Maybe "God Bless America."

I loved the radio serials. I was digesting botany and anatomy and Milankovitch's hypothesis along with "The Thin Man," "The Green Hornet," and "The Phantom." Orson Welles was a precocious talent; his adaptation of "War of the Worlds" in 1938 caused a national panic and earned him a standing ovation from the men of Emory-at-Oxford. "The Shadow" left you in goosebumps. Or if you wanted a laugh there was "Amos and Andy," a comedy whose stereotypes were not yet perceived as bigoted.

Emory's professors did as much as they could to engage students in the larger affairs of the world. Dr. Aenid certainly engaged me. But I had several pressures in addition to the usual ones that encouraged myopia. I was first of all pursuing a curriculum in stealth, substituting courses in botany and horticulture for courses necessary to a medical occupation. I was chronically short of money. And, finally, I was writing Dave Ogilvie's daughter.

Actually, I should say I was responding to letters that Julia sent from my first week back at school. The first one, I've saved them all, was very short:

> Carter,
> I know you'll be pressed with studies, please feel no need to reply to this letter, but I wanted you to know how much I enjoyed our visit at Doc's drugstore. The cherry Coke and conversation were very much something I needed at the time—I'm not so courageous, you see, as I let on.
> Mother tells me that she saw *your* mother briefly in town two weeks ago and that your father is recovering extremely well from his brutal wound.
> I will pray for his continued recovery, and your continued health—
> Julia

Characteristically there was no mention in this missive of Julia's pursuits or accomplishments. Getting that kind of information, I was to discover, was harder than pulling hens' teeth. Julia, for instance, made the dean's list every term at FSCW, a distinction I couldn't claim from my own institution. She was working at a newspaper, part time, and was tutoring youngsters in a downtown church. "Their schools are not sufficient," she wrote me once. "Most of these children cannot even read." It took another couple of letters for me to realize that the children Julia was leading to literacy were black.

I got that first letter in 1937. Received my last one in December of '39. During that time Julia and I never saw each other.

We both had to work to pay for our schooling. Holidays with our families were rare and never coordinated, and summers were spent at occupations that, praise God, were not related to the stringhorse or the tobacco field.

Julia's newspaper gave her full-time employment between terms. I took jobs over holidays so that I could spend summers with Dr. Aenid. Tink thought I was earning cash during these summer occupations. I wasn't.

In the fall of 1938 I relocated from Emory-at-Oxford to the larger, more settled campus in Atlanta. Emory to this day does not provide a four-year curriculum at its Oxford or Valdosta extensions. Once you finish your sophomore year at either of those colleges you have to complete your degree, if from Emory, at her Atlanta campus.

I chose Atlanta because of Dr. Aenid. Dr. Aenid approached me during my final term at the Oxford campus to tell me he'd been invited to join Emory's faculty at Atlanta. He asked if I'd be interested in pursuing some long-term experiments in hybridization there. "I won't be able to pay you," he warned. "But you can live in the dorm and eat free at the cafeteria. You'll be my research assistant."

That sounded like hog heaven to me, and so in the fall of '38 I took a westbound train from Covington forty miles to Atlanta. Atlanta was a large, breathlessly busy place. There were libraries and museums and architecture. I discovered salons and cold beer in Atlanta, and movie houses, voluptuous palaces in which to linger on Colbert or Cagney, Marlene Dietrich or Humphrey Bogart.

If radio provided the hearth around which families might congregate in those years, the cinema provided a Caligari cabinet where, cloaked in darkness, your imagination ran riot in solitary privacy. All the movie houses were characterized by an architecture and decor too outrageous to be called baroque. It was like being inside a Greek vase swarming with intimations of sex, scrolled columns and half-glimpsed satyrs peeking from behind pods of grapes and seashells.

My favorite houses were the Rialto and the Fox. The Fox particularly made an impression, the long, gracious stair working up a whole story to the mezzanine. Music introduced feature films in those years, a holdover from silent flicks. I will never forget the first time I saw the Fox's organ, lifting like an enormous erection from the orchestra pit, filling that house with Bach or Beethoven or some other classical arrangement.

I loved the movies, but I loved work even more. Not that work was always a place of magic. "Research assistant" was an impressive title, but sometimes it meant following a mule and plow. Sometimes it meant cutting crossties to make a rooting bed for aerial propagation. My favorite chores took me to the greenhouse. Here, in a miniature Eden, I saw developing hybrids of everything from azaleas to slash pine. We had a new strain of cotton showing promise in that greenhouse. Even a tarless tobacco!

It was amazing to see evolution short-circuited. To see varieties of life developed in months that, left to Eden's own design, might, if created at all, take millennia. Modern geneticists smile benignly on those first crude experiments. But I imagined myself a new Adam directing Creation toward a garden not yet named.

I benefited hugely from my Emory experience. But in some ways, ways I only began to face much later, I did not learn all that I should.

An instance will illustrate. The incident occurred the term before I left my Oxford campus. It was the dead of winter, I'm certain of that, and certain too that I was dead broke. In addition to my summer labors at Oxford, I received a stipend for tutoring, worked in the cafeteria, and slopped hogs, but an ambitious project in the greenhouse left me strapped.

I was not at first overly concerned. I'd just write Daddy and ask him to sell a few hogs or some extra timber. I penned a letter to that effect, sent it home. I got a letter back from my mother. I still have that labored correspondence.

> Dearst Carter,
> I am surtan you did not send your papa for money with out considerd need. Even so Tink has calclated your stay at collige to cost him so far in xces of a thowsan dollars. That is more by a long shot than he ever

rekoned it would take to get you threw your schooling and it comes when just now it is hard for your daddy to spare any cash at all.

Tink has the chance to take over a fare peece of grownd. It will cost him a kings ransum but he is determin to do it. We are eating deer meet killed out of season and fish out of the lake, just so you no, hording cash since the people running the bank refews to lind your daddy a dime toward his purpos.

I do not wont you to think your father does not love you, son, but this propertee hes after is taking all his time, all of his strinth and for right now all his ernings.

I have sent you three dollars and fifty cints matress money and I have not showed your letter to your daddy.

Please do not make me giv your letter to Tink as I'm fearfull with his present mind he might deecide to pull you out of school all together.

We love you,

P.S. Don't think hard of papa. It's the land. He cant think of anything else.

She signed this remarkable correspondence, "Your Mother." I had always known that whatever ambition I had or was assigned would be secondary to my father's desire for land. I was certain I knew what particular plot of dirt it was whose owner my mother was so careful not to mention.

But in the short run I didn't care. Having obtained and spent all of the financial aid that Emory officially provided, I feared I might be kicked out of school for debt. I finally confessed my penury to Dr. Aenid. He graciously assured me that mine was not an unusual (let alone shameful) situation, that I would not be dismissed, and that I was right to ask for help. "I'll look into it," he said.

The next day Dr. Aenid took me aside to say that a loan might be obtained through the head of Emory's maintenance department.

"Who do I talk to?" I asked.

"'*To whom* shall I speak,'" Aenid corrected me first. "Just ask for Billy Mitchell. Anybody can take you."

I thought I was being sent to an army aviator to seek a loan. I took a handwritten note as bona fides from my professor and went down to the back side of the campus where a spread of sheds kept everything you'd need to patch, plumb, or weld a small city.

The wind blew steady and wet from the north. The thermometer was indicating less than thirty degrees Fahrenheit above a column of mercury that seemed to drop as you looked. I didn't own any gloves at the time so I stuffed my paws into the thin pockets of my cotton jacket and made a beeline for the only open door I could see. Figured that was as good a way to get to the head of maintenance as any.

Inside, the odor of manure mixed with gasoline and iron and old hay. Tools were hung from pegs all over one wall. Lumber stacked to the rear. Parts of machines scattered about. Oxford's maintenance department did not use trucks or gasoline-powered conveyances of any kind. So you'd see a coffee grinder needed fixing, or a sewing machine. Part of a cotton gin, perhaps. A variety of farm implements.

Only one man working, though, a black man, old as cypress, bent at the hip in soiled bib overalls over a mule's harness. He had the harness propped in the rear of a wagon, using the wagon's bed for a workbench. A hane was torn, the strap that mates the harness's trace to its collar.

"Dr. Aenid told me to see the head of maintenance," I announced loudly, producing as I did so my crumpled piece of paper.

He didn't even turn his head. Just kept on. "Billy Mitchell," I said again, freezing cold and irritated. "Dr. Aenid sent me."

Still no response.

"See here, Uncle, I've been sent to Mr. Mitchell," I declared sharply.

A long moment passed before the old fellah pulled himself up from the place of his labor. He looked even older facing the light, his face seamed with countless rivulets, his teeth a broken row of ivory, his gums bright and scarlet inside a black, black face.

He regarded me steadily, amused it seemed to me behind a pair of calm brown eyes.

"You-all enna hurry?" the old man asked.

There was no "mister" here. No deference.

I raised my piece of paper.

"Dr. Aenid sent me."

"Didn't axe who sent you. Axed if you was in a hurry."

I felt my face going scarlet.

"You see," the old man laid down his knife and awl and wiped his hands on his overalls, "most people come in here, they real polite. But you, now, you come in here interruptin' a man at work. Don't even make a proper announcement. Don't even give out yo' name— that sound right to you?"

"Maybe you better just get me to Mr. Mitchell." I could hear my voice shaking.

"I'm Billy Mitchell," the old man said as calmly as could be. "An' you don't require no paper; Virgil done tole' me whatchu need."

Virgil?

Then the old man reached into a pocket big as a marsupial's pouch stitched over his chest. A faint alarm sounded somewhere. I backed away and felt my foot catch on a piece of lumber. I stumbled.

"Where you goin', Mr. Buchanan?"

Not Mr. Carter—Mr. *Buchanan*! Never had a black man or woman addressed me so! He strolled up to me. A wallet opened in those black hands. A slew of wrinkled bills molded inside. He wet his thumb, carefully selected what seemed a bushel.

"One hundred twenty dollahs," he said as he placed the money in my hand.

"I think I'm supposed to get a loan," I finally stammered. "Or something."

"Or somethin' is whatchu got," Mr. Mitchell told me quietly and headed back to his work.

I felt a rage such as I had never felt before. But I had sensed it before, felt the edge of it somewhere secondhand before. But where? When?

I saw a cross burning in my mind's eye, a pine-tarred cross blazing distantly at the edge of my father's land. But I was not one of those people beneath that crucifix! With sheets and cocked rifles. Bootleg whiskey. I was not such as those!

"Come around next week or two." Billy Mitchell was back to his harness. "I'll find some way to let you work that off."

I did not even give the man the courtesy of a reply.

After I took my light jacket and cardboard suitcase to Atlanta, I seldom thought about Billy Mitchell. In fact, I seldom thought about anything not related to my new role as student researcher. Dr. Aenid was familiar with my tendency toward narrow horizons and enrolled me in classes outside biology to broaden it. A seminar of what was called the New Physics exposed me to Einstein's Special and General Theories of Relativity. Max Planck and Niels Bohr were inventing something called quantum mechanics. There was even some crazy Italian who would soon split the atom!

It seemed pointless to me. Who could guess what might come of such ephemeral, disinterested inquiries into nature?

And if I was dim to perceive the consequences flowing from the pursuit of physics, I was opaque to consequences flowing from the entanglements of principalities overseas. "BRITAIN AND FRANCE DECLARE WAR ON GERMANY"—had to be the corker for 1939, but like the character in Hemingway's story, I lived in the movies.

Gone with the Wind was my favorite; I saw the first screening not a half mile from the railyard that David O. Selznick and Tecumseh Sherman made famous. I wallowed in that moving picture, embracing Rhett and Scarlett as hero and heroine of a noble South.

Clearly there remained gaps in my education. And they were

not yet filled when, in early January of 1940, being only a single quarter short of completing my baccalaureate, Tink called me home.

Chapter eleven

Cupid's Shaving Brush, *Emilia fosbergii*

The summons came by telegraph: "NEED YOU HERE LAND AT STAKE STOP RIGHT AWAY TINK STOP." There was no recourse. I needed something over a thousand dollars to settle my debts and pay the tuition and fees necessary to complete my last quarter at Emory. With every scrap of work and loan available I couldn't come up with that kind of money. Even if I could, it would have been impossible to refuse my father's urgent request for help. Though I had no idea what Tink could possibly need me *for*.

I packed and made ready to leave. Dr. Aenid drove me from Druid Hills to the Atlanta train station.

"Here," Aenid said after I was satisfied that my tickets and luggage were in order.

It was the fragment of a leaf, not much bigger than my thumb, an ancient artifact of fern preserved a hundred million years inside a dollop of amber.

"It will always be there for you, Carter." Dr. Aenid looked me in the eye. "It's never too late to finish."

I took the train south to Jacksonville. Then west and south back to Live Oak. When people think of January in Florida they generally have visions of palm trees and Holiday Inns. Of beaches and mild temperatures. But January in northern Florida, particularly away from the coast, can be bitterly cold. The wind doesn't come out of the south for another two months, generally, and the temperatures, influenced by masses of cold Canadian air, combine with the region's humidity to make things pretty miserable.

Today was not a day like that. The wind was still. The sun was high in a sky so blue it hurt your eyes. I saw lots of farmland coming home. Near Live Oak I saw a farmer working alongside a boy, pulling cheesecloth over a tobacco bed.

I saw fields being broken for cotton and corn. Saw a good bit of pasture. A dairy or two. The cultivated land brought aromas of damp earth and fecundity into my Pullman car. The terrain was tame, pleasant, easy on the eye; it made me realize how much I missed the tangle and wild of flatwoods and timber. I liked a certain degree of chaos in landscape, I realized, a ballast to the order I otherwise sought. I liked to see riots of unscheduled growth. I liked trees. I'd heard how glorious the original forests were along the East Coast, in Pennsylvania (. . . sylvan . . . sylvania .. . Through a place of forests? I'd have to ask Dr. Aenid) or New England. The terrain bordering Live Oak's station offered mostly water oak and scrub. A pair of dogwood trees off the tracks would bloom nicely come spring. And someone years ago had planted a tree not common to that region, a sugar maple *(Acer saccharum)* that had taken root right beside the station, had survived, and was now resting, waiting for the leaves that would return in just a few short weeks to give the tree nourishment and sustain life.

What triggered new growth in the spring? I wondered. What caused the maple's glorious, autumnal transformation? Something else left unfinished.

Tink arrived within the half hour. He wore his woodsman's attire, khakis and Stetson hat with only a light jacket to break the morning's chill. He was walking well and had good color, but his right arm was constricted in movement, a consequence of the bullet wound.

"Son. Sorry to pull you out so sudden." He took my bag instead of offering me his hand.

"It's all right," I said, even though it wasn't.

"I 'spect you're a mite disappointed."

"Was close to finishing is all."

"You'll finish." He bobbed his head toward the truck. "This here's just a hitch in yer git-along."

"How much of a hitch?"

"Year about. Then you can go on back and get ready for doctoring."

"If I can find a way to pay for it." I fished for sympathy, still pretending my father's ambition was my own.

"This year goes right, you won't never have to worry about money. Not never again."

"Telegraph said something about land," I said as we headed for the truck.

"That's right."

"What land? Whose land?"

"Good land," he glowered. *"Our* land."

So Tink confirmed what I already knew, that the land for which he had ransomed his future, and mine, belonged to Dave Ogilvie. What other piece of property could prompt such a desperate dash for possession? It was the land that held Tink's birthright hostage without hope, but it lay now within his grasp.

"How can that be?" I asked as we began our long drive home. "Dave's rich, for crying out loud! He can buy and sell us twice over."

"Not no more. Sugarcane?"

He offered me a sweet length.

"No, thank you," I declined.

Tink eyed me briefly. "Don't sulk, Carter, that's a woman's way. You're mad, tell me so. I been mad at before. Been mad *with* a time or two."

"I just don't want to quit school over a dream."

I waited for Tink to explode. He didn't.

"Year ago it would've been a dream," Tink responded mildly. "Dave Ogilvie wouldn't part with that property on any terms. 'Specially to me. Hell, I'm sure Dave'd rather give his whole place away for a spit than see me buy my little part for a million dollars. But the dice is turned. He ain't gonna have no choice."

I learned that Dave Ogilvie, the man who had dodged the Great Fall of '29, was now hopelessly in debt. In debt to the feed store, to the hardware store. In danger of being in debt to the county for taxes and deeply in debt, ironically, to the bank he had once saved.

"Dave's got hisself in a tight, sure enough." Tink grinned at the thought. "And too broke to pay attention."

Roosevelt's New Deal had, to rummage the words of a contemporary journalist, done a great deal to clean up the damn deals made daily on Wall Street. But nothing can turn a bad investment into a good one, and Dave Ogilvie had speculated in the most mercurial of markets, buying and selling futures on the commodities market. Dave probably imagined himself a sophisticated trader. Who, after all, was better to judge the price of wheat and corn and pork bellies than a shrewd and successful agriculturist?

Dave staked his sucess on his ability to intuit the not-yet-known prices of grains and beef and pork. He bought shares in volumes much larger than common sense ought to have allowed, and he lost money. Then was exposed the deacon's tragic flaw, a secret urge to gamble, to throw the dice. Far from cutting his losses, Dave skirted the new bank regulations. He doubled his bets, threw good money after bad, buoyed in his race against fortune by the advice of brokers, lawyers, and middlemen whom he barely knew.

People nowadays feel free to throw money into an investment or business knowing that a variety of nets exist to break their fall. Make a bad decision, you can still keep your home, your car, at least part of a salary. Lawyers file for bankruptcy, debts are settled or forgiven, and life starts over. There were no such mechanisms extant during the Depression. It's bad enough to have things go south in good times; in 1940 it was devastating.

The Lord giveth and the Lord taketh away. Dave Ogilvie's portfolio, valued at something over two hundred thousand dollars in 1929, was by 1940 worthless. The Greeks spoke often of hubris, my recent education made me recall. And the makings of a tragedy seemed present here, a man in a high place who, too confident in his own abilities, was poised for a great fall.

"He's mortgaged to the bank for something like forty thousand." Cane juice ran down Tink's cheek as he supplied that information.

Forty *thousand dollars?*

"Dave's gonna have to have himself one hell of a year just to pay the interest," Tink went on.

"But Dave saved that bank, didn't he?" I was not yet willing to cheer the deacon's imminent fall from grace.

"I'm sure Leroy remembers," Tink allowed cryptically.

And I was sure Dave would remind Mr. Sessions of that time only nine years past when twenty thousand of the deacon's own dollars stopped a county of farmers crazy with fear and tub whiskey from emptying Leroy's stone-broke vault at the points of their guns.

"I can see Dave cutting a deal with Leroy that would take twenty thousand off what he owes," I mused. "But that would still leave him twenty in the red."

"Damn fortune for any man," Tink agreed. "Much less a farmer. Twenty thousand dollars, hell—you could buy every acre Dave's got."

Yes, you could. In addition to the one hundred forty acres that originally belonged to my grandfather, Dave had accumulated in rough numbers another nine hundred. A thousand acres of property. Land coming in plots that large was selling for anywhere from ten to twenty dollars an acre. So what was a thousand acres times ten dollars an acre? Or a thousand times twenty? You didn't have to be Spence MacGrue to cipher that one in your head.

"How much interest you figure Dave would need to service his mortgage?" I asked.

"Twenty-four hundred," Tink answered promptly, and I began to wonder where my father was getting his information.

"How much tobacco would it take to pay that off?" I asked.

"Biggest crop Dave ever made," Tink said tersely. "Biggest crop ever growed that I know of."

Tobacco had not yet displaced cotton and peanuts as the cash crop in Lafayette County, as it soon would. A farmer could expect to get fifteen or twenty cents a pound for flue-cured tobacco. A good harvest in the late '30s might average fifteen hundred pounds an acre, about half what you can get nowadays. Most fields were very small, one to three acres.

Labor, not land, restricted the size of cultivation. Tobacco isn't like soy or wheat; it requires endless hours of hand labor, and even at a quarter or fifty cents a day, labor was expensive.

Dave Ogilvie avoided paying farm hands when possible by bartering his children's labor. This was a common practice. Families of eight or ten children were not unusual. A man with eight children to lend out for handing and cropping and stringing could expect during his own harvest to get eight free hands from other families in return. Dave and Sarah, having only three surviving children and one of them crippled, were considered unlucky in this regard.

But Dave worked his three offspring as if they were a legion, raising each year eight, sometimes ten acres of tobacco. It took a toll on his family, especially Sarah. And it earned Dave a reputation for being a hard taskmaster. Dave didn't mind that reputation. His concern was for profit.

But not even Dave Ogilvie could count on twenty-four hundred dollars from ten acres of tobacco.

"He'll have to raise twenty acres just to make sure of the interest he owes the bank." It was obvious Tink had run these calculations far ahead of me. "I don't even know how he's gonna start. Where's he gonna git money for fertilizer? For seed? He's gonna need at least one extra barn, and even working his children to death he's gonna have to pay for labor. No way around it for a crop that big. Where's he gettin' the cash? He's so short of help he's not even plantin' peanuts."

Tink stared over the steering wheel, now almost talking to himself.

"Man that farms, he's awful vulnerable. Worms. Drought. One barn catches fire, it can kill you. Or a flood. Takes a lucky son of a bitch to get past all that and show a profit too. And I think Dave Ogilvie's luck has just about played out."

A flush of mallards skimmed low across the water, stayed low over a hedge of palmetto, and then circled back as if to strafe our truck.

"What are you planning to do, Daddy?"

"I'm going to buy Dave's mortgage," Tink replied.

It took a moment to sink in. His *mortgage?* It's very difficult in modern times for a transaction of this kind to occur, an individual buying a mortgage from a bank; a variety of statutes and regulations make it almost impossible. And even now, when a mortgage is transferred between institutions, from, say, one bank to another, the owner of the mortgaged property normally must give consent.

You could buy a man's mortgage in 1940. There was nothing in the terms of Dave Ogilvie's lien that tied Leroy Sessions's hands regarding its disposition. If Tink wanted to buy the mortgage and Leroy wanted to get rid of it, Dave Ogilvie would be powerless to prevent it. That was Tink's plan: to buy Dave's mortgage, and when the deacon missed a payment or two—to toss Dave out on his ass.

But the money required!

"You're talking about twenty thousand dollars!" I stammered.

"Forty," Tink amended calmly. "Leroy might cut Dave a deal; he ain't gonna cut me one. If I buy the mortgage it's got to be for the whole hog or nothing."

"We don't have forty thousand dollars!"

"We got twenty." Tink smiled as if I would be pleased to hear it. "Twenty thousand in cash."

Twenty *thousand* dollars? In *cash*? Here I had been reduced to slopping hogs and begging from darkies for food and board and books, and all the while my father had twenty thousand dollars!

My knuckles were white on my suitcase. Tink apparently didn't notice.

"Leroy ain't ready to sign it over just yet," he was going on. "I don't blame him; I can't walk in today and buy the note, after all, and who knows? Dave might call in a miracle or two this summer and pay off his interest. That's if you count on miracles . . .

"I ain't. Come the end of summer, when Dave's scratchin' for pennies I'm gonna be shoveling dollars. Then I'm going to walk into Leroy's office and buy that note, and there won't be a goddamn thing Dave Ogilvie can do to stop it."

Tink pulled himself another chew of cane from his jacket.

"Be interesting to see Dave turned out. See him shit in the woods with his boys. His girl."

My bones ached with a sudden chill.

"Forty thousand dollars." Tink repeated the sum serenely. "Which means that right now I'm only twenty short."

"Where are you going to get twenty thousand dollars?" I asked incredulously.

"We got us an opportunity, Carter." He pulled a legal-sized envelope from his jacket, a stiff manila envelope. "Showing Leroy tomorrow. You'll be there. Here—" he cut me off a chew of cane. "Don't you want some?"

I hesitated, remembered Julia on her porch. A tan of skin along a shoulder half bared from its cotton shift. Or in the drugstore. Her laugh, her smell, a cherry Coke.

"Carter?" My father extended me an inch of cane. "Have some?"

"Sure," I said, plucking the sweet, sticky cylinder he offered. "Why not?"

Chapter twelve

Hog Plum,
Ximenia americana

The exact nature of my father's opportunity would not be discussed until we met Leroy Sessions the next day at the bank. Tink and I arrived home the night before tired, stiff, and in my case constipated. Mother, beyond a brief embrace for us both and a homemade laxative for me, had little to say.

Next morning I shivered and shaved beside my father on a back porch open to whatever weather was in season. We relieved ourselves in an outhouse that before an ingenious renovation had been a chicken coop.

As much as I despised being pulled from Emory, there was a welcome sense of familiarity, sitting there in the kitchen with my parents in good health, drinking strong coffee and watching the sun come up pink through the dawn.

I was surprised, though, to see that some of the most familiar things about our cypress-planked house now seemed wonderfully and strangely unfamiliar. Take the hemlock, for example. There was a water hemlock outside our kitchen window waiting for warm weather to bloom. Mother had planted that hemlock when I was a boy, warning me often to stay away.

Now I realized I was looking at the plant some variety of which killed Socrates. I knew now that this particular hemlock was a water hemlock *(Cicuta mexicana)*. I knew it came from the Apiaceae family, the same family under which we find celery. I observed that the hemlock's whitish-green flowers were stalked in compound terminal and lateral umbels. I knew its leaves alternated on a main stem, leaflets opposite, lanceolate, toothed, stalked. I knew that the plant's poison worked on the nervous system and that this particular plant had a synonym: *Cicuta curtissii*.

I had seen mother's hemlock thousands of times, but until I studied the science of description for flowers and stems and leaves I really had none but the vaguest experience of the plant, which, after all, had not changed *its* appearance outside our kitchen window.

I have come to believe that knowledge can never diminish the freshness of experience. In fact, I realized that morning that botany and horticulture had given me a new set of lenses with which to observe the world. Everything of plant life that I observed and experienced was new. I saw familiar things in unfamiliar ways. Not just differently, mind you. The hemlock I saw that morning was a category of being before unknown to me. It was as if I had never seen it before.

I wished at the moment of my unplanned homecoming that I had time to name all the things I could see, name their parts, classify them, relate them. Each flower and shrub and tree and weed and fruit and berry and vine seemed to me now things no longer separate and discrete. They were threads in God's blanket. And if I could only learn enough I could weave His work entire.

"Come on, Carter." Tink brought me back to the kitchen table. "Time to go to the bank."

I saw water running everywhere as we made our way over wet, rutted roads to Laureate, a sign of generous and recent rainfall. I saw deer running even this late in the season through cabbage palm and palmetto near to the road. I saw meadows interrupted with swamp rose and sensitive briar. *Croton argyranthemus* and crepe myrtle hung waiting for March in unexpected brocades on fence lines sagging in ill repair. Cattle grazed on a variety of native grasses perennial to the region; mallards and coots burst from slews and hammocks bordering the bovines' pastures, their wings whistling in uninhibited flight.

But if the ride to Laureate was exhilarating, the town itself was depressing in its familiarity. Leroy met us at the bank, perspiration pitting his stiff-starched shirt even in winter, his tie spread over an ample gut and secured with a brass pin emblazoned, "Jesus Saves." He had a broad face, did Leroy, a dome of a head, and eyes like raisins pressed hastily into a skull of dough.

Tink and I were ushered through a swinging gate at the counter, past an iron-worked grille that pretended security, past the clerks and officers and a massive vault to reach Leroy's office. Gas hissed through a space heater set in the corner, one of the first of those I had seen. I noticed a can of water propped on top. But the centerpiece of that overheated room was Leroy's desk. It was crafted of cherrywood, waxed to a mirror finish, much too large for the space in which it was placed. There was a thick pad of India paper set with a blotter on the desk and a pair of fountain pens fashioned, so Leroy claimed, from the bone that extended a walrus's penis. Leroy had those curiously retooled pieces of anatomy mounted in permanent erection within fourteen-karat gold holders, which themselves were secured on a base of granite.

"You making it, Tink?"

"Steady by jerks."

Leroy settled his bulk into a high-backed chair. Tink and I had the five-minute seats, so named because, as Taff put it, after five minutes you were ready to get your ass up and leave.

Tink opened the large envelope he had shown me on the way home. There were a half-dozen documents inside. "Contracts," Tink summarized the contents.

Tink spread the separate sheets like a hand of cards across Leroy's hardwood desk. The fat man perused the documents one by one.

"Department of Defense," a letterhead first caught my eye. Wasn't hard then to figure from what hill my father's help was coming.

Some of my contemporaries seem to take for granted that FDR's New Deal ended the Depression. It didn't. The only thing that could generate the kind of economic activity necessary to bring the nation out of its cycle of low productivity and wages was represented by the pieces of paper that spread before me now on Leroy Sessions's desk.

We were preparing for war. I couldn't believe it. Almost weekly our president assured us there would be no war. The news was filled with Congress's passage of neutrality laws guaranteed to keep us out of Europe, yet here before me were contracts for crossties, turpentine, and dimension lumber in vast quantities, and all going to places such as the naval bases in Norfolk and Jacksonville, an army post in San Antonio, and Camp Blanding, near Jacksonville.

All lumber provided was to be cut and finished according to military specifications. The quality demanded even for a simple army barracks was much higher than what was needed to satisfy a civilian contractor. Basically, *all* dimension lumber had to be finished from clear wood. A single knot in a boxcar of two-by-fours, and the army could reject the load. There were specifications for packing and for shipping. Deadlines for quantity and constant, constant inspection.

The same sort of thing applied to shipments of turpentine and also to tung oil.

"Tung oil?" I took another look at that contract. "Are we in the tung oil business too?"

"Man's got a grove in Madison County," Tink nodded. "We're going halves."

Leroy leaned back in his chair.

"Where'd you get all this work?"

"Fleishel," Tink replied shortly.

M. L. Fleishel was president and general manager of Putnam Lumber Company, the company that had been my father's longtime employer. Putnam Lumber was the largest and most powerful timber company operating in northern Florida. One of the most profitable, I'm sure, in the whole southeast.

"M. L. told me there'd be a ton of work." Tink gauged the effect of those initials on Leroy. "Told me he'd pass along the smaller orders if I'd guarantee delivery and give him ten percent of gross. Make me kind of a subcontractor. I said that sounded just fine. He made some phone calls. Government man came down to see my operation."

Tink shrugged his shoulders.

"Here we are."

Leroy worked hard to make sure he appeared unimpressed.

"And how much you stand to make, you think? Just on these contracts here?"

Tink lifted one of Leroy's erotic pens from its golden chalice, scribbled a number onto his damp paper pad.

"That's after expenses," Tink said and turned the pad around.

Leroy scowled over that information a moment. "Twenty-seven thousand dollars?"

"By next September," Tink nodded. "That's being cautious. Doesn't count the twenty I've already put in your bank, and it doesn't count the contracts coming *next* year."

"If you get any," Leroy sniffed.

"Oh, we will." Tink smiled. "There ain't nobody backing out of this fight."

Leroy's domed head bobbed like a cork. "I think you're wrong about the fighting but I won't argue with what's sittin' in front of me."

No one said a word for a moment. I began to wonder what we were waiting for. Tink had demonstrated that he had the means to buy Dave Ogilvie's mortgage. There didn't seem to be any doubt about that. Why was Leroy hesitating?

A soft knock at the door provided the answer.

Leroy looked up from his desk. "Bennett, good. You timed it out just about right."

Bennett Sessions was Leroy's oldest son, a sloppier if more nattily attired whelp of his father. He was already obese, an old man's paunch bulging below his belt. He had eyes similar to his father's, two pissholes in a snowbank.

I wondered for a brief moment what interest Bennett could have in the Ogilvie mortgage. And then I remembered—Bennett Sessions had for as long as I could remember, probably since God made dirt, been tax assessor in Lafayette County. The tax assessor was an important office for landowners in any county, the one man (and always a man in those years) upon whom you depended to appraise your land at the lowest possible value. The lower your land was valued, the less you paid in taxes. A man who got behind on taxes lost his land. Period. You could owe the bank and get away with it, but owe the county and you lost your ox, your ass, and every acre they grazed on.

For years Tink had complained that Bennett overvalued our timberland while assessing the Ogilvie holdings at an artificially low level. Bennett always countered by saying that Dave's acreage was in the Suwannee River's floodplain. Dave liked the latter assessment, naturally, and so each election year joined his political influence with Leroy's pockets to make sure that Leroy's oldest, pussel-gutted son continued to occupy the office of tax assessor.

There was nothing clandestine about any of this. Everyone knew that Leroy Sessions's son got reelected term after term because his daddy brought cash and Dave brought votes.

"Tink, I 'spected to see you here. What about you, Carter?"

Truth is, at that point I didn't know.

"He's just taking a break from school to help me with some business affairs," Tink spoke up smiling.

"Must be some business."

"It's an opportunity," Tink allowed. "All the work we're going to be getting, turpentine, tung oil, and timber, I'm gonna need somebody to set in an office. Keep the books and invoices straight. Payroll."

"So Carter's gonna be your general manager?" Bennett seemed to think that was funny.

"Carter's gonna be a doctor, Bennett." The tone of Tink's voice did not change. "But for the business at hand I need somebody smart who I can trust. And I need 'em right away. Carter's taken a leave from Emory to help me out."

It was a lie. But it was a lie that saved me face, and I appreciated it. Leroy cleared his throat.

"We were just discussing Dave Ogilvie's situation, Bennett. I thought Tink might like to hear your concerns."

"Could have told me yourself, Leroy." The tone had changed now in my father's voice, and it did not bode well. "Don't take a real smart man to see Bennett's worried about his election. That about, it, Bennett? That why you're here?"

I decided if I was going to be appointed a general manager, I might as well act like one.

"I can see your problem, Mr. Sessions," I said, deferring of course to the elder Sessions. "You risk being caught between a rock and hard place."

"Well put," Leroy nodded.

"Make sure I got this right," I went on. "About the best Dave Ogilvie can hope to do this summer is meet the interest on his mortgage. If he can't do that, or worse, if he goes bust, you and this bank stand to lose forty thousand dollars."

If I was waiting for confirmation Leroy didn't give it. I directed my remarks then to Bennett. "The problem *you* have is that if Leroy sells Dave's mortgage to Tink, then come the election Dave Ogilvie will turn on you, won't he, Bennett? He'll call in every favor anybody ever owed him, and he'll make sure you don't get reelected to that tax assessor's office."

"Not sure that's *exactly* how I'd put it." Bennett shuffled.

"Why not?" Tink growled. "Plain talk's easy understood."

The election wasn't far off. Technically there were two primaries, but no Republican had declared for tax assessor since Reconstruction. Bennet would run as a Democrat. He'd have to announce his candidacy sometime in late March, much earlier than candidates today, because in those years elections for county offices were held toward the end of May. That meant folks would be voting just a few days before Dave Ogilvie started cropping tobacco.

Leroy laid his hands on the table. "Don't see how I can give you the mortgage without putting a tight on my boy, Tink."

"We had us an understanding, Leroy." I saw the ligaments in Tink's jaw go tight as cable.

"I know, I know," Leroy nodded. "It's just bad timing is all. I don't see any way around it."

I cleared my throat. "I might."

Tink seemed surprised at that bold remark. He looked at me as if I were a child caught doing something unexpectedly precocious.

"Well, let's hear it," Leroy seemed amused.

"You could draw up a confidential letter," I began. "A letter of agreement based on specified contingencies."

"The hell, Tink, is this boy studyin' the law?" Bennett guffawed.

"Easy, Bennett." This from Leroy. "Go ahead, son."

"Dave won't turn on Bennett unless he knows you've sold Tink the mortgage." I made that point first. "The letter should first specify that you will not sell the mortgage until after Bennett's election. When would that be, Bennett?"

"Be a Tuesday," Bennett answered sullenly. "May twenty-eighth."

"Fine. So the letter will say that any agreement between Leroy and Tink will not take effect until, say, June first. In that way the deed can't be transferred until *after* Bennett's election."

"Dave finds out we got a letter it won't make a damn bit of difference *when* its transferred," Bennett jeered. "He'll come after me tooth and tong anyhow!"

"Who's going to tell him?" I replied. "*We* aren't. Wouldn't be in Daddy's interest or mine to go shooting off our mouths. You can keep quiet. I know your daddy can."

Leroy's chair squeaked with his weight.

"What else?"

I took a deep breath.

"We need a straight answer, Mr. Sessions. To one question."

"Awright."

"If Dave Ogilvie comes up with enough money to pay the

interest on his loan this year, will you still be willing to sell Tink his mortgage?"

Leroy shifted in his chair a bit. I could see my father stretch taller in his five-minute chair.

"No," Leroy said finally. "No, I guess I wouldn't."

"Goddamnit, Leroy!" Tink was on his feet. "That's not what you told me!"

"You heard what you wanted to hear, Tink. I didn't guarantee nothing. Not a thing."

"You said if I could come up with the money I could *have Dave's mortgage.*"

"You don't have the money, Tink. All you've got is a bunch of government paper."

Tink reached his hands into his pockets. I knew if I didn't say something quickly my father would wear out two overweight men with a pair of brass knuckles. If he didn't shoot them first.

"Daddy," I stood to whisper at Tink's shoulder, "give me a chance to get something out of this."

A long, long moment passed before I saw the cable in his jaw release just a fraction. "Fine. Go on."

"Mr. Sessions," I addressed Leroy, "surely you'd rather have forty thousand dollars in your bank than foreclose on a thousand acres that's going to be damn near impossible to sell, if at all, for more than fifteen or twenty thousand."

"Well, yes," Leroy conceded.

"There's nothing says that once Tink *has* his forty thousand dollars you're going to see any of it. Oh, Daddy's hot to trot right now, but we all know that forty thousand dollars is a lot of money to spend on that piece of property. By summer Daddy might have come to his senses. He'll start counting all that cash, and he'll say, 'My God I'm rich! To hell with Dave Ogilvie *and* his property!' It could happen. God knows if it were left up to *me* it *would* happen!"

I had the man's attention. This had turned into a poker game, and Leroy had to decide whether or not to call my bluff. I leaned forward on Mr. Sessions's cherry desk.

"You need a letter as much as Tink does. More! 'Cause when Dave goes bust, and Daddy has even average success with these contracts, there is nothing, absolutely nothing, which binds him to give you forty thousand dollars *for anything*."

I let Leroy consider that fact for a moment.

"So to protect *your* interest, seems to me you need some kind of agreement. Nothing fancy. Just a confidential contract that, subject to Dave's failure and the other terms we've discussed, *obligates* Tink to pay you forty thousand dollars in return for the Ogilvie mortgage."

"I'd want it in writing that if Dave meets the interest on his note, I still keep the mortgage. Your daddy has no claim."

"Fair enough. Dave owes you in interest, what—? Something around two thousand four hundred dollars?"

"Something like that." Leroy's eyes narrowed to slits.

"So we all agree if he pays off that interest by the time specified, Dave's mortgage stays with your bank. If he doesn't, though, this letter will obligate you to sell the mortgage to Tink."

"What if they both come up short?" Leroy was dealing in earnest now. "What if Dave loses his crop and Tink's business goes bad? How do I get my money then?"

I didn't have a ready answer for that contingency. But Tink did.

"You can use *my* property as collateral," he said.

I was shocked. So, I could tell, was Leroy. Bennett was so unhappy with the general progress of affairs that I don't think he saw what a gold mine had just dropped into his daddy's lap.

Leroy began to work the clasp of his tie like a rosary.

"Let me get this straight." Leroy's head swiveled like a turret to Tink. "You will *guarantee* to buy Dave Ogilvie's mortgage under terms I specify, and I will have *your* property collateralized to ensure performance?"

"My land," Tink affirmed tersely. "Leaving out the mills and the turpentine. That's all rented acreage anyhow."

"You must be pretty damned confident you're going to have the money, Tink!" Bennett licked his lips nervously.

"Got half of it already," Tink answered mild as a milkmaid.

Leroy was perched by this time on the very edge of his fancy chair. Balanced precariously in his decision, a boulder propped atop a very narrow ridge. Looked to me like he needed just a nudge more. I leaned back in my hard-bottomed seat just as if it were the most comfortable couch in the world.

"Dave's been talking to you for months, hasn't he, Mr. Sessions? Jewing you down. Making you sweat your balls off for a favor more than ten years old. Well, Tink isn't asking any favors. He's coming in offering to pay off the whole forty thousand. He's already put up half in earnest money, in your bank by the way, and he's willing to put up *our* land in security for the rest. You can't get much more square than that."

A silence fell in the room. Only the sputter of the space heater intruded.

"Damned if I don't believe your boy could run for office hisself, Tink," Leroy finally said.

Then the elder Sessions quit worrying his tie. He took one of those penis pens in hand. Scrawled some numbers on his expensive pad of paper. Looked at the figures briefly. Put his pen back in its holder.

"We'll give Dave till September," Leroy declared. "That should give him time to sell every leaf he can grow. Give him every opportunity to make his interest. If you'll agree to a contract not to become effective until, say, September sixteenth, I can sign it."

"Daddy?"

"First I want to know where Dave Ogilvie's gettin' money to grow his twenty damn acres," Tink said. "Where's he gettin' money for his seed, Leroy? For fertilizer? For labor? Before I sign anything I want that answered, and I want it straight."

"We gave him some help," Leroy conceded stiffly. "Not a lot. Matter of fact, just between you and me and the lamppost, Dave came in here Friday looking for a loan to raise a barn. Didn't occur to him, I guess, that when you double your acreage you're gonna need to double your barn space."

"How much you figure he needs?" Bennett asked.

Leroy shrugged.

"Seems to think he can get by with one. Be a big one. Ten tiers plus a crow's nest. Eight rooms. That's what he came to borrow for, anyway."

"Did you help him with the barn?" Tink asked evenly. Leroy shook his bald head.

"No," he said tersely. "I told him we couldn't do no more. If he wanted lumber for a barn I told him he should think about making some kind of arrangement with a mill."

Bennett chuckled then, the kind of chuckle that comes from the spleen, the kind spurred at somebody else's expense.

"Hell, he might come lookin' to you, Tink! Come lookin' to you for lumber to build his barn!"

"I doubt that." Tink took his massive, misshapen hands out of his pockets. There was some kind of trash in those hands, I thought at first. Then I saw that it was the remains of a walnut. Perhaps a pair of walnuts. Tink dropped the crushed remains of shell and meat onto Leroy's cherrywood desk.

"Draw up your papers, Leroy. I ain't leaving town till they're signed and sealed."

"Fair enough," Leroy said.

They didn't bother to shake hands on the deal.

Chapter thirteen

Rabbit's Tobacco,
Gnaphalium obtusifolium

It must have been around a month and a half after my father and Leroy cemented their clandestine agreement that Dave Ogilvie began pulling plants from a tobacco bed to set his twenty-acre crop. I have sharp memories of Dave and his family working that winter and spring. By that time I was working for my father, organizing books and ledgers and payrolls. But from the Sand Pond I could spy on Dave's field. I would sometimes be granted on those occasions a pisgah sight of Julia as she bent to a familiar labor.

Dave tended his beds assiduously. The making of beds was the first of many hand-labor steps necessary to take tobacco from seed to cigarette. Start with the seed. Tobacco seed in your hand looks not much more substantial than dust; a mere sneeze will plant three or four acres of full-height, fleshy-leafed tobacco. And because its seed is so small tobacco can't be broadcast directly into a field. Unlike soy or corn or wheat, tobacco must germinate in a bed. Its young plants are then removed, one plant at a time, and replanted into the field.

As a youngster I had done all this work, of course, sometimes with Julia but many times without. Her father put down four beds that year, each more than a hundred yards long and perhaps thirty feet wide, stretching like long rectangles on level ground, bounded at the periphery by any old log or post that would suit the purpose.

Not easy to make a good bed. You broke the ground first, broke it very fine. Then you mixed your tobacco seed into a barrel of ashes and stirred until instinct or fatigue convinced you that the seed was well distributed within its ash-filled incubus. You next strewed those ashes up and down the broken ground. A cheesecloth would finally be stretched over stakes or hoops of palmetto to prevent the growing seedlings from being killed by the chill and frost that would surely come.

All the while that I sat with my father and Leroy and Bennett inside that overheated office Dave labored, pulling the plants that if set, weeded, watered, suckered, harvested, strung, hung, cured, unstrung, graded, packed, hauled, and sold successfully *might* give Dave an outside chance to pay Leroy Sessions the twenty-four hundred dollars necessary to keep his land.

I got away when I could, sneaking back to the Sand Pond, seeing Julia beside her father, their tall, aristocratic frames bent beneath a washboard sky in a sea of new growth, pulling plants with Sarah, and Wyatt, and little Caleb. And then sowing the bright-green plants, one by one, row after row, in the largest tobacco field ever attempted in Lafayette County. I saw that side of Dave Ogilvie. It was familiar to me.

But I did not see everything.

It was not until much later that Julia would recall for me her experience of that bitter February. Dave had required his daughter to interrupt her schooling, extending her winter break to help tend tobacco beds. Julia would tell me what it was like to be inside the family during that time, inside that forbidding home, how one frosty evening Dave burst in angry to roust Wyatt out of an hour's slumber.

You didn't cover the beds, he said.

Wyatt rose to that chastisement, his nightshirt stained with the evening. And then Julia cringed in her bed as her father fell on her brother with a leather strop. Julia and I were married before I actually saw that violent band of cowhide. It hung in the hall beside a display of china.

Only three children, people clucked sympathy for the one failing in their wealthy deacon. But they were not there, nor was I, when in a fit of anger Dave shoved Sarah down the back steps. Sarah, a saint beyond belief, Sarah small-boned, who, pregnant, broke her pelvis and gave birth to a boy deformed. Little Caleb.

He won't hit Caleb, Wyatt said later with malice, because he made him.

And Julia. That tan of skin. The blue along her neck. Along her thighs too, I only later found. Some transgression cited for cause. Any transgression, real or imagined, would do. Stripes along her flank. Not a young girl anymore. Made to stand arms stretched between two crib posts, blouse loose and down about her waist. The peach-tree switch.

Then the shame, him putting the blouse across her bleeding back. Holding her, cupping her. Sometimes seconds only. Sometimes minutes.

And then Sarah, small-boned Sarah, saying, Never again! Not even once! Or I will kill you, husband. I swear to my God I will.

I didn't see that side of Dave Ogilvie at all. For me, Dave was the church's deacon and the bank's savior. He was the man who, one cold night, took me in his Packard to fetch a doctor for my gunshot father. It was the public man I saw, and Dave was very careful to cultivate that persona.

He won you over like an actor. Every gesture was calculated, every opportunity exploited. The presentation of Caleb's birthday gift, for instance, reminds me. It was a Saturday. I was outside the feed store with perhaps a dozen others when Dave appeared, carrying an elaborate hand-wired cage. There was a wheel mounted inside, a tiny, immaculate merry-go-round, and on that fragile carousel a squirrel ran a million miles a minute.

Dave called across the street to little Caleb, a pleasant salutation, we all heard it. Nothing could appear more artless, Caleb turning to his father's voice, seeing the cage in his hand—"papa!" Then stumbling across the street. Tiny arms thrown about a father's neck.

"His name's Henry," Dave said. "He's yours."

He even had pecans ready at hand, already shelled. So that Caleb might feed his new pet.

That's the man I saw. That's the man we all saw. And coming home from Atlanta that January I was too busy to see anything else.

⁂

If I imagined studies of calculus and anatomy to be a challenge, I was totally unprepared for the curriculum that came with my promotion to general manager in my father's hay-baled assortment of business interests.

The four or five pepperbox mills Tink started upon leaving Putnam Lumber were portable. It was a lot easier to take the mill to the timber than to transport the timber to the mill. The one exception to that rule was our mill at Fort McKoon.

Fort McKoon was an old Confederate ruin sited on a flint bed beside the Suwannee. In low water you could almost cross the river on that shelf, walking its promontory to a point only yards away from the clay bank on the far side.

Tink loaded his turpentine barrels off the natural quay that Fort McKoon provided and used the river to bring trees to our mill. A barge would take the dimensioned lumber along with heavy barrels of turpentine to Branford, where both products would be transferred to rail for delivery to our military customers.

The sawmill was the center of it all. Nothing makes more racket. I worked no more than fifty yards from a six-foot, tungsten-toothed circular blade powered by an Allison engine that daily screamed vengeance on trunks of pine and cypress. The "office" where I worked was not much more than a tin lean-to with a kerosene stove and lamps. No electricity. We wouldn't have electricity until well after the war.

I had a hand-cranked calculator, a Remington manual type-writer, and lots of carpenter's pencils. We kept our books in chests of drawers. A floor safe secured our valuables. Padlock on the door. It was quite a change from the time, twelve or fifteen years earlier, when my father first brought me to this then-magical place.

I loved camping with Daddy at Fort McKoon. It was one of the few expeditions Tink required of me that I didn't actually dread. This wasn't a region at all like the flatwoods; here the river was broad and solemn and open. A mossy forest of water oaks rising all around. I scoured the area looking for Confederate coins and arrowheads and found them both by the dozens. You could imagine you were a Johnny Reb behind the ruins of the fort's cypress walls, taking aim with your minié ball rifle at the Union troops making their ragged assault from the river.

Or you could be an Indian, a young Creek or Seminole chipping the natural flint from McKoon's wide shelf, fashioning it to fit your arrow or your spear. Taking that finished weapon then to stalk and to kill.

The place was teeming with game of all sorts. Ducks and geese flew by the thousands down the warm river water on their migratory routes. You could get twenty-pound catfish right off the shelf with nothing more than a hook and a worm. And there was big game too. Deer and black bear. And panthers.

First panther I ever saw was at Fort McKoon. We had camped out. I woke early with Daddy shaking me by the shoulder. "Get up, Carter. You don't see this often."

At a point where the fort's flint shelf reached its most extreme extension across the river there was a deep narrows. The narrows got you to within thirty yards or so of the bank on the river's far side, a shallow wall of clay that rose fifteen or twenty feet above the slow-churning roll of river water.

I was scanning that far bank, trying to see whatever it was that my father seemed to believe was so unusual.

"Not on the bank, Carter," Daddy whispered. "In the water."

I looked and, yes! There he was! The first and biggest panther I ever saw, and swimming! Swimming across the narrows to reach Fort McKoon's flinty shelf. He got to that counter of ancient flint, pulled himself on easily, spotlighted golden in the just rising sun.

And then he walked a line almost directly toward our camp. Walked stiff-legged just as if he owned the shelf, the river, and the banks on either side. Couldn't have been more than fifty, sixty yards away.

He had a long, long tail that twitched back and forth like a kitchen cat getting ready to pounce on a sparrow. He even paused at one point to lick his paw, just like a giant-sized kitty. There was fog on the river that morning. Its damp tickled my throat as I crouched holding my breath beside my father to see this magnificent creature. There was not a sound in the forest or on the river beyond. Perhaps the gentle lap of the river rolling over the shelf of Fort McKoon.

The tickle wouldn't quit. It started in my chest. Worked to my throat.

"Be still," Daddy barely whispered.

I coughed.

I coughed, and that panther's tail went stiff as a stick. I held my breath. He searched the bank, brown eyes calm in that predator's skull. Barely sixty yards away he panned his head slowly, deliberately, I swear it to this day, until he came to rest looking me squarely in the eye.

A cloud of fog rolled up. He just held me there. Eye to eye. I blinked first, and in the space it took to look again—

He had vanished. Gone. Like a wraith into the fog.

"I'll be damn." Tink roughed his hand through my boy's head of hair. "I been in the woods all my life. Never seen an animal do that."

But a dozen years later I sat not twenty yards from that spot, balancing double-ledgered books, recording board feet of this and shipments of that. A six-foot saw now screamed where three generations before there was only the gentle chip of a stone axe shaping arrowheads of flint; I took aspirin to quell the headaches.

Winter slipped into spring at Fort McKoon. The Suwannee

River and its surrounding flora exploded into a riot of color and variety, and I barely noticed. I was too busy to see much of anything except the stacks of ledgers and correspondence that clamored at my desk for attention. Payroll was pretty straightforward, but each military consignment required a ton of paperwork. Forms in triplicate. Forms on top of forms. Letters to some procurement officer at Camp Blanding or Norfolk, Virginia, assuring them that, yes, the three thousand gallons of Grade I turpentine contracted for delivery in mid-March would be received no later than the nineteenth day of that month, transport being delayed due to... etc., etc., etc.

Anything could delay a shipment. Early rains wiped out fully half of the already limited roads that allowed mules to get our timber to their mills. Creeks and sloughs usually reliable for transport were too swollen to be usable. The Suwannee, similarly, was near to cresting, Fort McKoon's flint shelf now invisible beneath fifteen feet of brown water. If I spat hard enough out of my tin office I'd hit foam swirling like cotton candy downriver.

Then there was what might be politely described as labor difficulties. A turpentine camp was not the healthiest of environs, families and single men living in patched tents or rude cabins set beside outdoor privies. Sometimes water came from a well, sometimes from any clear-running stream that was handy. Any kind of illness contracted in such conditions communicated quickly throughout the closely gathered laborers and families.

Influenza was the gravest threat. Even healthy people contracting "the flu" died in the '20s and '30s by the millions. A single bout of influenza killed half the laborers bedded toe to head in one of our canvas camps, along with many children. We made caskets for them on site.

Even if an illness didn't kill your crew it could render them useless. It was not uncommon to have a hundred laborers stricken with diarrhea. Would you like a challenge for your general manager? Charge him to persuade some cracker getting forty cents a day to tap turpentine in a damp, bitter cold with shit running down his legs.

Malaria was a common malady even in winter. Tink took to

dosing the grownups with quinine daily as a prophylaxis. Put it in their coffee. And to dull whatever urge might prompt a man to adultery or rape, Tink also dosed the food with saltpeter. Keeps their dicks soft, Daddy insisted, though Doc West denied that claim.

Every delay, whether caused by weather or equipment or personnel, had to be explained. We were in constant fear that a larger supplier would take one of our precious contracts away. Or some government employee, irritated that twenty thousand board feet of fine-cut yellow-heart pine had been delivered at noon on the thirteenth instead of at noon on the twelfth, would cancel further requisitions from our mills.

To prevent such an occurrence I developed an ongoing correspondence with our military customers that was a masterpiece of officialese and sycophancy. But it took time.

Tink said I used up more trees typing than our gangs did cutting, and I believe he was pretty nearly right.

I could not have done it without Spence.

I was reunited with my boyhood friend at Fort McKoon by the demands of double-ledger accounting. It was obvious by now that Spence's gift for "ciphering" was not much short of phenomenal. A half-dozen adding machines with clerks to work them could not keep up with Spence MacGrue. The man was invaluable; he'd come in bone tired after a day in the woods and within an hour balance books that would take me half the day.

And he never made a mistake!

It was obvious to me after a couple of weeks that Spence could, with little guidance, reconcile all of our accounts by himself. I looked forward to his coming. I suppose I expected some easy familiarity to ensue. On the surface that was the case. I was "Mr. Carter" at work, of course, or sometimes "Boss," but I was sure those were formalities, second nature and unresented, merely a common deference and obligation between coloreds and whites.

Nevertheless, there was a reticence on his part. At first I attributed his silence to our long separation. I tried to take the initiative, provide Spence small seeds of conversation that would help him. I'd say, Morning, Spence, how's Eida Mae? Or, Daddy tells me you've got a winter garden bigger than Mother's. Or, You getting any bream out of that slough behind the Little House?

Spence would reply gregariously enough. Always with a smile that never varied. But he rarely volunteered anything. Our conversations were one-sided. Soon conversations consisted of the usual courtesies and inquiries related to the mill.

No resentment or temper. Spence never showed a temper. I didn't even know he could get angry until an incident in the yard crossed him with Red Walker.

I was in the yard looking for Red when it happened. Half the time Red's handwritten receipts needed deciphering as badly as his arithmetic; I had a receipt that indicated a shipment for thirty-two hundred feet of two-by-fours for a price that made sense only if we'd shipped thirty-two thousand. Thought I'd run that information past my sawyer. See if he felt a tenfold error was something we could afford.

I was near the mill pond. Spence was unloading some just-cut trunks into the water when Red jogged up. He was waving a sheet of paper in his hand and cursing MacGrue from forty yards away.

Spence levered a log into the pond with his peavey. A peavey is a heavy pole fitted at the end with what looks like a Swiss pike, something like the claw at the end of a dinosaur's arm. Before the heavy slap of the log's splash dissipated, Red was to the skids. Spence hefted his peavey and met Red halfway. When I got there Red was still cussing a streak and brandishing a limb that he appeared bound and determined to break over Spence's skull.

Spence showed no sign of retreat. By the time that fact registered with Red Walker, he was too far along to back down.

The whole yard came to a halt.

There were about as many blacks as whites working the Fort McKoon mill, and this was not good for either side to see.

Red threw down the limb in his hand, reached into his overalls, and pulled out a straight razor.

Spence didn't budge.

"You son-of-a-bitchin' nigger!" Red screamed. "You keepin' numbers on *me?* You got-damn jungle bunny? On *me?*"

Spence didn't say a word. Just held that peavey level and still. Red displayed his own weapon.

"Think you're apt to do something with that frogsticker, boy? Hah? I'll cut you down. I'll cut the soles off your black-ass feet!"

CRAAAAAAAACCKK. A shot rang out. Scared the shit out of everybody except Spence. Red jerked his head around. There was Tink, standing by the mill pond with his rifle.

"What you doin' with my man, Red?"

"This got-dam nigger picked up his peavey on me!" Red still had his razor raised.

"Not what I saw." Tink strolled over.

"Hell you say!"

"The hell I do say. What's this?" Tink picked up the paper Red had thrown to the ground.

"It's mine!" Red said, the belligerence suddenly gone from his voice.

"I'll keep it," Tink said.

"It's mine, got-damnit!"

"I'm just keepin' it for you, Red. End of the day you can pick it up."

Daddy said that just as accommodatingly as if he had volunteered to retrieve Red's snot rag.

"I won't have no nigger lookin' over me," Red blathered.

"He's my man, Red. He does what I say do."

Red stood there a moment, the lesions on his face stretched hideously like water spots on a foul parchment.

"You're gone push me too far one day, Tink."

"You're mine to push, Red. Don't like it, why, you can leave."

The whole camp held its breath.

"Fuck you," Red muttered, turning away.

"What was that?" Tink inclined his ear benignly in Red's general direction.

"You heard me," Red turned back. "I said—"

That's when Tink hit him. He didn't hit him with the octagonal barrel of his thirty-thirty because, Tink later explained, he didn't want to risk warping the true of a good rifle.

But he got Red with the stock.

That wooden butt came from the ground to catch Fort McKoon's sawyer in his crotch. Tink lifted Red from the ground, so hard did he hit. Gave Walker a hernia, an autopsy years later revealed, and I am certain Red would have been grateful in his agony to have qualified for a postmortem on the spot.

Red went down too hurt to scream. He clawed the dirt with his dirty nails. Puking.

"Take care of him, Taff." Tink walked away without a hint of rancor apparent.

I turned to see Spence's reaction.

He wasn't looking at Red. He was looking at me. Staring eye to eye just like that panther had so long ago. For the first time since his father died, Spence contemplated me openly and, more surprising, more unsettling, invited my gaze deeply into himself.

Why? Was he accusing me? What had I done? What *could* I do, run over there and take Red's razor away?

I glanced back briefly to see a couple of men drag Walker away. When I looked back—Spence was gone. He was there one moment, alive and unsettlingly eye-to-eye. And then he had vanished into the yard or beyond the mill pond or into thin air.

Tink would not elaborate on the incident or the paper that provoked it. Neither, in spite of my prodding, would Spence. Spence was taken out of the yard, put on a black gang, back out in the woods. After a hard day of labor he would come in as usual and in the course of days accomplish what I could in a week.

The books looked promising. In spite of influenza and the influence of government we were making money. Good money. But we weren't making quite what my month-to-month calculations indicated we should. Turpentine worked out about right. Tung oil was practically to the dime. But timber looked short. Not much, but some. More alarming, it looked to be some kind of recurring discrepancy.

Spence had told me years ago that Red Walker only made mistakes in his own favor.

"Daddy." I walked up to Tink a couple of weeks after the incident with Red, sleepless after a long night over the books. We had some privacy, standing alone beside a stack of clear-heart cypress.

"Son, you look tired."

"Yessir, well. Got some news I wish I didn't have to report."

"Won't get any better waitin', I don't expect."

"I think Red Walker is cheating you."

"Think?"

"I guess I know he is. Not the military contracts; they're too risky. But he's underreporting lumber milled for other customers, billing them for the full amount, and putting the difference in his pocket."

Tink nodded. "What Spence said."

"Spence—? That's what he had on that paper?"

"That's what you had too. You were just a little slower about seeing what it meant."

"But then—" A vague anger suddenly took sharp shape. "Why didn't you tell me? Why'd you let me do all that work? Why didn't you *do* something?"

"I had to see if you could figure it out for yourself, Carter."

"I could have missed it," I spat out.

"Could have," Tink averred. "Either way I had to see whether you could do the job."

"Well, I hope to hell you're satisfied!"

"Ain't no free rides in this enterprise, son. Not even for you."

Free ride? I wanted to hit him. I wanted to rear back and put my fist dead center in his sun-baked face! I'd never live to tell about it, of course. But, hell, I might. If I could find myself an equalizer. There had to be an axe handle around there somewhere! I think I might actually have been looking for one when Tink began to laugh.

"What are you laughing at?"

That *really* set him off. He collapsed onto that stack of lumber, sides fairly splitting with laughter.

"You laughing at me? Goddamnit, Daddy!"

Tears came to his face he was laughing so hard.

"Quit it, damnit!"

But it was getting harder to stay mad at him.

He gradually settled down. He stood—"Yeehaw!" Wiped the tears off his sunburned face. "You've done good, Carter."

"Good?" I wasn't sure I heard him correctly.

"You've worked like a Turk. Prob'ly saved our business. You slopped through hell without a sip of water, and now you're show-ing some sand to boot. That's about as much as a man can ask out of anybody, certainly of his own son."

He clamped his iron hand on my shoulder so hard I thought I'd faint.

"What say we go hunt something? Birds, maybe. I saw some mallards coming in."

"Mallard." I nodded, still shaken by the recent praise. "Sure. Why not?"

"One thing we got to do first, though." Tink's release was merciful.

"What would that be?"

"We got to fire Red Walker." Tink said.

"He'll be mad as hell." I had to smile. "Love to see the look on his face."

"You will," Tink replied. "You're firing him."

"ME?" I stumbled to a halt.

"Why the hell does it have to be me?!"

"Business ain't all bookwork, Carter—" He said this as kindly and gently as if he were telling me I had cancer. "Sometimes in busi-ness you got to be boss."

Red limped into the office around noon. I made sure I was standing. Tink was sipping coffee by the stove. I had my ledgers dis-played prominently on the desk.

"Taff said you need to see me?"

Red was talking to me, not to Tink. Tink mandated that I be responsible for the summons, that I be responsible for discovery of Red's theft and all consequences to follow.

Red at this time was making one hundred fifteen dollars each month, not counting what he stole, at a time when other men were making fifty cents a day. He was not going to make this easy.

I was surprised how reluctant I was to fire the man. Red had betrayed our trust, my trust. He had stolen. He had lied to me and to my father. And yet my heart was hammering in my chest as if I were guilty as sin myself.

"We got a problem here, Red," I began weakly. "Need to talk a minute."

"Ah-hah." Red just stood there, sneering.

"Do you have any idea how many skids we hauled in last month, Red?"

"I don't know. Two-forty, two-fifty. It's in the books."

"Two fifty-three. And how many feet did we cut out of that?"

"Hell, we cut what we haul."

I could see this song and dance wasn't getting me anywhere.

"We're losing money, Red. What I can tell there's between five and ten thousand feet of lumber going out the door every month that doesn't wind up on my books."

"You cain't tell that. You cain't tell for sure."

Tink dolloped some honey into his coffee. "He can tell when somebody's pissin' on his leg."

"Just what are you sayin'?" Red ignored Tink and stepped right up into my face.

"I'm gonna have to let you go, Red." I hoped my voice didn't sound tight.

"You've got nuthin' on me. Who in hell d'you think you are?"

"He's the boss man." Tink worked his bad shoulder as he rose from the stove.

"He wouldn't do this lessen you said so," Red came back.

"I don't know." Tink smiled. "He's gettin' awful independent."

"I paid you out for the week, Red." I had his cash ready in an envelope.

"You're gonna need a sawyer." Red snatched the cash away.

"Got a man," Tink said.

We did?

"Who you thinkin'?" Red asked, stone-faced.

"Spence MacGrue."

Red stood as if struck. When he finally spoke his voice was so broken it was hard to understand—"Spence. A got-dam *nigger?* A got-dam nigger *boy?* You son of a bitch! You ain't get'n away with this!"

"Already have, Red," Tink replied amiably. And then to me, "Draw his papers."

"Fuck the papers! You think you're the man, Tink?" Red backed away as he railed at my father. "Think you're King Shit? Put a nigger over a white man? I'll tell Tarrant Sullivan he's got a boy down here needs correctin'!"

"Best speak up, then," Tink said softly. "I hear Tarrant's hard of hearing."

"They won't miss twice," Red came back.

My blood chilled. I looked at Tink. What would he do?

"Somethin' you wanta tell me, Red?"

Red snarled something indecipherable and took the door off its hinges as he stormed out of that tin shed and into the yard.

Daddy was quiet for a moment after Red left. I cleared my throat. "He's just talking."

No reply.

"Red's just mouthing off, Daddy. The Klan! Just tryin' to sound big."

"Maybe." Tink sipped his coffee. "Maybe not."

I wondered then—should I tell him about Stanton Lee? Should I risk it?

"Last time Red went on about the Klan was when I had Saint set up to sawyer," Tink mused. "We had that little trouble."

That little trouble is what got you shot, I thought. How much should I tell him? I decided to take an in-between path.

"Maybe you should watch out for Tarrant and that whole bunch," I said. "Just to be safe."

"Play it safe. That what you'd do, son?"

Of course that's what I'd do!

"Come on." Tink rose abruptly to his feet.

"Where we going?" I asked, startled.

"Hunting." Tink seemed amused. "Don't you remember? See can we get ourselves some duck for supper."

Killing birds was the last thing I wanted to do. I did not want to wait stiff in the cold, craning to hear that peculiar whistle of wing. I did not want to look into eyes green in death or red with blood still pumping.

Wring his neck, son, would come the command. That's best, just a good, hard wrench.

I did not want to wrench anything. I did not want to remain a moment longer in this shed, in the din of this place, on this now spoiled site of distant memories of coins and arrowheads and magical animals.

I wanted to be away. Gone. Back to Emory or any place unspoiled by my father's grand obsession. In fairness to Tink, I should have told him that. I should have said, I want to go. I want to strike out on my own. I should have done it the man's way.

"Give me a minute to close up," I told my father. "I'll be right on."

Tink left. I stowed the receipts and ledgers in our makeshift cabinet. Secured our on-hand cash in the safe. The mail remained. Requisitions to be courted or concerns to be allayed. But there was one letter in the pouch that Taff had delivered that seemed of a gentler stationery. I pulled that envelope from the rest.

It was from Julia. She had left Tallahassee for a teaching job. In Laureate.

Chapter fourteen

Bedstraw,
Galium tinctorium

Laureate's school attempted to educate the first grade through the twelfth in one building. The building was only recently constructed, a project completed by FDR's Works Progress Administration. There was probably enough rebar and cement in that thing to lay a runway. The classrooms themselves were bunkers placed at Roman intervals inside the school's H-shaped interior. Tiers of louvered windows provided the summer's only air-conditioning. We had radiators for heat.

An unplanned opening in the faculty brought Julia to the new facility. Christie Gayle Land, the English teacher for seventh, eighth, and ninth grades, had been struck hard with strep throat, which escalated to scarlet fever. She was not expected to survive. I had been a classmate of Christie Gayle's; I hated to think of that fine figure and face diminished in any way by illness. And I had some mixed feelings about Julia's return.

In her letter to me, Julia made it clear that she was not leaving

Florida State College for Women and Tallahassee by choice. Dave had told her that he could not afford to keep her in school. Worse, he would not let her finish on her own, even though Julia had the means. She was ordered to come home, to work on the farm as well as at Laureate's school, and to contribute half of her forty-dollar-a-month salary to Dave's save-the-farm coffer. Julia was drafted, as she wrote in her letter, "to serve in Papa's infantry." She was one year short of graduating with a bachelor's degree in education.

It wasn't long after I received Julia's correspondence that Tink's presence was required at the bank. I made sure I rode along.

There was a political rally of sorts when we got to town. Bennett Sessions was convening his supporters in Edward Land's store, shoring up support for the coming May election. Candidates had to announce for the one useful primary by March 28. As yet Bennett was unopposed.

Tink was to make a deposit at the bank to reassure Leroy that cash was coming in quantity and on schedule. While they did their business, I needed to square a bill with Edward, then meet Tink around noon at the drugstore. That itinerary gave me time to walk up to the school and see Julia.

I settled with Edward and was headed out the door when Bennett nodded me off to one side conspiratorially.

"Dave Ogilvie was by the bank this morning," Bennett's eyes seemed even more radically recessed than usual. "Looking for money to build that barn."

"I'll tell Tink." I accepted the information lamely.

"Tell him we didn't extend anything," Bennett seemed to think this most urgent. "Not a dime."

"I'll tell him," I promised, but the only thing I gave a damn about was Julia.

"If the Lord sees fit to put me in this place at this time, perhaps there is a reason," Julia's words burned through the letter in my pocket. "Perhaps we are the reason, Carter. You and I."

She was nearby, a five minute walk away. But with her father so vigilant, and my own, I'd have to be careful.

"Be sure and tell him," Bennett seemed dimly to sense my preoccupation.

"I'll tell him." I shook his hand for emphasis. "Thank you much, Bennett."

The school was open to anyone, so I walked right in. A gaggle of first graders marched by on their way to the cafeteria. I knew the high schoolers wouldn't be far behind. I hurried down that Roman hall to find—"RM 12, Miss Ogilvie." There was a square of glass gridded with wire set about eye level into Julia's door. I peeked in.

I didn't see her at first. What I saw was a shock of teenagers, fifteen, twenty, or more, displaying even in winter the distinction and demands of sex. You could see the signs of the times in their thin dresses, their patched trousers and worn footwear.

A wooden desk up front was littered with pencils and paper and an empty vase. I could see a portrait of George Washington on the wall, and a poster proclaiming the Pledge of Allegiance. Something was chalked large across the blackboard, a blown-up version of the cursive with which I had become familiar: "Fire and Ice."

"A poem has a voice," I heard her say. Julia came into view near her desk and empty vase.

"A voice," she repeated. "The same as you and I have. But we have to train ourselves to hear a poem's voice because without our own voice to give it life, it cannot be heard. That is one of the many mysteries of poetry. How it has a voice, and yet without ours has not."

She brushed a lock from her face. That plain panhandler's face. And yet the russet hair, that gorevan raiment, shone like gold. Eyes green as a hoard of jade. And her carriage so tall. She wore a sweater over a long-sleeved cotton blouse. Dark knee socks disappeared up into a wool skirt that came nearly to the floor to wisp over scuffed brown leather shoes. She cradled her book to a swell of breast as if it were an infant.

She was glorious.

"Fire and Ice," she began to read. "By Robert Frost."

Her voice a croon. A beckoning. An invitation.

> *"Some say the world will end in fire.*
> *Some say in ice.*
> *Front what I've tasted of desire,*
> *I hold with those who favor fire.*
> *But if I had to perish twice,*
> *I think I know enough of hate*
> *To say that for destruction ice*
> *Is also great*
> *And would suffice."*

The bell rang, that familiar release from pedantry. But the children sat still. Immobile for a countless moment. Like snow clinging to the incline of a steep tin roof.

But then the spell broke. The students burst rambunctious from their uncrowded desks and coursed through the door like a stream of salmon. Julia was left alone to see me remaining in its frame. Caught as in a picture or net.

"Carter!"

A smile warmer than spring turned that ordinary face into a countenance of distinction.

"Carter, you came!"

"Of course."

She closed the door. "Oh, God, thank you for coming!"

She embraced me. For the first time I felt her breasts firm and full on my chest. I had imagined before what they might feel like, her breath, her breasts. Caught in her arms, I realized I had a poor imagination.

"Of course I did." I didn't even know how to hold her. "I couldn't stay away!"

"Come with me." She took my hand.

"Julia?" I glanced to the door, its wire-rimmed glass a peephole to the hall outside as well as in.

"Don't worry," she said. "We have the cloakroom, remember? And we have an hour."

We didn't have a full hour, of course. Miss Ogilvie would be expected to supervise the cafeteria. There would be the necessity for me to leave before the bell. Say we had forty minutes.

How much can you say in forty minutes? How much can you do? We had until this point only a single hour of conversation between us, and I had only movies to guide what I should do next. But in the event, as with most important things, I found Julia much more experienced than I.

We had been together in the cloakroom once before, I recalled. I remembered the smells—of damp wool, warm bodies, and perspiration. I left after forty minutes, or forty years, I can't recall. She held my hand at the door.

"I was foolish. Too risky."

"No," I said. "I'm glad you did."

"Don't leave me alone, Carter." The woman so confident only moments earlier seemed now as helpless as an orphan.

"I won't," I said. "I want to see you again. Not here! This is insane!"

She laughed, and some of her natural confidence seemed instantly to return.

But where to meet? And how? We knew we couldn't keep an ongoing tryst secret, not in Laureate. And the last thing either of us wanted was to have our fathers discover our courtship through gossip. On the other hand, if I went to Dave's front porch and asked him if I might see his daughter for a social, say, or take her to a movie, we both knew he would say no.

We still lived in an age, community, and circumstance where a father's "no" carried the force of law. The fact that Julia was twenty years old would cut no ice. Dave had her under his roof and under his thumb, a situation more horrific for Julia than I understood at the time.

We needed some way to court in Dave's presence that did not require his permission.

"The county sing." Julia came up with the perfect solution. "Midway Church, this Sunday. We're going. Can you come?"

"I'll be there," I promised.

"Bring your trombone." She squeezed my hand as I left. "Maybe we can talk somebody into some ragtime."

I floated the rest of the day and worked all that week thinking only of Julia and Sunday and the coming sing. A county sing was a grand affair. It was the one time during the year that the highly evangelical churches of the region cooperated to do anything evangelic. Well over a thousand people would convene at the Midway Baptist Church, fully a third of those coming from outside Lafayette County. They would stay from sunup till sundown, the primary activity, as you might expect, being gospel singing. But this was country gospel, not the staid, solid German and English rhythms that Lutherans and Whiskeypalions mistake for fervor but the kind of gospel you can still hear in hardshell Southern churches, black or white. A simple music, easy to play, often with quick, vibrant, almost colloquial verses, more akin to B. B. King and rhythm and blues, and before that to Negro spirituals, than to the solemn cadences of mainstream tradition. It was ironic, considering the roots of the music, that there would be no black people singing it.

Every white congregation would send a group, usually selected from the best of its choir, to perform. But there were featured groups too, professional traveling salvation shows with names like "The Dixie Travelers" or "Sadie and the Mount Zion Spirits."

There was always a tenor who could sing higher than a castrated cat and a bass who could get deeper than a coal mine. We loved them all.

In the breaks between sets the gathered faithful would sing en masse. People would pray, dance, or speak in tongues. Women prostrated themselves in the aisles, and men otherwise distinguished for their restraint and rectitude would buck dance in ecstasies of salvation. I've often wondered if our county sings weren't the truest precursor to rock concerts.

Except we had food. I mean real food. Pilau and mullet and swamp cabbage. Hams and sausages and barbecue beyond description. And desserts! You've never had a peach cobbler or banana pie or homemade ice cream till you've tried Miss Mamie's pie on a chilly day with "Precious Memories" swelling from a thousand fervent voices beyond. I've heard lots of preachers in lots of churches, but I never heard anybody invoke the Holy Ghost any better than Miss Mamie could with a slice of pie, or chicken and rice.

Everyone who came brought something, could be lima beans or venison, didn't matter. Nowadays people coordinate these affairs, paranoid that two folks or families might actually bring the same thing. Freed from that concern or pretense, we brought whatever we wanted, and miracles never ceased to happen. Loaves and fishes were indeed multiplied at our county sings, and the people were well fed.

The gathered dishes were served in common on a field fence pulled tight as a corset and forty yards in length between oak trees or posts anchored for the purpose. You'd put sawhorses beneath the heavy fence at intervals of ten or twelve feet to bear the weight of cast-iron pots or simple plates. Bed sheets thrown over the fence kept the covered dishes from falling through the heavy squares of wire. I've seen a hundred and twenty feet of fence so crowded with dishes you couldn't put a glass of iced tea, always sugared, between them.

I came early to Midway's Baptist church. The fence was just being pulled to its anchor when I arrived in Tink's truck. I was lucky to be driving; I had almost had to walk.

I had gotten up for Sunday breakfast as usual. Sunday was Tink's favorite day. Unburdened by business or religious obligation, Sundays gave Tink the chance to smoke or fish or fire-hunt for deer. Sometimes he'd sit on the porch swing and slice a pear while my mother sat alongside knitting. That was an odd sight, my father's giant, disproportioned hands doing their rude work next to Mother's slender and adroit occupation.

They could see the lake from our front porch, Tink and Martha. They'd talk to the sway of the swing and the click of her knitting, combining a necessary task with the notion of leisure and relaxation, spend most of the day on that porch. I did too, usually. I had no friends nearer than Cross City and was too tired after a week of Tink's business to go sparking anyplace distant. So Tink was surprised when he looked up from his slice of pear to see me dressed for church.

"Somebody die?" he asked me.

"I'm going to the sing," I replied.

"The county sing? How nice." Martha smiled beside my father. "I used to go when I was little. Tink, you need to take me sometime."

"Could do, could do." Tink frowned over his Barlow. "Don't ever remember Carter being interested before."

"Guess I got religion." I tried to joke my way out of it.

"I been to a sing or two myself, when I was younger," Tink declared, pocketing his knife. "'Course, when I went it didn't have a thing to do with religion. Nossir. When I went to a county sing it was 'cause I wanted to see some girl."

"That a fact?" I edged for the steps.

"Why, surely," Tink responded innocently. "You take a girl you want to see, but you were worried about her daddy, he might run you off his porch with a whip, why, you'd just meet her at a sing, right there in front of God and everybody. What could her old man do then?"

"Not much, I guess."

"Improved the odds at any rate," Tink agreed, and then he quit the pretense of ignorance altogether. "So who are you seeing, Carter? Or hope to see?"

I glanced to Mother, but this was my fight.

I cleared my throat.

"Julia Ogilvie," I answered Tink loudly. "Dave pulled her out of FSCW."

Tink just grunted.

"Dave needs her for the tobacco," I went on. "She gives him half her salary too."

"Salary?" Martha inquired.

"From teaching. She's teaching now, Julia is. Up at the school."

"Sounds like you two have a lot in common." Martha spoke lightly enough, but Tink wasn't having it.

"There's all kinds of women to sharpen yer pencil, Carter. Doesn't have to be Dave Ogilvie's daughter."

Equal parts rage and embarrassment confused my reply. But Mother's was quick and hard. "Tink, I don't want to hear you ever talk about that girl that way, do you hear? Nor Carter. They're both good children. They've been loyal, both of them, to their daddies. Just because you and Dave can't get along—!"

With that my mother flew out of that porch swing, all six foot three of her, and damn near dumped Tink onto the porch. He looked after her, amazed.

"I don't think Martha's been that put out with me in twenty years."

I didn't say anything. Tink covered the swing's arms with those great, great hands.

"Go on, then," he finally sighed heavily. "You're gonna go anyway. Just don't forget who's family."

"That'd be pretty hard to do," I said and left with the truck.

Edward Land's wife was singing "Just a Closer Walk with Thee" when Dave Ogilvie's Packard came purring up to join the hundred other vehicles already massed around Midway's church and cemetery. Caleb was the first one out, sweet and eager and awkward as usual. Wyatt trailed sullenly behind, already fetching a cigarette from his shirt pocket.

Then Dave got out, tall and straight in a Sunday suit immaculately pressed. His shoes were, as usual, brightly polished and soft. He wore rimless glasses that morning. He was the only man wearing gloves, calfskin. A gold-plated watch chain drooped prominently in an arc below Dave's vest pocket; when Dave took off a glove to wind his Hamilton's stem, you could have mistaken him for J. P. Morgan.

Once his timepiece was reconciled and his entrance grandly assured, Dave circled the Packard's hood to let Sarah out, not a gesture expected of men. He was halfway around that block-long car when Julia stepped out from the sedan's rear seat.

She had a wrap against the chill but otherwise was dressed plainly as an Amish housewife in a chambray dress that covered her from neck to foot. A belt at her waist gave you an idea of her figure, though. And her hair was down, lighter and more russet than tobacco when it's cured. Long, like tulipwood laid against the blue of her dress. She had on the same scuffed shoes that I remembered from our cloakroom reunion.

My legs took off toward Julia before my brain fully realized the depth of that commitment. Dave saw me before she did.

"Carter," the challenge came before I was two strides toward the car. "Didn't know you liked to sing."

"Oh, yessir, Mr. Ogilvie," I replied like an idiot. "That is, I like the singers. The people. I like the food too. Hullo, Mrs. Ogilvie."

"Why, Carter, how nice to see you. Look, Julia, it's Carter."

"Morning." Julia tried to find some posture between encouraging me and pacifying her father.

"Morning, Julia. Good to see you."

"I thought you were at the university, Carter." Sarah distracted Dave by offering him her arm.

"Daddy needed help with the business." I was half honest. "I hope to go back within the year and finish up."

"Julia is in a similar circumstance." Sarah offered that as much for her husband's censure as to inform me. "You two should have a lot to talk about."

"We're here for the gospel, Mother."

"Of course we are, Dave. Come on inside, Carter. Sit with us."

And so with one civil stroke Sarah saw to it that Julia and I sat that whole morning side by side. It wasn't like the cloakroom. But in some ways the absolute impossibility of any but the most timid physical contact made that gospel communion all the more erotic. I could drink her in, and her father could find no possible excuse for offense.

It was stuffy inside that overheated church. All around us voices rose to God as cardboard fans flapped back and forth like outsized butterflies, cooling our faces and reminding us in gaudy advertisement of the comfort to be derived from Broward Homestead's sleek black hearses and waterproof caskets.

Julia's hand guided mine to find the correct verse in the hymnal we shared. I do not remember the song. Didn't know it then. But to be so near her, so near! To see, to touch. And to smell a gentle dab of lilac water on her wrist, smell her freshly washed hair, the stiff clean of her soft chambray. I could feel the Holy Spirit rising hard, and only the absolute terror of embarrassment allowed that crisis to pass.

Finally we broke for our midday meal.

"Mrs. Ogilvie?" I do remember turning to Sarah before stealing away.

"Yes, Carter?"

"Do you think I might take Julia to church on Sunday? Would that be all right?"

"I can't imagine why not." She smiled, and I saw in the mother's small face and eyes some palimpsest of the daughter's.

"Do you need help getting a plate?" I asked, almost as an afterthought.

"Let Dave." She smiled almost mischievously. "Gives him something to do."

Julia and I were left to our own devices. Sarah kept her husband unobtrusively occupied. It wasn't hard. Many of the families at the sing were from Dave's uptown church; they all had to say hello. Many other families came too, eager to speak with or be introduced to the man still renowned for bailing out Laureate's bank and saving the town from financial disaster.

It was only natural that voices so intimately entwined would at some point turn from song to socializing. These weren't strangers, after all. Practically everyone who came to a sing was kin or dog-kin. It was inevitable in that setting for children to play, for women to congregate, and for men to talk politics.

Leroy Sessions and Bennett had journeyed to the sing for no other purpose. March 28 was not far off, the last day for a Democrat to declare against Leroy's son. Having Bennett so amicably near Dave's side at the county sing was a good way to discourage any would-be contestee for the tax assessor's seat. And so Leroy was making sure Bennett prominently displayed himself beside if not actually inside

Dave's vest pocket, smiling to the gathered pilgrims who came to pay homage to Julia's father.

There they were. Bennett affecting a politician's smile beneath eyes set into that skull of dough, a small-town candidate for a small county office. Dave adopting the perfect pose of a man of means, tolerant of lesser mortals, slightly preoccupied with the demands of some plane of consideration not accessible to the plebeians who pressed in khakis and gingham for his attention.

I wondered how many other people besides Leroy and Bennett and I knew that Dave was broke? I felt an urge at that moment, an incredible, insane impulse to tell them all, to scream at the sycophants gathered at Dave Ogilvie's feet—He's finished! He's broke! Leroy's already plotting to sell Dave's mortgage! And *my* father's buying it! Tink Buchanan! Boy, would that make some jaws drop. Would *that* shake up the political equation.

What I didn't know, busy as I was with Julia and bowls of banana pudding, was that the political equation was already changing in ways that would involve us both.

Ray Henderson probably started things. Ray owned the farm and cold water that bounded the east side of our property. Lounging with Ray beneath an enormous water oak was Sheriff Frank Folsom. Judge Blacksheer was there too, a long-ago transplant from Virginia known for his political acumen and accuracy with firearms. These were the men who lived on politics. In years past all three had received considerable compensation for supporting Leroy Sessions's son in his runs for office. Sometimes the compensation came in cash, sometimes land or livestock. Always it had come from Dave Ogilvie.

But this year there had been nothing. I can imagine their deliberations, the farmer, the sheriff, and the judge, pondering beneath Midway's generous oaken shade why it was that the tribute normally delivered for supporting Bennett Sessions was this year withheld.

"Nobody running against him, what Bennett told me," Ray might have put the situation to the sheriff and Judge Blacksheer. "'Leroy said pretty much the same thing. No point in spending money on Bennett this year seein' as how he's running unopposed."

"Unopposed so far," the judge rumbled. He was always dressed in black. Like some hanging judge, though too intelligent and passionless for that rough analogy.

"Not sure I woulda supported Bennett this year anyhow," the Sheriff rationalized uneasily. *"You take a look at property values—they've stayed steady, am I right? Whole country's going to hell, you cain't sell an acre of land for a fleas fart, and here's Bennett talkin' 'bout millages and assessed values and taxes just as if we was all rich."*

"You think he can be beaten?" Ray would have taken that initiative.

"I b'lieve so," Sheriff Folsom declared with the certainty of a man whose political support was always for sale. *"Thing is—we ain't got much time. And we ain't got a candidate."*

"We might have." Ray always voiced dissent gently.

"Where?" the judge asked.

"Right over there."

That's most likely when I saw Ray nod in my direction. Just a friendly, neighborly gesture. I smiled politely in return.

The sheriff and the judge followed Ray's nod.

"I'll be damned." The judge roused in pleasant surprise, *"Is that Tink Buchanan's boy? With Dave's little girl?"*

"She don't look too little to me," the sheriff objected through a pinch of snuff.

"Is this a recent assignation?" the judge inquired.

"Don't know about that, but Carter's been up to her school; I seen him walkin'," the sheriff chuckled salaciously. *"Reckon he could've struck himself a lick or two."*

"Not on that flint," Ray shook his head positively.

"My, my, my." Blacksheer's response withheld judgment for evidence. *"And how'd this-all come about?"*

"Tink brought his boy home, what I heard." Ray smiled. *"He's running about three businesses at once. Reckon he needs all the free help he can get."*

"How about Julia? I heard she was up in Tallahassee. Doing well."

"*I don't know less it has somethin' to do with money,*" *Ray replied conspiratorially.*

"*You know something, Ray?*"

"*Don't know. Just heard. But what I hear Dave's got money problems.*" *Ray letting it all out quietly. A little nugget at a time.* "*Miss Mamie's been working at the bank over a year tole me she ain't never seen a cent Dave's paid toward his mortgage. He's come twice lookin' for barn money, got turned down. And then the other day Mamie says she's pulling Dave's file for the auditor, Leroy just takes it from her, pulls it right outen her hand and tells her, 'I handle Mr. Ogilvie's accounts, Miss Mamie. My personal responsibility.' 'His personal responsibility!' Ain't that a crock of living shit?*"

"*Ever hear Dave say why Julia left the university?*" *This from the judge.*

"*High school needed her to teach, what I heard,*" *Sheriff Folsom supplied.*

"*Could be,*" *Ray nodded.* "*Or could be Dave cain't afford to keep her up there.*"

"*My, my, my,*" *the judge rumbled again.* "*I wonder if there is some advantage to be gained here?*"

"*What you think I'm sayin'?*" *Ray retorted quickly, not wanting his genius to go unnoticed.* "*What you think I'm tryin' to point out?*"

"*Interesting, interesting,*" *Judge Blacksheer narrowed his eyes.* "*If we can't get something out of Bennett's race, we might as well have a man of our own.*"

"*But even with money, Carter'd need Dave's support to win.*" *The sheriff shook his head.* "*Ol' Dave controls a block of votes right by hisself—why would he give 'em to Carter Buchanan? It ain't likely he's gonna forget Carter is Tink Buchanan's son.*"

"*Don't look to me like he's too concerned about it,*" *Ray declared.*

They might have seen the way Julia leaned quickly to my ear.

"The cemetery. Give me a minute."

The brush of her lips against my ear could have been an accident. So I told myself. But that did not fool for a moment the older eyes that regarded Julia and me yards away beneath the shade.

⁂

The county sing would end with sunset; already the sun was low and hidden behind a bank of indigo clouds. Welcome shadows. Julia skirted the crowd as she took leave of me. She rounded the yard, her chambray skirt lifted to prevent its dragging in the sand. A quick look round. Sarah had already guided Dave back into the church for a final "Rock of Ages." A simple thing then to round the church, to follow the barbed wire to a place where every boy and girl knows there is a break in the fence. A place where lovers can step unseen from the lane into deep shadows and the backgrounds of the cemetery. Beneath and behind a shield of cypress dense enough so that we can steal kisses pent up over a day of hallelujahs. Quick, urgent kisses.

We find a headstone set over a monument laid flat and wide to shelter the coffin beneath. We settle together. The granite's chill is unexpected on my skin, hers damp now and hot, and I smell something new to me, something different to mix with the aroma of lilacs and water. I fumble for a way inside.

"Here. Here!" Julia traps my hands with her own. And then laughing, breathless, reaches for me.

When we left separately from that yard of the dead, we were certain our rendezvous had passed unobserved. For weeks afterward we enjoyed the illusion that our secret was well kept.

⁂

Our courtship bloomed with a hasty spring. Generally in our region you can look for February to be cold, warm days not coming often before Easter. It varies, of course; I have seen peach trees blooming in January or even earlier, though usually a late frost will kill any attempt at new life that comes so early. Fortunately for Julia, for me, for the peach trees, and for Dave Ogilvie's twenty planted acres, spring came early in 1940, and there was no frost to spoil it.

By the first week of March fish began running the creeks

and slews, their roe once again rising with hyacinth from the water. Honeysuckle and cow dung mingled damply aromatic above fallow fields and new-ground broken in rows of corn and cotton and tobacco. You could smell spring in the dew that clung to the pickerelweed. You could smell the iron in the pump handle. You could smell the moss.

Beyond the aromas of spring there came also the acoustics. Cattle bellow and stamp. Horses whinny, dogs yelp. All seeking mates and procreation. I never believed *all* that racket was for the advancement of the species. Birds chirp for any excuse if they have sunshine. Cardinals and mockingbirds and blue jays nesting in trees or barns cackle and cry and whistle all day long and into the evening. Hawks cry solitary and vigilant in the lofty heavens, while buzzards' mutterings can only be imagined, dark, brooding specks that they are.

Even so, it was apparent that nature was copulating, sowing herself in seeds and spores and pollen and eggs and sperm to create a pattern more complex than any mosaic in a movie house.

And then of course there were the flora for me to see, immeasurably enriched by my introduction to botany and chemistry and science. Everything from the common cattail to the pineland hibiscus burst to life in a spontaneous combustion. The common names were wonderful: bloodleaf and alligator weed and crow poison growing wild in hammocks and ponds and swamps. Deer tongue and goldenrod, both *fistulosa* and *odora* more common to the dry, open pinelands. Rambling through the woods near Fort McKoon I'd see Turk's turban nine feet tall crowding some abandoned sharecropper's shack, or Florida violets brocading some farmer's sugarcane kettle. On the lakes you'd see mingled with the fragrance of roe and hyacinth floating hearts weaving like yellow valentines between the hyacinth's brilliant magnolia blossom.

I fashioned a wreath of passionflower for Julia one Sunday morning. Reverend O'Steen had just labored an hour and a half trying to describe the ineffable majesty of the coming Passion; it seemed to me that a more moving and concrete testimony pointed toward resurrection and crawled on a vine right up the side of his church.

I cut a bouquet from that creeping beauty, the blossoms uniform, five lavender petals, flowers fringed with a finely toothed corona close to purple in hue. Jesus' robe was said to be purple, a royal color.

When Sarah saw the wreath I'd made for Julia she smiled. "I hear you have a fondness for plants, Carter."

"Yes, ma'am."

"Is there a proper name for that one?"

"Yes, ma'am, *Passilflora incarnata*. Still means 'passion flower.' Just in Latin."

"Do you know all the Latin names?"

"Oh, no, ma'am. Only a few. I have books, though. If you'd like me to look something up."

Julia rounded the corner, then, her father holding court on the front lawn. In her mother's presence, I presented the wreath. If not a declaration of love or intent, it at least signified that our Sunday meetings were not trivial.

Julia and I imagined all of this to be secret, of course. Young people falling in love always believe they are invisible. And immortal.

Judge Blacksheer was watching. Ray and the sheriff too. I still don't know if I imagined that Dave himself was blind to Julia and me. I had no choice, really, except to act as if that were the case. I wasn't strong enough to confront the man or take his daughter away. Easier to believe that he didn't know we were intimate. Perhaps he didn't—why else would Dave tolerate my Sunday courtship?

In the short run it didn't seem to matter. I made every Sunday service between the county sing and Easter. I paid a price for it at home.

"My, God, Martha, I do believe our boy's done got religion," Tink complained when I asked once more for the truck.

"Not particularly," I said.

"What is it then—pallbearer? Goddamn, you're never home."

"He's goin' to see Julia, Tink." Martha was frying tomatoes to take the rust off her skillet. "You know it, I know it, Carter knows it. Let's not act like squaws."

"Well put, Mother." Tink was capable of accepting discipline. Then to me—"The last time I set foot in church was to bury your grandpa."

"Wouldn't hurt to visit now and then," I made bold.

"At Dave's church? Dave Ogilvie's?"

"You don't have to fight him all the time, do you?" I adopted the pose of peacemaker.

"I'm not fightin'. If I was fightin', you'd know. *He'd* know for damn sure."

"Sunday's the only day Julia gets free." I unwisely pressed my case. "It's the only time we can see each other. What would you do?"

"If I had to pray beside that son of a bitch I'd do without."

"Tink!"

"Who are you courtin' anyhow? The girl—or her daddy?"

Have you ever swallowed a glass of iced water too fast on a summer day? That's what it felt like, hearing those words. I wondered even then whether Tink might know my heart better than I knew it myself.

But I resented being trapped in my father's grand design. Here I was free, white, twenty-one, and *educated!* Educated, by God, and having to ask my daddy if I could see my girl! If I could please, Daddy, please borrow the truck for a few moments of practically Puritan intercourse? A grown man, only one quarter shy of graduating from Emory and on my own, and shut of everything, *everything* in his god-forsaken business, and yet I was still being treated like a boy!

I rose from our kitchen table.

"Is there something needs doing at the mill? Because if there's not, it is Sunday, and I'd like to take the truck to church."

⁂

I quickly realized that much as I disliked my own situation, Julia's was even worse. Julia was also indentured to her father, but Julia looked to the end of her teaching year with special dread. The end of term for Julia meant a hard summer in her father's tobacco field.

It's hard to explain to someone never exposed to hard labor what dread its return can provoke. I've often thought the only thing worse than being condemned to the gulag is being freed from it long enough to trust the luxury of a good meal or a warm bed or a full night's sleep and then being sent *back!*

I began to hate my father's mill with a passion. I began to conjure daily the small luxuries I had so recently enjoyed in Atlanta and the time I had to enjoy them. Time to read a book or buy a drink or stay in bed till seven in the morning. Time to see a movie or sit with friends. And then to stay up till ten, have a nightcap, or maybe just go home and listen to the radio.

God, how I longed for just one day of that other life, *my* other life! And for Julia the return to the hard labor was worse.

Julia and I shared our disappointments and our dreads. It was during our Sunday assignations that we started planning in stolen whispers on the church lawn for a way to be free forever.

We could elope. But that would mean offending both our families, something Julia and I were unwilling to do. Julia just might be able to stay on at the school if she left her father's house, but without my father's employment I'd be scrapping for work right alongside all the other homeless, jobless, desperate men.

We both owed money. In addition to the fifty dollars I still owed Emory's Oxford campus, I had accumulated another seven hundred dollars in Atlanta, which the bursar would soon press to collect. Today debts like these, especially for a student, would present little dilemma. But in 1940 a seven-hundred-fifty-dollar debt was onerous. Until I found a way to pay Emory what I owed I could not return to complete my degree. I could not finish my education without my father's help.

Looking back, maybe I wasn't brave enough. Maybe *we* weren't brave enough. Maybe Julia and I should have cut loose from the security or promise of our fathers' separate fortunes. Maybe we should have tried it alone. But Thomas Jefferson said that people will willingly tolerate a situation that is intolerable, so long as it is familiar.

Those were the things over which Julia and I agonized all that incredibly beautiful spring. Why should the children's future be held hostage to the war their fathers waged? Why should *we* be made to pay for our father's sins?

And then Spence got married.

Chapter fifteen

Fiddle Dock, *Rumex pulcher*

If I needed another indicator of the impotence of my own situation, Spence's freedom to wife could not have been better chosen. She was a sloe-eyed woman, a high yellow, the result it was assumed of massah's good time with Polly's grandmother or great-grandmother. A hybrid. She seemed to glow in the dark, the patina from that smooth skin reminding me of strong coffee mixed with a rich cream.

She was only an inch or two shorter than Spence, about Julia's height, I realized when I glimpsed her over the sea of guests who arranged dishes of food on Eida Mae's porch. She was supple in frame and movements, more slender than I would have expected. High cheekbones. She came with a family ready-made, a boy. Her first husband was killed when fishing; he slipped into a twine of water moccasins. Polly understood Eida Mae's fear of snakes. The yard would be raked even more religiously than was customary.

Polly's little boy had a name, but everyone took to calling him Little Saint because of the startling coincidence that the youngster had one blue eye and one brown one, just as Saint MacGrue had. That sparked some gossip among the whites in the camps. Spence's father was now accused around fireplaces and whiskey bottles of having nearly two decades earlier bedded with either the paternal or maternal grandmother of Spence's new wife, thereby siring Polly's father or mother. How else, ran these discussions, could Polly's pickaninny get Saint's eyes?

Such convoluted lines of completely unfounded speculation lead to others, of course, chief among them that Spence was mating in sin with his quarter-sister.

Gossip among black people tended more toward superstition. Saint MacGrue for many Negroes, especially the elderly, had long been thought to have died unnaturally. Seeing Saint's eyes in Spence's stepson, many black men and women were convinced that the dead man's spirit had returned to seek vengeance against his murderers.

Spence treated Little Saint just as if the boy were his own. He had sparkle, no doubt about it, had Little Saint. Only six years of age and already a pistol. Even Eida Mae would stop her ceaseless rocking to watch him catch a lizard or run around the house, tirelessly, as Spence used to with me, chasing a barrel hoop with a tobacco stick.

I resented Spence's wedding. Black people I didn't know descended on the Little House. As I watched from a place not far outside the yard I could barely make out Spence, let alone his bride, through the throngs of Negroes milling about the place, their cheaply shod feet scuffing out Eida Mae's sandy labor.

I guess I expected Spence to come out. To leave his wedding party and to extend, however briefly, a courtesy. Something like—

Mr. Carter, how 'bout some swamp cabbage?

Or—

Thanks, Boss, comin' see my Polly.

Any recognition would have sufficed. But as I waited on the outside of that fenced-in celebration, I could see that there would be none coming.

Here, I thought, is a nigger living on my daddy's land, and he has more to say about his life than I do.

Mother was there. She walked right in, mounted the steps, said something that got Polly blushing and brought a smile to her face. Mother left a plate heaped with venison sausage; I saw Spence thank her for that.

Then I saw my mother's tall, proud frame move easily out of the yard, speaking as she went, acknowledging pleasantries and greetings as if she'd known these people all her life.

Somebody brought a broomstick, extended it across the door. Spence and Polly jumped over easily and disappeared inside to gifts of music and eggs and chickens.

I knew what he soon would be doing with that light-skinned, well-toned woman. I could imagine the feel of that supple belly, those golden breasts. I knew the desire. I don't know how long it was before I noticed a boy regarding me calmly from a point just outside the fence.

He was a small boy. Six years or so.

I saw the one blue eye.

"Who'a you?" Spence's new-got son asked me.

"Nobody," I said and left. No one noticed my leaving except the boy. I was well outside the circle Spence had drawn for himself, his family, and his friends. As I walked home I realized there might never be a way back in.

Still I looked back. One long, last look. There was Little Saint now dancing with some black man on the porch. Eida Mae clapping time with one hand, the other still seeking, even now, the yo-yo that would never come.

I turned away, quickly, and quickly walked back to the Big House and my own empty bed.

For weeks I had wrestled with my fears, my doubts, my intentions. I decided I had to try and make an honorable arrangement with my father. One morning early I got my opportunity.

"Git yer coffee an' grab your eats, Carter," Tink boomed the greeting at breakfast. "We're goin' fishing."

Generally when Tink took a pole and worm it was to some secluded locale distant from the house, usually to some unmarked hole or hammock in the flatwoods. Today my father walked me right off our front porch and out to the lake that defined the southern extent of our property.

It was Wednesday. Ought to have been a work day.

"Shouldn't we be at the mill?"

"Spence can handle it for a day," Tink replied cheerfully.

That was true. Spence could handle the mill, the office, and everything else so far as I was concerned.

"I figured you could use some time off," Tink said.

"What brings this on?"

"Seems to me you're wound a little tight," Tink replied. "Nothing like a day on the water to fix that."

The sun was still hidden behind a ridge of cypress and pine. A fog clung like silk to the skin of the water. We had a boat, a kind of long John, that you could pole or paddle to some likely ambush of bass or perch.

The lake was clear and brown as coffee. You could see the bass beds in the shallows, irregular patches on the white sandy bottom looking yellow through the lens of water.

"Gators." Tink pointed casually ahead. About a hundred yards to starboard you could see twin wakes of gators' snouts approaching each other from opposite sides of the lake. The reptiles hunted in tandem, each chasing fish and turtles into the jaws of its mate.

"Should be a good day," Tink's baited hook fell with a lead shot and cork beside a cypress knee.

I used the activity necessary to prepare my line as an excuse for silence. I clamped the lead shot onto my line with a pair of pliers and sliced the cork halfway to slide in the line and set the depth of my still unbaked hook.

"Something you wanta say, Carter?"

This overture came unexpectedly. I tried to take advantage of it.

"I don't want to manage mills and timber all my life," I said. "I want to get done with school. Have my own life."

"You will, Carter. Things go well, you'll be back in Atlanta in time for the fall term."

"That's assuming Dave can't stay ahead of his mortgage. What if he can? What if he makes his crop and pays off every dime of interest?"

"That ain't likely."

"You don't know. For all you know he'll make his crop, throw the dice again on Wall Street, and be right back in business."

"I'll still have the mortgage," Tink shrugged. "Worst comes to worst we can try again next year."

"I don't want to try again next year. I didn't want to try *this* year!"

"Did it ever occur you might be owing *me* something, Carter?"

"I've done everything you wanted. Everything. But I can't do this."

He sighed. "It's Julia, isn't it? Dave's little girl."

"She's not little. You don't have to be so damned patronizing."

Tink's cork bobbed with a bite. He didn't take that first tease. Just nudged the line, slowly. And waited.

"You aim to marry that girl, Carter?"

Another question I didn't expect.

"We've talked around it some. I guess, sure. But Dave won't let her go. Not till he's free of the mortgage."

"Well, he ain't never goin' to be free of that," Tink declared softly. "Not so long as I've got breath to breathe."

"Why can't you just leave me out of this, Daddy? I don't want a quarrel with Dave Ogilvie. Julia doesn't want to think badly of you."

"Julia wants to get away from her daddy," Tink popped his cork gently as a soda pop top on the water. "I don't blame her."

"Let me go, then. Let me go; give me money to finish school. I'll marry her, and you and Dave can finish your business by yourselves."

My own line dipped sharply then. A big strike. I paid no attention. Tink seemed focused on some distant point across the lake.

"You ever notice that sawgrass? On our lake?"

"Sawgrass? How'd we get on sawgrass?"

"You ever notice?"

"Sure I have. 'Course I have. Why?"

"Surprised you haven't asked about it is all."

"What do you mean?"

"You're studyin' plants, aren't you, Carter? I know I'm not an educated man, but I *can* make out a transcript. School sends 'em to us, you know. Ever' term. You're studyin' plants a lot."

"Well, yes, I am."

"Mmm hmm. Well, then, don't you ever ask yourself—how'd it get here? How'd it get here onto our lake?"

"No. Damned if I see what you're driving at."

"Well, sawgrass is a saltwater plant, Carter. Brackish, at least. And this here lake's freshwater, true enough?"

"Yes, sir."

"So how'd the sawgrass get on our lake?"

"God put it here!"

"No. He didn't."

Tink pulled in his line. Cast again.

"I put in the sawgrass."

"You did?"

I looked again to the ragged boundary of our lake. There was indeed sawgrass everywhere. *Cladium jamaicense.* Our lake was well inland and relatively elevated; we certainly had no saltwater. And yet there was sawgrass plainly visible and familiar all about me.

But it should not be here.

How had such a contradiction escaped me? Why had I not seen this for myself?

"You planted the sawgrass?" I asked my father.

"It was years ago," Tink affirmed. "'Bout the time you was born, actually, I brought some sawgrass back from the coastline. Picked me a mess right there near Deserters' Island, near to the

Gulf. I always loved the smell of salt on the water. And the sight of sawgrass."

"So you came back to our lake and, what—just stuck it in the muck?"

"Ah hah. In a little corner. Right over on that point. Where those gators are trollin'. Right over there."

"It's growing fine," I observed.

"That's the problem." Tink spat. "It's growin' too good. That rascal started out in a little patch on that point. Now it's takin' over the whole lake. I even tried burning it out once. No good. And sooner or later I'm goin' to lose my fishing hole because of it."

Just about that time I got a hit on my line that nearly jerked my pole from my hand.

"HOLD ON, CARTER!"

Just that quickly we were back to being fishermen. The line sang like a bowstring. Tink grabbed a paddle.

"DON'T LET 'IM FOUL THE LINE."

A thrust of the paddle and our small craft skidded away from the path of my singing thread.

"Keep the tension, keep the tension!"

I was standing by now, my bamboo pole bowed like a pole-vaulter's, Tink backing the boat away to deeper water.

"That's good, keep workin' him."

I had never had a fish of this size on my line before. Never. And I was bringing him in. I was bringing him in! A whoop of pure joy burst from my throat.

"That's my boy!"

I worked him closer, closer. He leaped thrashing from the water! Giant leaps! My God, he was beautiful! Fighting me! Fighting me with a fury I never imagined! Fighting me and trying all the while to throw the claw, which even as we struggled was working its way into his gills and gut!

"KEEP 'IM COMING!"

That fish plunged, then, as if to charge the boat. I heaved back sharply, the pole wrenched to the stern.

"I'm losing him!"

That's when Tink plunged the net over the side—

"GOT HIM!'

Next thing I know the biggest bigmouth bass I've ever seen was drumming the bottom of our flatbottomed boat like a jazz man on Saturday night. He was huge, over twelve pounds huge. His eye glared at me angrily, this old monster, scarred and veteran of countless encounters with fishermen, with turtles, gators, and heron and moccasins and God knows what all else. And brought in by *me?*

I had to sympathize with the old fellow's condition.

The hook was caught all the way back to his gills.

"He's a beauty isn't he?"

"Yes, sir, gentlemen." Tink smiled broadly.

There was a pause then. A brief respite as Tink worked the hook free.

"There," he said, his hands bloody with the work.

"Say, Daddy."

"Yes, Carter?"

"Why did you tell me about the sawgrass?"

Tink rinsed his hands in the cool water.

"It reminds me who's responsible. Why the lake will die one day. Reminds me too that I can't change what's happened. No one can."

Then that bass thrashed suddenly, violently in the bed of our boat. A final bid for freedom. I leaped to keep him from getting away, jammed my hand down his throat to the gill.

I cut myself badly in the cove between thumb and finger. The blood ran, but I didn't care. That old fish fought on, chewing on me until the last of the oxygen left his powder-dry gills and that old, bright-glaring eye went slack.

I wanted to keep him fresh. I dipped our catch-pail into the water. Watched him revive feebly.

"You could let him go, Carter," Tink said softly.

I looked at the prize at my feet. Magnificent and subdued.

"You could just let 'im go," Tink said again.

"Why?" I asked.

"Ah hah," Tink smiled and nodded his satisfaction.

I realized then that there would be no middle way for Julia or for me.

We went ashore. I kept my bigmouth bass captive and fresh in one of mother's washtubs. That night we killed, scaled, and cleaned him. Then Mother made grits and hush puppies and we ate my trophy whole.

Next morning I went into town. To the courthouse.

Chapter sixteen

Cooley's Justicia,
Justida cooleyi

J udge Blacksheer in?" Ed Land's mama was the judge's gatekeeper, what we might now call an executive secretary. She was, however, expected to make the coffee and fetch (if not actually cook) the judge's meals.

Mrs. Land looked doubtful. "I don't know, Carter. The judge usually don't take callers without some kind of—"

"It's all right, Miz Land." The judge stood there stark and black as a crow. "Carter. How are you?"

"Doing fine, sir."

"What can I do for you."

"I've got fifty dollars, Judge Blacksheer."

"I'm willing to accept it."

"It's not for you, sir."

"No? Who then?"

"Don't know exactly. But it's March twenty-eighth, Judge. Last day to declare, I understand."

"For what office?"

"Tax assessor. I believe the fee is fifty dollars."

Judge Blacksheer smiled the darkest smile I've ever seen. "Why don't you come into my study, Carter. Miz Land—? Get the sheriff over here, would you, please? And Ray Henderson too. He's over at Doc's. You hurry you can catch them both."

By the time Ray and Sheriff Folsom arrived, Judge Blacksheer had pretty well sounded out my purpose.

"I can see why you'd want some independent means, Carter." The judge did not offer me refreshment from the pitcher or bottle plainly visible. "Independent of Tink, that is. And I can see why a young man with education would find a political office appealing. Especially in these hard times. But that's not enough to make people vote for you."

"No, sir," I said. "I expect it isn't."

"Bennett Sessions is a well-supported candidate."

"*Was* well fixed, Judge. But not now."

"Oh? Do you know something I don't?"

"I doubt it, sir, to be honest."

The judge laughed.

"Oh, honesty has its uses, I suppose. Let me see. You figure Bennett is vulnerable because Dave's too broke to support him. Is that about it?"

"Partially."

"But outside of fifty dollars, I don't see any money burning a hole in your pockets. Unless Tink—?"

"No, sir, he's not supporting me. 'Fact, when he finds out what I'm doing I'll most likely be thrown out of his house."

"Indeed," the judge agreed icily. "Well, then. If you don't have your daddy's support you're going to need Dave's. But Dave's broke, Carter."

"He still commands votes, Judge. All he has to do is sit on that church lawn and say the word and those votes will go as they have every election to Bennett Sessions."

"Some obligation to Leroy compels it, I imagine." The judge smiled like a Cheshire cat. "Some quid pro quo."

He paused as if waiting for me to amplify. I didn't.

"Of course, now," Judge Blacksheer finally resorted to something like candor, "there may be other reasons for Dave to switch his allegiance from Bennett to you. Something I have yet no ken of?"

"If you mean Julia, sir, yes, it's true I've been seeing her. But I can't say Dave altogether approves of Julia and me."

"Can't blame him. Your daddy and Dave have looked for each other's throats a long time now. Can't be easy for Dave to see you making advances toward his daughter."

I tried to control the crimson spreading over my face. Blacksheer laughed again. More like a bark, really. Then he stopped, abruptly.

"So what makes you think you can turn Dave Ogilvie from Bennett's camp to yours, Master Carter? What is it that you know you are not telling me?"

So I told him. Blacksheer listened greedily while I explained Dave's financial straits and the secret contract obligating Leroy to sell Ogilvie's mortgage to my father.

"Come September Daddy will be holding Dave Ogilvie's mortgage," I told Judge Blacksheer, adding, "He's paying the whole forty thousand."

"Tink *has* that kind of money?" Blacksheer was truly astounded.

"He's got most of it," I said. "And getting the rest."

"My, my, my."

"So you see, Judge, I think once Dave knows that Leroy's selling him out, Dave isn't going to be backing Leroy's son financially or otherwise."

"And how is Mr. Ogilvie going to find out?"

I took a deep breath. "I'm going to tell him."

Blacksheer leaned back. Then, the ice for the barest moment thawed. "Do *that* and you *will* be on your own. Unless Tink shoots you first."

"Yes, sir, I know."

The judge's chair squeaked as he leaned far back. Far back. He reached over lazily to a coffee table and chessboard, lifted an ivory knight, considered the field of play. He placed it back.

"Might work. But I wouldn't count on Dave's gratitude. Just because you tell him what your daddy's up to doesn't mean he'll like you for it."

"Well, he sure as hell won't be happy with Leroy and Bennett. And neither of those two care about his daughter."

"That's how you mean to present it—!" Blacksheer straightened suddenly in his creaking chair. "You mean to say you're doing this for Julia, is that it? For her love and her hand!"

"That is why I'm doing it!" I protested hotly.

Blacksheer chuckled gleefully. "Oh, yes. It's a pretty plot you're hatching for yourself, Carter. Beat Bennett. Get Julia. Be free of your daddy. What then? A term as tax assessor, perhaps, and then back to Atlanta? Let Julia work while you finish up at Emory, that about it? And noble all the while."

My ears burned.

"It's the only way I see I can be my own man."

"Your own man. Well. We'll have to talk more about that. Hello, Ray. Sheriff."

I turned in my wing-backed chair to see my neighbor and Sheriff Folsom in the judge's warm chambers.

"Come in, gentlemen. Find a seat. We may just have ourselves a candidate."

Chapter seventeen

False Hoarhound,
Eupatorium rotundifolium

I had to make an excuse that evening that would allow me to leave for the night. Tink was in a fine mood at supper. Since firing Red Walker, the sawmills' books looked to be balancing, and Spence was proving as fine an accountant as he was a sawyer.

"If I had two of Spence, I wouldn't need you," Tink joked.

"Oh, you could replace me," I said. "I'm not much more than a clerk."

Tink seemed to take my response as high humor. Martha didn't, though. I could see her watching me closely, like you'd watch a toddler trying his first set of stairs.

"Think I could borrow the truck?"

"My God, is it Sunday already?"

"I miss the radio." I mixed the truth and a lie to get the worst of both. "Thought I'd go up to Doc's. See if I can catch something good."

"We should buy a radio," Mother said. "We could listen to the president."

It struck me then that Roosevelt was openly seeking his third term in office just as I was trying to conceal my first attempt. The war in Europe was raging; Hitler was already massing the end-sweep around France's Maginot Line that would take him by June to Paris; but in Lafayette County political discussion centered with remarkable insouciance or indifference on taxes, taxes, taxes.

"Have to use batteries to run a radio." Daddy shook his head. We had no electricity, recall. "And I hear those things suck up the juice."

"I heard some talk about putting a dam on the Suwannee," I made small talk. "Like the TVA? We could have all the electricity we want."

"Seems a high price," Tink mused. "Lose a river so you can listen to Roosevelt."

Sometimes the best way to get permission to do a thing is to act as if you already have it. I rose from the table, took my plate and utensils to the sink.

"Good supper," I told Mother.

"You didn't eat any," she observed quietly.

I wasn't so used to playing the role of Judas that I was adroit at it. I just hoped Martha assumed that my lie was meant to cover a visit to Julia.

In a way I suppose it was.

I took the truck unopposed, drove down our long lane to the new county road, which the WPA had only recently finished. Took at least twenty minutes off the drive to town, I figured. Made Dave Ogilvie's wide front porch practically around the corner.

I drove across the cattlegap that led to the Ogilvies' fenced-in yard. The hounds waited for me to open the truck's door before they started raising hell. Dave was on the porch, ramrod straight with his Bible on a straight-backed chair. Julia looked up astounded beside her mother on the porch swing.

"Be still, boys," Dave commanded the dogs. He appeared unsurprised at my arrival.

"Good evening, Mr. Ogilvie."

"Sarah. Julia. Why don't ya'll go on inside." Dave issued his commands without acknowledging me.

I was so frightened I didn't even meet Julia's eyes as she retreated inside with her mother.

"Well, don't just stand there, son. Come on."

I opened the gate gingerly to run a gauntlet between his dogs, certain every moment they'd tear me to pieces. I was still naive about what constituted a real danger.

"Your daddy shot again?" Dave inquired as I reached the porch. He remained seated.

"No, sir."

I remained standing. He didn't ask me to do otherwise.

"I'm reading the Book of Job." Dave surprised me with that non sequitur. "You ever read the Book of Job, Carter?"

"I've read the story," I evaded.

"That's not the book." Dave laid his Bible aside. "That's only part."

"Yes, sir."

"Read it sometime. Whole thing."

"I will, sir. Yes, sir."

"'I will, sir. Yes, sir.' Are you here to sing, Carter?"

I almost turned my back. I began to see dimly in what contempt this man held me, ordering his wife and daughter inside. Keeping me standing while reminding me of the plight of righteous men.

"I have something you need to know, Mr. Ogilvie."

"No more than you need to tell it, I imagine."

I had not expected this. I hadn't expected to be greeted warmly, of course. I was steeled to overcome an initial stern admonition to leave but not this toying, calculated indifference!

"Daddy's planning on taking your mortgage," I blurted out.

"Leroy's bound to sell if you don't make your interest this season. I've seen the contract. Hell, I helped write the contract!"

"Don't curse, boy. Not under my roof."

"No, sir, but—don't you see, sir? If you don't make the interest on your loan, and do it *this* season, Daddy will own your mortgage. That happens, he'll foreclose, Mr. Ogilvie, I know he will. That's what he means to do."

"I know what Tink means to do," Dave smiled coldly beside his Bible. "Thing I don't know is—*whatyou* mean to do."

"Me? Why, I don't want anything, Mr. Ogilvie. Not for myself."

"That a fact?"

"Well, I certainly don't want your land," I declared. "And I don't want to be any part of taking it, either."

"Good Lord, boy, how you make that sound righteous."

I didn't know to reply.

"Know what I think?" He was standing now. An arm's length away.

"No, sir."

"I think the only difference between you and your daddy is that Tink calls you out straight and hits you in the face, whereas you, Master Carter, are a Judas. A coward. Just some little snake in the grass gets what he wants by goin' behind people's backs."

It wasn't the response I expected.

"That's not true, sir!"

"Oh, it's not? Did you tell Tink you were coming over here to see me? To tell me about the plot him and Leroy and Bennett hatched to take my land?"

"Well, no, sir, of course I didn't."

"'Of course'! There you have it, then. The difference between you and your daddy."

"I didn't have to come at all!" I declared, my face and neck gone scarlet.

"You must have had to, boy," Dave snarled into my face. "Else you wouldn't have."

He backed away then. Regarding me as some interesting if slightly repugnant breed of bacteria.

"So why don't you tell me what you want, Carter? Tell me straight."

"I want to be on my own," I began.

He laughed. "Liar."

"I do want to be on my own, Mr. Ogilvie." I tried to mouth conviction that was fast slipping away.

"You weren't worried about independence so long as your daddy was paying your way at Emory." Dave turned his back.

"I want to finish college, sure," I said. "What's wrong with that?"

"Nothing, nothing." Ogilvie faced me again. "But you could wait a year and do that. If chance goes your way. Goes your daddy's way."

"But what if it doesn't?" I almost whispered in reply.

For the first time Julia's father smiled. "Exactly. You see, Carter, I'm a gambler myself. I know when somebody's bluffing. I know when a man's hedging his bet. That's what you're doing, Carter."

"Not much of a hedge." I tried to retreat, but he only laughed.

"Don't backtrack, son. You were doin' good there for just a minute; don't give it up."

Then the smile left the old man's face, and there was nothing but cold. "What do you want out of me?"

"I want to see Julia, sir. With your permission."

"You're seein' her already. Every time I turn around, I see you with her."

"Not just at church, sir."

"Don't give me that 'sir' crap, boy. You think I'm blind? Think I'm a fool? Think you're the only Johnny took some Sally behind the cemetery?"

My God, how much did he know?

All pretense at civility was dropped now. Dave was raging, towering over me on his wide front porch. I felt for the steps behind.

A dog growled. Dave Ogilvie reached out, shackled both my wrists in a fast grip.

"You don't think I know where these hands have been, boy?"

"Mr. Ogilvie, we haven't—!"

"SILENCE." He threw my hands practically into my own face. "You lie to me again, I'm takin' that belt down. You know the one I mean, boy? One lie, or even the *piece* of a lie, and I'm gonna get that strop and beat you crippled for *fucking* my daughter, you think I won't—?"

Had I heard him right?

"—I'll tan your hide, and when your daddy comes looking to right that wrong, I'll tell him how you came over here. You his only son, a JUDAS! Selling out his daddy for a few months of college and a piece of ass! That what you want, Carter? That what you came over to my house thinking to get?"

I fought a sudden urge to vomit.

"I better go," I mouthed weakly, resigned to fighting dogs all the way to the truck.

"I say you could go?" Dave growled.

"No, sir."

"One thing you got to learn, boy. Once you put your hand to the plough . . . don't never turn back."

I stood there numb.

"Sit down."

I edged over to the swing. The chain's squeak startled me. I tried to perch perfectly still.

"I don't care *what* you do with my daughter, boy. You and Julia, why, ya'll can do anything, *anything* your carnal natures can conjure. You can fuck dog-fashion if you want to!"

This was not the Dave Ogilvie I knew, not the deacon I had seen!

"That's right," he hissed into my ear. "You can take her on a tombstone, in an *outhouse,* I don't care! You can screw in the mud. Run buck naked in the streets, makes no matter to me. But you want to marry her, boy? Do you?"

I tried to swallow the lump that prevented my reply.

"DO YOU?"

"YES, SIR!"

He had me in tears, twenty-one years old and crying on his porch.

Dave smiled, satisfied.

"Y'see, you can *have* her anytime you want. But by God, if you intend to take my daughter to wife you best do everything, and I do mean *every single thing*, it takes to keep me my land. Do you understand, Master Carter? Or you will *never* see my daughter in a lawful bed. NEVER. I'll sell her for a whore first."

He paused for breath before continuing.

"And then I'll go to your daddy, tell him everything you told me on this porch tonight, *everything*, and what do you imagine he will do then? Say, Carter Buchanan? What do you imagine Tink will do to you when he finds out you betrayed him to *me?*"

I couldn't imagine.

Dave chuckled. "Truth is, Carter, all you really want is to finish school. Go back to Atlanta, to Emory. Get that sheepskin. If you knew for sure your daddy would let you go at the end of the season, pay off your debts and let you go, you wouldn't be talkin' to me. I'd bet even odds you wouldn't be interested in Julia, either, nosir. Not if it got in the way of your damned ambition."

I wanted to say it wasn't true. But I didn't.

"Your daddy finds out what you did here, he'll cut you off like a hangnail, you know that."

"Yes, sir." I swallowed.

"So you've pretty well left your fate in my hands, haven't you, son? And drove over here to do it."

I didn't know what to say. Seemed every time I opened my mouth I just made things worse. But then I thought—confess! Confess it all! Show how it all started, how the lie came to be, how it grew from hard necessity.

"I'm declared for tax assessor—" I began.

"I know that," he cut me off. "Knew two hours after you walked out of that courthouse."

"Then did you—?" I couldn't finish the question.

"Know the rest?" He seemed amused. "Know about your daddy and Leroy and Bennett? You'd like to be relieved on that point, wouldn't you, boy? If I knew all along, that would ease your piddling conscience, wouldn't it? That'd make it all right!"

I didn't answer, and he laughed. A laugh, I'm sure, like Satan's.

"Get off my land," he said at last. "If you hurry I won't sic the dogs."

I ran filled with shame and humiliation through his gate. I drove home crying curses and prayers, and when I rolled to a ragged stop beneath the pecan tree that shaded our porch, I stayed outside, very late, so there would be no chance that I would have to face Tink with the sign of traitor on my face.

Chapter eighteen

Eyebane,
Chamanaesyce hyssopifolia

Next morning it seemed Mother was paying me undue attention. Tink seemed happily preoccupied in contemplation of the day's labor. We'd be going to Fort McKoon, he told me. But first we'd need to drive to town. Some tungsten teeth had come by mail for the mill's circular saw. We'd collect a package waiting at Land's.

"Then maybe we'll stop by Doc's." Tink massaged the scar over his shoulder. "Get a Co-Cola. Pick up my medicine early."

God doesn't always give us a chance to right a wrong, but He gave me one chance. I could have made a real confession to my father that very morning on the way into town. I could have called him aside any time that day, told him what I had done. I had chances. In the truck. At the hardware store. Along the street.

But I kept hearing Dave Ogilvie reminding me of my ambition and warning me that Tink would have no pity on a traitor. I had never seen my father reward an injury with mercy in my life. I had seen him beat a man in trade for an insult. Seen him put the butt of his carbine into a man's codsack just for talking back. And I knew he had cut off a Klansman's ear for burning a cross on our property. How much deeper was my own sin?

I had to tell Tink about running against Bennett Sessions, of course, but that was something I'd planned for, something I'd rehearsed. In my imaginary dialogues I simply told my father that I wanted a career of my own. That I wanted to be my own man.

The business didn't need me anymore, I would point out reasonably. Tink had already brought up a pair of sawyers from his pepperboxes to take Spence's place at Fort McKoon so that Spence was now full time in the office, balancing the books and supervising the entire timber operation. And as for Tink's contract with Leroy, I would remind Daddy that although my bid for elected office violated the spirit of his agreement with Leroy and Bennett, there was absolutely nothing, legally, they could do.

Tink might even get a kick out of that, outfoxing Leroy and his pussel-gutted son. At least that's what I'd convinced myself. I couldn't tell Tink how I planned to beat Bennett Sessions, could not reveal the manner in which I'd tried to persuade Dave Ogilvie to my cause.

There was much more for Tink to hear. Things I should tell him. Confess. Plead. But sitting beside him, with the night's work done and Dave's voice still in my ear, I could not manufacture a word.

We got the teeth for our saw without incident or revelation. Tink was uncommonly loquacious, engaging Edward and his wife in small talk. I wanted to avoid all extraneous conversation. I needed to get my father away from these people and out of town so that I could think of what I should tell him. What I should say. I dreaded going to the drugstore—what would Doc say? What chance remark might destroy the careless alibi I had only the night before fabricated for myself?

"Why don't we skip the drugstore, Daddy?" I made the attempt. "I don't really need a soda."

"Well, I do," Tink declared brightly. "Besides, Doc owes me a checker game."

Tink played checkers with Doc probably three or four games

per presidential administration. My luck he should on this particular morning experience the urge to improve his average.

Fractured sunlight spilled across Doc's well-polished pine floor, but it gave me no comfort. It was so warm the stove was not stoked. As we entered I saw Doc West tapping a powdered elixir onto a set of scales.

"Hullo, young man," Tink boomed in greeting.

"Tink. Come in," Doc replied without looking up from his work. "What can I do you for?"

"Co-Cola. Two of 'em."

"Can do. Want a cherry, Carter?"

"'Cherry'?" Tink turned to me, grinning. "Since when have you taken a shine to *cherries?*"

That got chuckles from Doc's customers. There were three or four men at the counter. One or two children. A veritable crowd. I recognized Mac Morgan and his little boy. Tommy Spikes was there, in uniform! I wasn't familiar with the crossed rifles of his insignia. Punk McCray was taking a coffee break from his barbershop. Taff was there too, Taff Calhoun, nursing a hangover with equal parts coffee and nicotine. Oblivious it seemed to everyone and everything about him.

Tink granted Taff his hangover and greeted everyone else. Tommy stuck out his hand to me.

"Carter."

"Tommy. It's been a while. Too long."

"Heard you wuz working with your daddy."

"For now, yeah," I said uncomfortably.

Tink was already dragging out a checkerboard.

"You owe me a game, Doc."

"Let's see, that would be the second, third game this decade?"

"Mondays are for payin' debts," Tink replied. "Black or red?"

"Black," Doc replied, filling the roles of waiter, soda jerk, conversationalist, and checker player with singular aplomb.

"I can never remember who goes first." Tink scratched his head with a gargantuan hand.

"Black." A familiar voice supplied that clarification from Doc's front door.

It was Dave Ogilvie. He was dressed in work clothes that morning. A pair of broadcloth trousers, as I recall, tucked above brogans.

A thick chambray shirt. He strolled straight toward Tink and me at the counter. The door swung shut behind him.

"Smoke before fire. That about it, Tink?"

"Dave." Tink touched the brim of his Stetson to acknowledge the deacon's presence, and then, "Can you get some music on that radio, Doc?"

"Sure." Doc nodded then to his newest customer. "Dave, what'll you have?"

"Coffee'll do."

"Coffee it is."

Dave took a seat right beside Tink. Didn't even look at me. He nodded to the newspaper Doc had left spread on the counter. "What you think, Tink? Roosevelt gonna keep us out of this mess?"

"Beats me."

Roy Acuff, it might have been, picking and playing on the radio.

"Paper says everybody in Washington's getting ready for war." Dave seemed determined to make conversation. My gut went into spasm.

"That's just the papers," Tink replied, oblivious to my discomfort. "They got to write about something."

"Talk, hell!" Tommy spoke up. "There *is* a war going on. And we're getting ready for it too, mark my word. You just have to know where to look."

"Oh, I expect Tink could show you a place or two, am I right, Tink?"

"Nobody's business if I can, Dave."

"Except your own. Not that I blame you. If there's going to be a war, man might as well make himself some money out of it. Yes, sir."

"Seems like you know more about my business than I do," Tink snapped a checker down on the board.

"Well, I hear things." Dave smiled directly at me.

"Don't be so small-mouthed, Tink," Punk urged from the counter. How like a barber to encourage conversation.

"Tell everybody you meet about your business pretty soon it ain't your business." Tink refused Punk's bait affably.

"False modesty becomes no man." Dave slurped his coffee. "Why, I hear between the railroad and the army you're busy as a bee in a tar bucket."

"The army?" Tommy perked up. And then to me, "Ya'll are workin' for the D.O.D.?"

"Sure he is." Dave gave me a wink. "Railroads are laying new lines all over. Putting in a brand-new line to that post near Jacksonville, aren't they?"

"Camp Blanding." Tommy was pleased to display his specialized knowledge.

"That's it," Dave nodded. "Big job. So Tink sells crossties to the Loping Gopher. And two-by heavies to Uncle Sam for barracks and mess halls and God knows what all else. Doin' that kind of thing all over the Southeast, what I heard. Up Georgia. Virginia. Not a bad fracas for you, is it, Tink?"

"Beats whoring on Wall Street," Tink replied almost absently, and I saw for the second time Dave Ogilvie's cultured smile go rigid in his face.

Doc saw it too and tried to ease things up. "Well, Mrs. Roosevelt says we shouldn't have boot camps for our boys, and Mr. Roosevelt says we *should!* Wonder who'll win that one?"

"I wonder who's president," Mac Morgan declared and broke the tension gathering along the counter.

"There's gonna be a draft. Mark my word," Tommy Spikes spoke up.

"Waste of good men. Got a jump there, Doc." Tink gave up a man to take two off Doc's side of the board.

"Be hard on farmers, I 'magine." Doc frowned over his pieces. "Losing all those boys."

"There'll be deferments," Dave countered.

"You'd best hope so," Tink responded. "Else you might actually have to pay wages to get your crop."

I saw the lines tighten across Dave's face. His eyes were bright and terrible and fixed squarely on my own. I was terrified that Dave was about to tell my father where I had been the previous evening.

That I had not been anywhere near the drugstore or Doc West's radio.

But instead he turned to Tink and in a voice barely above a whisper said—

"I aim to keep my land, Tink."

In the instant of that declaration, conversation everywhere else along the counter came to a halt. Everyone hushed as if on command, their Cokes and doughnuts and coffee cups suspended in midair.

Only the radio mewed on. Some hillbilly song. Tink quit all pretense then of enjoying his Coca-Cola and checkers.

"You do remember *my* pa's place, don't you, Dave? He had a couple of bad years. Just like you. But ya'll tightened up just the same."

"I don't need no slack," Dave bit it off.

"That's good," Tink replied grimly. "'Cause you sure as hell ain't gettin' any."

Dave rose stiffly from the counter and dropped a dime. "For the coffee, Doc."

"Thank you, Dave."

I didn't breathe until Julia's father was out the door. It was almost heady then, the dread and tension of the previous minutes evaporating in an instant.

"'Bout time we went home," Tink growled.

"Yes, sir," I too eagerly agreed.

We were about halfway to the door when Taff Calhoun roused from his stupor to hail from the counter, "Say, Carter—"

"Yes, Taff?"

"What's this I hear about you running for tax assessor?"

❧

"You hated it that bad, you should've told me," Tink finally said after we were well distant from town.

I hadn't told Tink I hated anything at all. Had not said much at all, in fact, except to mumble that of course I had planned to tell him of my determination to strike out on my own, to challenge Bennett Sessions for the tax assessor's well-salaried office. My new ambition.

I had tried on the lake to make plain how I hated his mill and the whole business tied up with throwing Dave Ogilvie off his land. I had at least been honest in that.

Best now to play defense. Just respond to whatever Tink had to say. Or do.

I jammed as far to the passenger side of the truck as possible, waiting for a fist to come flying across that short space into my jaw.

"Goddamn, Carter, what are you afraid of?"

I didn't know how to reply.

Tink sighed heavily. "My God, my God."

We drove a while in silence.

"You wanted to run for office, you should've just told me," Tink started again. "I'd have let you go."

"Not without making me pay a price, you wouldn't." The reply came out before I had time to stop it.

"Of course you'd pay a price." Tink seemed genuinely puzzled. "Goddamn, there's a price for everything, Carter. There's a price for grits!"

A price for every man too.

"Are you courtin' the girl for her daddy, Carter? Or courtin' Dave for the girl?"

I didn't answer.

"'Cause I think I'd rather believe you're doin' this stupid goddamn thing for love. If you could tell me it's for love I wouldn't like it, but I'd understand. Just tell me if it wasn't for that little girl you wouldn't be doin' this. Tell me it's Julia. Whether it's true or not."

"It was both," I said, adding, "and some other things."

Thus committing what I believe Catholics call a sin of omission.

"You think if you take her daddy's farm she won't have you?" Tink asked me.

This wasn't what I expected. I expected a beating, and instead here my father was trying to place some honorable gloss on my defection, trying to assign some motivation that would make my desertion less onerous than we both knew it was.

"Who are you courtin', Carter? The girl? Or her daddy?"

It was a shifting balance. Exactly how much of this was I doing for Julia? How much for myself and my real ambition? How much had I done because I hated my father's mill? Perhaps even hated my father himself? Or was I, as Dave Ogilvie said, simply hedging a bet?

"It's all mixed up," I answered finally.

Probably the only truthful thing I said that day.

"Why tax assessor?"

"I think I can beat Bennett," I replied. "Plus with Julia working, we can save enough in four years for me to go back to Atlanta. Finish up school."

"Finish our business and you can go back anyhow," Tink pointed out. "Go back inside the year. That's what I said. That's what I meant."

"You'll be broke, Daddy. My God, you're talking about giving Leroy forty thousand dollars! In *cash!* That's *if* Dave doesn't make his crop. You'll be land rich, sure, but you'll owe taxes on two thousand acres of land, plus operating expenses, plus labor for the mills and the turpentine and the rung oil. Where's the money for school? I can't take the chance that when it's all said and done there won't be anything left for me."

"The hell are you talkin'? It's *all* for you!" Tink stared at me, amazed. "Can't you see that? The mills, the turpentine, the land—who do you think it's all for?"

"Thought you wanted me to be a doctor," I replied.

"You can be a doctor *and* have the land, the mills, the tung oil, the turpentine. What's wrong with being rich, son?"

"Not that way; it's not what I want." I risked then looking my father frankly in the eye. "It's not what I ever wanted."

We drove a while longer in silence, Tink working the steering wheel in those big hands, grinding gears at the shift.

"Leroy's gonna have a shit fit," he sighed.

"He can't do anything about it," I said in a voice meant to reassure. "You've got the contract."

Tink just shook his head.

"You ought to'a told me," he said finally. "You ought to 'ajust come flat out and told me. Paid the price."

He exhaled slowly. "Maybe you can win this election, Carter. I don't know. But if you're counting on Dave Ogilvie's support, you better understand this: He's gonna want something back. And one way or another, it's gonna come back to the land."

I swallowed hard. "Yes, sir."

"I know this man, Carter. If Dave Ogilvie gets his back to the wall, he'll turn on you or Julia or Sarah or Wyatt just as soon as spit. Hell, he'd cut off little Caleb's one good leg if it meant keeping his farm. Make no mistake, son, Julia's papa wants that land just as bad as I do. And he'll do anything to keep it."

"Well, that's the heart of the problem, isn't it, Daddy?" I replied bitterly. "For Julia and for me."

We rattled off our WPA-built road to the rougher, rutted path leading to Fort McKoon.

"You gonna stay on till September?" Tink finally asked. "Help Spence with the bookwork?"

"I don't know," I equivocated. "Election's May twenty-eighth. But even if I win I won't be taking office till January of next year, so I 'spose from June till January I could be at the mill. If you needed me."

"What you plan on doing between now and then?" Tink growled.

"Shake some hands. Stay out of your way," I tried to joke feebly.

It didn't sit well.

"We'll just see how it goes," he said finally. "See how it goes."

Even after the turnoff it took the best part of a long half hour to reach Fort McKoon and the sawmill. I sat in silence beside a father showing unexpected mercy to a son who had not yet exposed the full breadth of his treachery.

I should have told him. Maybe even in the light of his unexpected moderation I believed I *could* tell Tink that Dave Ogilvie was alerted to the contract that in September would put the Ogilvies' land under my father's thumb. Maybe I *could* even admit that it was I who had alerted the deacon. Maybe I was beginning to think I could do that.

But on that active day yet another incident arose to derail any consideration so reckless.

When we reached the mill Spence came striding urgently to the truck. He glistened with sweat in the unseasonably warm April sun.

"What is it, Spence?" Tink saw right off that something was amiss.

"Somebody done got into the yard. Last night." Spence seemed ready to blame himself. "They took some timber, Boss. Prolly round three thousand feet all together. Diff'ent dimensions."

"Been a day for surprises." Tink didn't sound surprised at all. "Don't s'pose there's any quick way to know who did it."

"Maybe not." Spence hesitated.

"Spence, if you got something to say, say it."

"Well, Mr. Tink, whoever done it been around a lumber yard before, I can tell that. And look to me like they came wantin' somethin' particular, you know? Like for a house or something? Or maybe—?"

"A barn," I finished the thought. "You think the lumber's for a barn, is that it, Spence?"

"They's nuthin' took but rough lumber. Everything from four-by-sixes to two-by-fours. Big dimensions too. Bigger than a house."

"Marked?" Tink asked.

Most mills had some kind of identifying mark on finished lumber; ours was a double-diamond stenciled along with the grade.

"Hadn't marked 'em, nosir." Spence shook his head. "Hadn't yet got 'em to the drying shed."

Tink turned to me. "There's a shotgun in the office. Get it."

"Daddy, wait!"

"Don't you 'wait' me. Not after how you've tested me this morning. Go get that gun. See if you can act like a man's son."

The new road got us to Dave's house in fifteen minutes. Tink didn't bother to go by the house, though. Instead we skirted the cattlegap that marked the way to Dave's Cerberus-guarded gate and took a dirt road that wound beneath a grove of live oak trees on the far side.

The truck broke out of that densely forested grove like a plane breaking through a bank of clouds. There was new-ground around us now, stumps still burning, the smell of pine and water oak heavy in the air. This was where Dave had placed his final bet, this stretch of riverbottom, this newly broken ground. This was where in early April his planted tobacco would rise green as emerald in half-mile rows.

Our Ford truck bounced along a badly rutted trail that hooked off the smoother dirt road. Within minutes we could see the crows' nests of Dave Ogilvie's twin barns.

A flue-curing tobacco barn looks just like an enormous tar-papered box stood on end. A gently sloped tin roof and carefully placed vents top the barn. A wide door allows sticks laden with tobacco to be passed inside for hanging. Tobacco sticks hang on tier poles mounted parallel with the ground. Each tier of poles has a little over two feet of vertical separation; the tiers start around six feet above the barn's dirt floor and run all the way to the crow's nest at the top. Large barns like Dave's could accommodate six rooms of tiers in their interior.

It was something to watch a barn being hung. Tierpoles swayed as barn help skilled as acrobats tossed sticks heavy with tobacco from the "poker" on the ground through relays to the "hanger" above, the sticks lilting ever upward from man to man, tier to tier, until hung a fist or two apart from the topmost tiers to the bottom. Air heated to a hundred seventy degrees or more would rise from burners on the floor to circulate through the tarry leaves, killing out the green and the moisture slowly so that within a week a harvest taken green from Dave's field would hang golden in his barn.

But now the barns were empty. Empty of tobacco, that is. Tink nodded to the car whose familiar hood was partially concealed by the fresh stack of lumber drying on crude skids in the late-afternoon sun.

"That's a Packard, ain't it? Settin' by that pile of lumber?"

"That pile of lumber"—as if he didn't already know it was our lumber.

I nodded. "Looks like Dave's car."

"I don't see Dave."

"Maybe he's inside a barn."

Tink stopped our Ford on the lumber's side of the barn, not a spit from an opened door. Then Tink opened the truck's complaining door. But not before he pocketed his knuckles and revolver.

"Let's go, Carter. It ain't gonna get better by waitin'."

We stepped into the barn, into the smell of sweat and mold. The floor was laced with wires and huge tin pipes for the kerosene burners. I banged my leg against a pipe and sent echoes through the barn.

"Who goes?" a voice floated down. I craned my neck back as far as I could; it was like looking from the bottom of a dark pool to see something near the surface. I peered through motes of dust to see two figures silhouetted against the tierpoles above.

"It's me, Dave," Tink said.

"Tink." The disembodied voice did not seem nonplussed.

"We're almost done," Dave went on. "Meet you outside."

"That we will," Tink answered.

Dave emerged from his barn to see Tink running his hands over the high-grade timber as if it were a newborn calf.

"You got some business out here, Tink?"

Dave strolled up as calmly as you please. Wyatt trailed behind, feral and excited.

"Seein' as how you got my lumber, yes, Dave, we do have some small business to conduct."

"I paid a fair price for this lumber. Fair and square."

"With what?"

"None of yer business!" This from Wyatt.

"Shut up," Dave snarled at his son.

Wyatt cowered.

Tink relaxed an elbow on the stack of lumber.

"You got a bill of sale, Dave?"

"I do."

"That's good. 'Cause you can go to whoever sold you this lumber and sue 'em for passing along stolen goods."

"I don't aim to sue anybody. Never."

"Wouldn't do any good to sue Red Walker anyway, would it, Dave? He's got nothing to take."

Dave remained poker-faced.

"I don't concern myself with Red Walker."

"But you did business with him, didn't you, Dave? You too broke to buy a box of seegars. Him drunker'n a shithouse rat and out of work. My guess is you told him you'd pay when yer tobaccer comes in. Sound about right, Dave?"

"How I pay for my lumber's my business."

"It's not your lumber. It's mine."

"You're pretty sure of what's yours, aren't you, Tink? What's yours and what's not?" Dave said this looking directly at me.

My heart hammered in my chest. No, God, no; don't let Daddy find out from Dave Ogilvie.

"I know my when I see it." Tink slipped his hand into his pocket.

Dave let me squirm a long moment before he turned to face my father. "Get off my place, Tink. And don't come back."

"Don't plan to, Dave. As long as it *is* your place."

Dave smiled. "I know about the mortgage, Tink. I know about

Leroy and Bennett. Not like you, Tink—making deals in closed rooms. Keeping secrets."

Tink remained stone-faced.

"Didn't figure Leroy could keep a secret forever," he said, and Dave laughed. Wyatt laughed too, an aping caricature of his father's evil delight.

Did Wyatt know me for a Judas too?

Dave's laugh cut short abruptly. "I see you on my place again, I'm callin' the sheriff."

Tink took his hand out of his pocket. I followed him past Dave's smirking smile, past Wyatt's. We found our truck, cranked up, and turned back down the rough, rutted road that would take us away from Dave and his tobacco field.

"Daddy—" I tried to start.

"Don't," Tink cut me off. "Don't say anything. Don't tell me anything. I don't want to know."

And so I didn't.

"What are you going to do?" I asked.

"'We,'" Daddy replied. "*We* are going to do something together, Carter. You and me. Give you a chance to act like a man."

"Anything," I promised. "I'll do anything."

Tink smiled grimly.

"We'll see."

Chapter nineteen

Skullcap,
Scutellaria arenicola

We passed beneath the grove of silent trees, rocked in that truck's metal cab past Dave's cattlegap, up the smooth dirt road, catching the rays of a falling sun on that good farm-to-market road.

"He probably got a bill of sale." I made conversation awkwardly. "Just in case we brought the sheriff."

"Won't do him any good," Tink grunted. And then, "There'll be a time. There'll be a place."

We rode the short distance to the turnoff that would put us on our own lane. Except Tink didn't turn off.

"Where we going?" I asked dryly.

"What shells you got for that shotgun?" He didn't answer my question.

We had two shotguns, an old Ithaca double-barrel, rabbit-ear hammers, and a Remington pump. Both twelve gauge. The pump rested on the gun rack behind us; I brought that weapon around awkwardly in the cab's cramped space and pumped out a shell.

"Number eights," I reported, reloading the round.

"Bird shot," he grunted. "Well. Have to do."

"Do what? What are we doing?"

"You said you'd do anything."

"Yes, sir."

"Then what does it matter?"

Red Walker lived in a sharecropper's shack near Cook's Hammock. He had a wife and four children. I mention this because those seeking rough justice seldom take into account the effects of their business on the innocent. I know my father certainly did not.

Daddy ignored the flea-bitten mongrel who passed for a sentry at Red's rickety front porch. He strolled to the front steps without challenge. Red's wife was on the porch shelling peas.

"Tink. Evenin'."

"Need to see Red, Clara Sue."

"He's out."

"Out fire-huntin'? Or out drinkin'?"

She shrugged with weary indifference, the peas reporting off the bottom of her tin pail like shots from a derringer. "Could be drinking', ah don't know. But he was happy 'bout somethin'."

"I'll guess drinking," Tink said. When we climbed back into the truck, I knew where we were headed.

Even though nationwide Prohibition had been discarded, Lafayette County was still dry. You couldn't get a legal drink unless you went clear to Taylor County. The closest thing to a bar was more than fifteen miles from Red's place, a mere half mile inside the Lafayette County line. It wasn't legal, but it was out of the way, and the sheriff's first cousin owned it, so Leb Folsom's cantina was tolerated. Tink knew Leb's establishment was the place where Red would celebrate a fortune of any land or amount, however distant or deferred.

When we turned east out of Red's place and hit the hard road leading north, I knew my hunch was right.

My hands began to sweat on the shotgun. "What are we gonna do, Daddy?"

"Settle with Red," was all Tink would say.

"You can't kill a man for stealing!" I'm sure I stammered.

"Maybe not," Tink allowed. "But I can make him wish he was dead."

I have hung on to that last exchange through the years to mitigate, if not justify, what took place that night. Tink did not go to Leb's to kill; I am sure of that.

The bar was a corrugated lean-to with an outhouse backed up to the south side, the bar's south-facing wall providing a merciful barrier against the winter wind for the inebriated who stumbled in to bleed their lizards or puke their guts out from the rotgut Leb passed off as bourbon and gin. No scotch. I don't think anyone had ever heard of scotch whiskey in that place.

On a busy night there might be five, maybe ten trucks or beat-up sedans parked asunder beneath the straight pines that surrounded the place. That night there were at least twenty vehicles and a couple of horses.

"Hot time in the old town tonight," Tink remarked. "You see Red's automobile?"

Red owned a Model-T that, even in 1940, was getting to be ragged. I rolled down my window, craned for a look.

I pointed to the back side of the bar.

"I see it," Tink said.

He opened his door.

"What do you want me to do?" I asked.

"Follow me. Keep quiet," Tink replied shortly. "Things get rowdy, watch my back. You got a shell in the chamber?"

I did.

He nodded. "All right, then. Let's see if Leb's improved his entertainment."

As we walked straight toward the bar, I tried to figure out a way to conceal my shotgun. People carried weapons openly in those days. Rifles, shotguns, or handguns. Even in bars. But it didn't feel natural to me.

"Round back." My father's quick command took me unaware.

My foot caught on a pine root.

"You all right?" Tink didn't even look back.

"Fine," I said and scrambled to catch up.

We began our reconnoiter from the shithouse side of Leb's bar. The early heat made for a terrible stench. That ensured at least that we wouldn't have too much company. There were no windows in the bar, only shutters propped open with sawed-off tobacco sticks. The place had seen its share of ungentlemanly encounters. The walls winked constellations from the kerosene lamps inside, their patterns determined by the random explosion of tempers and buckshot.

Tink walked without any particular effort at concealment to a shutter that opened behind the bar and allowed a view inside. I took a position opposite him. Night had fallen. We could see inside while remaining virtually invisible.

I saw Red. He lollygagged at the bar not ten feet away from our vantage point, a shit-eating grin splitting his leper's face. Beside him stood a man unfamiliar to me, a better-dressed man, his hair pomaded flat to his head like a seal. When he turned to tap a smoke from a pack on the bar, I saw the horribly mutilated ear.

Holy shit.

I looked at Daddy.

"Shhh," he warned me softly. "Quiet."

Just like that time with the panther.

Tarrant Sullivan smiled beside Red Walker, the king of all he surveyed. Conversation mixed with curses, coughs, and laughter floated out of that dismal place seined through whiskey or gin. Leb Folsom's laughter was genuine, however; he delighted to have such distinguished company and in such numbers patronizing his establishment. I could make out only one woman in the bar, but there were at least thirty men, a score of them lounging protectively around Tarrant Sullivan. Half the Klan in Taylor County must have been in that hooch house.

I leaned close to Daddy. "Let's leave!"

"Easy, son."

"It's too dangerous!"

"Just wait. Listen. We'll get our opportunity."

I held vigil with my father, downwind from the defecation and micturition of drunken men, expecting each moment to be surprised or confronted by some pistol-packing Klansman. An eternity seemed to pass. Then another.

"Listen," Tink said as I squirmed.

I placed my head close to Leb's open shutter. Tarrant Sullivan was talking. "… and by God, Red, you *shouldn't* give a damn! Man fires you! Puts you out of work for a *nigger*, why—he *owes* you a barn's worth of timber. Hell, you could have burnt his damn mill straight to the ground while you were at it, and God hisself would call it justice!"

A chorus of drunks seconded that motion.

"Whole thing started with Spence's daddy," Red's voice was by now sluggish, and I stiffened at my listening post.

"Saint Mac-fuckin'-Grue." Red took a shot of sourmash before completing his thought. "I figured with Saint gone Tink'd *haf* to hire a white man. Didn' *haf to* be *me,* you unnerstan'!"

No, no, the gathered brood chimed confidence in Red's sincerity.

Tarrant just smiled.

Red pushed his shot glass back to Leb.

"Need to see some green, Mr. Sullivan," Leb apologized.

"Sure," Tarrant said and peeled off a bill. "Let him have the bottle."

"Got-damnit, you'a good man!" Red declared.

A ragged toast then to the Klan's top fellow.

"But I wont to know how ye did it!" The query came from somewhere in the back.

"You mean Saint?" Red became suddenly coy. "Watn't nuthin' to it. Just a little accident."

"What's wrong, Red? Don't you trust us?" Tarrant had to work his mouth in a peculiar way to force a smile.

"Sure I do!" Red blustered.

"Ain't no Klansman ever, *never* turned on another, am I right, boys?"

Cheers all around for that one.

"So how'd you manage with Saint?"

Red took another shot of whiskey. A slow grin competed with the slur the alcohol had induced in his voice and face.

"I waited for Tink to go up the line," Red said.

I shivered as if it were the dead of winter and turned slowly to see my father's reaction.

There was none. Nothing. He just stood there, patient and quiet against the shithouse wall, just as if he were listening to some distant and not particularly interesting account.

"I saw Saint step inside that line, an', like Tink's always sayin', I took my opportunity."

"Why'd he step inside the cable, Red?"

"Just a stupid nigger, I guess. Saw some stump he thought might spoil the pull on that log."

"Naw," Tarrant teased, "they was more to it than that. What say, Red? You didn't offer 'im a little encouragement, did you now?"

Whoops of laughter, then Red toying for a moment with his Jack Daniels.

"All right," Red played to his crowd. "Whole story."

I looked to my father. Impassive. No sign at all.

Red began his chronicle.

"Ol' Saint, he tells me, 'Have Hank put some slack on the line, Red.' That's what he says. Orderin' me around like I's some kind of nigger myself. 'Have him cut her some slack so's I can clear that lightard out the way.'

"Just some stump or another." Red shrugged as if the whole parable turned on that hinge. "Hell, it watn't even that big, but Saint he was worried about foulin' the fuckin' line, so I turns and I waves my flag. But I could see Tink's got his back to me. Hell, he ain't even lookin'. But, by God, just about that time there comes a little slack in the line. Happens all the time, line straightens out a kink or maybe slips on the capstan. Jumps a log. But ol' Saint, he thinks it's Hank took some of the tight outa that cable, you see?

"Still, he should've waited. He should've. But he didn't, and that was his mistake. He saw a little give in that line, mistook it for some slack comin' in, thinkin' that Red's done sent the signal to the skidder, so he steps inside the pull of that big steel wire, and when he does I take the head of my axe and tap that pin outen that block, that clevis pin—? Outen that snatchblock—?"

The bar sucked in a collective breath of anticipation.

"Just tapped it once. 'Ping!'" Red declared, delighted with the effect his story was having. "And then that steel cable twanged like a bandsaw and cut Saint MacGrue in two. His ass over here." Red was laughing now. Huge joke. "His feet over yonder. Looked like *two* niggers rollin' red in that mud!"

The bar roared with that comic touch. Red smiled through his hooch. "Yes, sir, I killed Tink's best got-damn nigger. Killed his sorry ass dead."

Throughout this monologue my father remained motionless as a statue. Not a quiver on his face or eye to signify what he heard, or what he felt. Or what he intended to do about it.

"Daddy—" I reached out to touch my father.

"There's a screen door other side of the shitter," he said, turning briskly away from the shutter.

"Daddy, please."

"I'm going in, Carter."

I'd already betrayed him once. This was my opportunity for reconciliation. Or punishment.

Tink took out his revolver, opened the cylinder. Six slugs. He snapped the cylinder to quietly. Then he reached into his pocket and pulled those brass knuckles over his left hand.

"You decide to come in, just shoot hip level," he said quietly. "It's only bird shot, but they won't know that."

We went in.

We didn't crash in, or bang in, or run in. Just shoved a rear screen door aside and walked in. Tink went first, shouldering without pause past some drunken cracker scratching his balls on the way to the outhouse. It wasn't till the old boy saw me that he realized we weren't regular customers.

"TARRANT!" the ball-scratcher yelled.

The shotgun seemed to jump on its own. Bucked like a mad damn mule. I probably took half that man's head off as I walked in behind my father. He squawked, a terrible sound, like a chicken held to the block. Then just slid down the tin wall.

The whole bar froze. People who think music is the universal language have never heard the action of a pump shotgun—*rack-rack*, I chambered another shell, triggered a second explosion, and the dam broke. People started jumping everywhere. Out the doors. Out the shuttered windows. One big man slammed his chair straight through Leb's corrugated wall and followed it outside.

Once I had them moving, it was just a matter of pump and pull, pump and pull, pump and pull, and whatever you do don't stop. With the plug out I had six shells. Spending two, I only had four left. Those last four shells felt like a hundred and forty.

Leb just stood there terrified the whole time. Frozen. So did Tarrant. And so did Red Walker.

Daddy walked right down the bar, unconcerned apparently by the carnage around him.

"Heard your little tale, Red," my father spoke loudly and then shot him. Wasn't three feet away when he fired. The .38 slug caught Red right beneath the heart. He was dead before he hit the ground.

Tarrant was scrambling down the bar now.

Pleading. Begging.

"Please! PLEASE DON'T I GOT FAMILY!"

"I could give a goddamn," Tink said and fired the gun practically in Tarrant's face.

The slug skipped through an eye and out the side of the man's skull.

"Messed with my business once too often, Tarrant," Tink said and shot the Grand Wizard again.

Leb was edging his hands beneath the bar.

"Don't do it," I waved Leb from behind his bar with an empty shotgun.

Tink grinned widely. "Now, that's my boy. Come on, son."

We walked out the way we had walked in.

"You'd best tell your cousin this was self-defense, Leb," Daddy suggested casually over his shoulder as we found the back door. "I'd hate to have to come back."

I expected to find an army waiting for us out front, but in that dark panic it was every man for himself, and those brave Klansmen were exercising the better part of valor with a vigor that would have made a pacifist proud.

We walked right past a couple of wounded men. One fellow came straight at us with a knife. Tink stepped aside and punched him viciously across the temple. That was the only impediment we encountered between the bar and our truck. The only bump in the road on our long way home.

I got sick. I was fine so long as the paroxysm of activity was there. But about five miles down the hard road—"Daddy—!"

"I know."

He stopped. Let me puke at leisure. Was almost tender helping me back into the truck.

"Daddy, I'm sorry!" I was bawling like a baby. "I'm sorry, I'm sorry!"

"It's all right," he said again. Kindly. Gently. "You did good in there tonight. It'll help me remember."

I didn't know what my brutal accomplishment was supposed to help my father remember until the next morning when Mother leaned across my bed.

She had let me sleep in; that was unusual. Unusual, too, to have my mother there, that tall mix of Creek and convict, so close to me in bed, so intimate, her long hair brushing my face.

Her aspect was sad and immobile.

"Carter, are you up to breakfast?"

"Yes, ma'am."

I was. In fact, I was ravenous.

"Ouch!"

The bruise on my hip was purple and sore. The result of that steel mule's kick. Martha kissed me on the forehead.

"I'll make you a poultice," she said. "You can eat. After that you'll need to pack."

"Pack?"

My hip was a distraction.

"What for?"

"You're on your own, Carter. Tink's put you out of his house."

Chapter twenty

Deer Tongue, *Carphephorus paniculatus*

I remember numbly gathering my things, placing them in that cardboard suitcase for a journey never imagined, and waiting with my mother for Taff to take me to town.

I don't think Mother and I said good-bye. I suppose I figured Tink was in a fit of anger that when cooled would see me repacking my bags to come home. I must have been at the Boatwright Hotel across from the courthouse for a week before I fully realized I'd been turned out for good. It was only then that I realized what my father's parting remarks meant: Tink would rather remember me dead or a murderer than as a son who betrayed his father.

Tink took me to Folsom's bar hoping for a penance of sorts, but Red Walker's confession offered a chance at redemption. I did what Tink hoped I would do. Better, probably, than he expected me to do it. That's what he would hang on to. That's what he would remember.

But there was a price; there was always a price. And after a week's banishment I realized that, even redeemed, my father would not have me again in his big house.

I was on my own. Duly qualified and declared as a candidate for tax assessor of Lafayette County. Living out of a suitcase in a livery that had been converted into a boarding house and later graced with the garnish of "Hotel."

Taff handed me back pay sent by Tink for the months I had worked at Fort McKoon. It was a fair sum, four or five hundred dollars, as I recall. Enough to cover my room and board for a good while. Plenty if I wound up rooming and boarding in jail.

I had, after all, killed at least one man, blinded and wounded others, and collaborated in the deaths of Red Walker and Tarrant Sullivan. You'd think that would be a liability for a man running for public office.

Didn't work out that way. For one thing, all the Klan killed or wounded were from Taylor County. Sheriff Frank Folsom had always been uneasy at the free hand Tarrant took with his hooded men in Lafayette County. Not that the sheriff cared about black people, mind. It was a matter of Tarrant's getting high-handed, dismissive of local authority.

The sheriff, in other words, didn't give a damn how Tarrant Sullivan had been killed. Not that Frank would allow his personal feelings to interfere with justice. No, sir. But it gave him considerable leeway in its implementation.

The sheriff acted swiftly. He met me the morning after the shootings as I was checking into the Boatwright. Collared me right there. But there was no arrest.

"We need to see Judge Blacksheer," was all Folsom would tell me in the hotel.

"Son of a raving bitch, Carter. I didn't think you had it in you," he said as we crossed the street.

"It was self-defense," I replied automatically.

"What Leb said," the sheriff chuckled. "Yessir, that's exactly what Leb said too."

I met with Judge Blacksheer for an hour or so.

"Just tell me the truth," he admonished, and then, without a hint of irony, "You can feel free; we aren't in court."

So I told the judge exactly how the evening had gone. From Dave to Red to murder. The judge reached back to pour himself a modicum.

"If this is how you planned to announce your candidacy," he regarded me dryly, "I have to tell you it's somewhat more spectacular than I might have advised."

There was an inquest of sorts. Again, it was held very quickly. Four or five days, as I recall. The hearing was for the purpose of determining whether an arrest should be made or a grand jury convened to determine whether a crime had been committed.

Hearing the coroner's report, I figured Daddy and I were going to prison. I was sure we deserved it. The reality of what I had done began to sink in. I saw the man I had killed in every face on the street. I woke from nightmares like Macbeth's wife, wringing blood from my hands. I was culpable, I knew, and fully expected punishment for my deeds.

But I was not tried in the court of conscience, and neither was Tink. Red's wife testified that on the night in question Tink seemed friendly and that Red was in good spirits too, and celebrating. When asked why Tink wanted to see Red, Clara Sue replied that it had something to do with a job at the mill. She thought maybe Tink was going to hire Red back.

Leb Folsom was one of four witnesses present at the scene besides Tink and me to be called to make a statement before the court. Leb went on record to declare that Tink and I acted in self-defense.

"Tink came in with some question 'bout some lumber." Leb fidgeted on the stand as he answered questions addressed to him by the judge. "Soon as Tink cleared the corner of the bar, why—Red went for his gun. Soon's he did that, the Klan thought Tink was after Tarrant. Next thing I know ever'body's shootin' ever'body else."

"So in your opinion, Mr. Folsom, Tink Buchanan and Carter Buchanan acted only in defense of their lives?"

"Sorry, Judge, what—?"

"Self-defense, Leb." The judge leaned like a carrion bird from his high seat. "I'm asking you if your testimony insists that Tink and Carter used their weapons solely in self-defense."

"Self-defense, right, Judge, ah, Your Honor. They hadn't been armed, why, they'd both be dead for sure."

There was no discussion about Dave Ogilvie or stolen lumber. No curiosity about why Tink for the mere purpose of polite conversation would track Red Walker to a bar at the county line. Nothing like that.

The court did hear three other witnesses, all pronounced present when the shooting started. None of them could identify Tink or me.

"It happened too fast," one turpentiner declared. "An' it was dark. Leb's place is *always* too dark."

"The court will do what it properly can to encourage illumination," Judge Blacksheer assured and dismissed the man.

All this in open court. The Honorable Judge William Jackson Blacksheer presiding. No one was charged with a crime. No grand jury was convened to determine whether a crime had been committed; Judge Blacksheer was within his jurisdiction after a careful review of the facts to make that determination on his own.

"Court finds that Tink Buchanan and Carter Buchanan, men, the court notes, who are not at present accused of any wrongdoing, shall not be charged with a crime here."

With the rap of a gavel Tink and I were free as birds. There was no mention of compensation for Red's wife and family. No provision for Tarrant's family either, or for the family of the man I murdered. FDR initiated Social Security with widows and orphans in mind, so I cast away my responsibility by saying that the government would take care of the survivors. That was what we paid taxes for, wasn't it?

I made myself forget the name of the man I murdered that April. But later, much later, I went back to the courthouse and found his name. He had a wife. No children.

I tried during the hearing to get a word with Daddy, but I was rebuffed. It was hard. Everybody in the courthouse was talking about us, yet Tink and I, who were not three rows apart the entire hearing, exchanged scarcely a dozen words.

Tink did not seem to be angry with me. He was polite but cool. Indifferent. Indifferent to the proceedings too, apparently unconcerned at the prospect of arrest or indictment. Unfrightened by the price of slaughter. Even more astounding, Tink did not seem particularly grateful for Leb's perjury and complaisance, which got us both off scot-free.

I remarked on that odd passivity to Taff Calhoun as he walked me from the courthouse to my new residence across the street.

"Your daddy don't gamble," Taff told me.

"What do you mean by that, Taff? Taff—?"

But for probably the only time in his life Taff kept his mouth shut.

It wasn't until the following week, when I was summoned by Judge Blacksheer for the ostensible purpose of discussing my candidacy, that I learned what Taff meant.

I had barely walked into the judge's chambers when he put two hundred dollars in cash into my hand.

"What's this?" I asked.

"Campaign contribution," the judge answered. "You don't have long till May twenty-eighth. We lost a week already."

"Who gave it?" I asked. "Who's it from?"

"Why, your father, Carter."

"Daddy?"

So I wasn't abandoned!

"I needed three thousand to clear up that business at the bar," the judge went on smoothly. "Two thousand went to Leb. Well worth it, I'm sure you'll agree. Two hundred goes to your war chest. The rest—Sheriff Folsom and myself. We have to run for office too, y'know."

I must have looked downcast.

"Come, come, boy. You wanted to be a man of your own, didn't you? Well, put that money in your pocket. You won't stand alone long without it."

I was free now to campaign against Bennett Sessions. The incident at Leb's bar made that task quite a bit easier. Everyone, whether outraged or intrigued, had an opinion about the shootout at Leb's bar. A totally unearned aura of respect, or notoriety, now clung, however flimsily, to me—older folks stepping aside in deference when I'd go into the feed store or Doc's pharmacy. People got up out of their chairs at Punk's so I might get a quicker haircut.

It's very seductive, that kind of deference. At first you refuse it. Then you graciously accept it. Then you begin to expect it.

But it didn't last. If I had been able to call the election right after my dramatic exemption from prosecution or even within a few weeks, still near to Easter, I probably could have cashed in my momentary fame for an easy victory. But by the middle of May the story began to tire in competition with a daily barrage of news clips reporting strife domestic and foreign. Within a month it was obvious that unless some new source of support emerged, old habits would prevail and Bennett Sessions would win the election.

Such was the gloomy verdict Judge Blacksheer and Frank Folsom passed on one night toward the end of May in the judge's study.

"Is it a matter of money?" I was no longer naive in these affairs.

"Money might do it, certainly," the judge nodded. "But you don't have any, Carter. And the interest that followed your little shoot-out, well, let's just say it was not sustainable."

So there I was, thrown out of my home and my father's business, without a job and with no prospect of getting one. I went to my hotel room considering whether I might, like Julia, find work teaching. I had started drafting letters requesting recommendations for such a pursuit when a knock sounded at my door.

"Come in."

It was Dave Ogilvie.

I stood when he entered, pulled up from my chair like a marionette. Dave smiled at that automatic response.

"Sit down, boy."

I did.

"Not quite like the Big House, is it, Carter?"

"Not quite, no, sir."

"Can't be easy. Living with a man like Tink. Putting your own reputation, your own life on the line and then—being cast out. Just like Satan cast from Heaven. Do you know why Satan was cast out, Carter? Why, really?"

"Because he was evil?" I ventured.

"No. Because he was *beautiful.*"

A gust of breeze through my opened window chilled the perspiration that bathed me. Dave worried the watch in his vest pocket.

"I've been thinking about your campaign."

"Yes, sir," was all I could manage.

"You do remember our last conversation, don't you, Carter?"

"Yes, sir, I remember."

"Well, then. You tell me. What are you willing to do for my support? My support and Julia's hand in marriage?"

"I guess anything," I said. "Anything that has to be done."

He nodded gravely. "I have to be honest with you, son; I didn't think you were capable of very much before. Nothing worthwhile, anyhow. I didn't think 'anything' really meant a whole lot to a boy spoiled rotten. But you may have shown some potential. May have."

I decided to keep silent. He nodded approval of that decision before going on.

"I'm going to announce my support for you publicly." Dave seemed to relish the prospect. "I'm going to pull every vote from every deacon in every pulpit I can manage, and then I'm going to have them do the same. In return for that—"

"Yes, sir?"

"You answer to me. You work for me. You belong to me. You'll be my bootblack, my field hand, my house nigger—anything I want you to be until my crop gets made this summer, and then if, *if* I keep my land, you can take Julia and your real purpose, whatever it is, and go on about your life."

"What if you don't make it?" I asked. "What if I do everything you tell me and it just doesn't make? What then?"

"Then I'll ask you to do one more thing, Carter. One easy, straightforward thing. And unless you can tell me now that you will do it, I will walk out this door and make *certain* you never gain respect or employment *ever* in this county again. Nor my daughter's hand."

Did Faust hesitate over his oath? I didn't.

"Yes, sir," I said. "Anything you say."

"That's my boy," Dave Ogilvie pursed thin lips into a kind of grimace, and I gave up whatever pretence I had of standing alone.

I wanted to talk to Julia, to tell her what had happened, to see what it might mean for us. From my hotel window I watched Dave leave the Boatwright and drive away. I ignored the car lent me by Judge Blacksheer and dashed across sandy lots filled with stinging nettles to reach the school.

I caught Julia between bells. I came in winded and flushed, bearing the news both wonderful and terrible.

I expected her to be glad to see me. It had been weeks since we were together. But when I entered the room, she paled and pressed her hands to my chest—"Not here!"

"What? Why?"

"Tonight. Meet me tonight," she said. I saw a welt beneath the sleeve of her blouse.

"Where?" I asked.

"The Sand Pond," she replied.

I was surprised. "The Sand Pond? *Where?*"

"The mayhaw grove," she said. "Nine o'clock."

"Nine it is," I agreed and tried to warm her with a smile.

"Now go!" She pushed me out the door.

"Julia?"

"GO!"

⁊⋲

I had always entered the Sand Pond from my father's land. But being recently disowned, that approach did not seem advisable. I couldn't enter from Dave's land; I was sure he had not approved our late-night rendezvous, and if I drove onto Ray Henderson's property I'd have to ask his permission or risk buckshot.

I decided in the end to park Judge Blacksheer's car on a road east of my father's property, from there to hike across the fields and scrub growth to the pond.

It was not yet dark at eight when I began my stealthy journey. I could not see the lake from my approach, nor my father's house. I could see Spence's shack, though. A pair of lanterns lit up the porch, and Polly was singing some African spiritual. She was singing to the dusk. The sun had already lowered below the treetops. Only the last vestiges of ocher light were left to play on the bellies of clouds nestled near the horizon.

She sang to that canopy of scarlet, Spence beside her shirtless in his chair. It took me a moment to make out Little Saint at his dad's feet. Playing with some kind of toy, a top, maybe? Something Spence had improved with whittling, I could tell that.

The father carving a toy for a child. The boy trying with young hands to master the snap that would spin the carved spool on its point, the father, my one-time friend, laughing over his little saint's tireless play.

I thought for a moment Spence spotted me. A dog padded up the cypress planks, and Spence seemed to pause a moment, to step out of his tranquil cocoon and stare out from the bib of his porch. To search that fiery horizon for intruders.

There were no threats this evening. No obvious ones, anyway.

I loped along a fence line, Polly's siren song going mute in my ears, and within minutes slipped into the skirt of live oaks that signi-fied the Sand Pond's boundary.

I had to cross two streams and skirt the southernmost pond to reach the mayhaw grove. The trees were so thick I could barely break through, and it was falling dark fast. No moon tonight. I could barely make out the mayhaw trees themselves, their pink berries almost gone. A few still floating in the water.

"Julia!" I called out, not knowing what to expect. Whether she was there to love me or to tell me to go to hell.

"Carter!" she cried, and I turned to the sound as she launched into the stream that divided us.

We met halfway across, knee deep in water. A long embrace. Hot in the night. Staggering then from water to virgin sand. We neither of us had thought to bring a blanket or bedding. So we braved red bugs by gathering moss.

I had never enjoyed the leisure of undressing her slowly, or she me, and now that we had time we did not take it, stripping our things frantically, throwing them onto the moss, murmuring, it's been so long, been so long, been so long!

I could not see her small, firm breasts in the cloak of our arbor, but I could feel them, erect and taut. I could feel her flat belly and firm thighs.

"Lie down," she commanded. "On your back."

Always more experienced than I. Knowing more. Risking more. And when I had exploded into her and found myself rock hard yet again, she laughing, laughing—

But with a bitter desperation.

"Now me," she said. "Behind."

I did not know at first what she meant.

She went on all fours, her back arched like a cat. Her breasts barely swaying beneath, so tight, so firm.

I lay across her back, damp with sweat, and I felt something I did not expect, something along her back, like sandpaper. Coursing her backside like the stripes of a zebra.

"Julia—?" I hesitated.

"Don't pull away, don't!" She gathered herself viciously to me. "It doesn't happen much. Not anymore."

"My God, Julia!"

"Come on!" she commanded, taking me.

My belly slid along her back. I could feel every fresh welt. Every abrasion.

"My breasts!" She practically yanked my hand from her flank to cup her. Nipples hard. Aroused.

"Hold them—hold them both!" she cried, I behind all the while. My stomach cramping in ecstasy on her long back, she on all fours carrying me.

It took longer than the other times. Much longer, and whatever hesitation or fear I had disappeared in the rhythm of our copulation.

She came before me this time, something I had never experienced.

"Don't stop, don't stop, don't stop!" she commanded urgently, desperately, and then I felt that feeling just before the dam breaks, just when you know it's coming and there's nothing you can do.

I came, and she collapsed, her spent arms buckling so that I fell on top of her.

"Don't leave me." She was crying now. "Just tell me that, please! Tell me you'll never leave!"

We stayed that way the better part of an hour, I suppose. We had come to that virgin sand, virgins ourselves in many important ways, but we both knew as we turned our backs to find clothing that we were now Adam and Eve, newly shamed. A serpent had rudely risen between us in this our garden. He would not be easily scourged.

I did not walk Julia all the way home that night, only partway, to the place where I could see the crows' nests of the barns behind her house. She assured me when prompted that she could make it the rest of the way and agreed it was prudent that I not risk seeing her to the gate.

❧

Being a puppet candidate and unemployed had its advantages. From the end of April until almost the end of May I had little to do other than attend the occasional meeting with this church or that civic organization. Judge Blacksheer even brought me to speak with the Masons.

Not in their lodge, of course. Not in that windowless room above Doc West's drugstore, rumored to be the home of ancient Coptic ritual.

We met in Clarence Simms's cafe. I mouthed the necessity to cut taxes on farm owners and small businessmen while promising to raise the valuation on the vast stretches of timber owned by Putnam Lumber. It's always easy to tax one big man when running for the votes of lots of little men. Easy to champion the underdog even when the underdog isn't particularly repressed. But even in these myopic settings someone or another might ask my opinion or position on a subject related to the world outside Lafayette County.

We were not immune from national or global affairs, only insulated from them. The life my community lived, filled with wash days and tobacco and timber, was already anachronistic to the thousands of men and single women fleeing to the cities for work in department stores or factories. The people I courted for votes knew this in an abstract, untutored way. They wondered occasionally how such shifts of people, money, and power might eventually impact the flatwoods and farmlands of our region.

But mostly we were simply disconnected from urban life. People were talking about television as early as 1940, but farmers around Laureate didn't even get electricity until 1953. Howard Hughes had flown around the world in record time in 1938; by 1940 you could find advertisements for United Airlines and the radio boasted of something even newer in aviation—a jet engine!— yet no one in Lafayette County had ever seen an airplane until the Army Air Corps began training pilots in Cross City.

Kids in New York and Los Angeles were reading about spaceships and ray guns in comic books and *Buck Rogers*. Children in Lafayette County were still raised on the Bible and *Pilgrim's Progress*.

The world outside Lafayette County seeped in through radio and printed advertisements. Had it not been for these, most of us never would have heard of Dentyne chewing gum or Bromo-Seltzer or Johnson's Baby Powder. It was advertisement that brought ready-made cleansers to our kitchen sinks and back-porch pumps. And movie stars such as Jackie Cooper and Irene Dunne and Claudette Colbert endorsed everything from cigarettes to toilet soap.

By the time I began to take the pulse of my small body politic, I could see the affairs of city, nation, and world color if not crowd the drift of everyday conversation. I began to hear words like *concentration camp* and *blitzkrieg* as well as *millage* and *valuation.*

The world insinuated itself into our rural life. Africa, formerly regarded as the sole province of missionaries, was now known to be a killing field for the Germans and British fighting there. The Balkans had a romantic ring, something to do with Xanadu and opulent trains, diamonded potentates in sybaritic pursuits, until you saw movie clips displaying a poorly mounted cavalry being mowed down with machine guns.

There were occasional rumors about Stalin and Communists. After an evening propped beside the wireless I might briefly try to conjure up a battlefield in my imagination, "Right against Wrong," pitted across a field filled with Tommy guns and tanks, contested in the gray skies above by Spitfires and Hurricanes and Messerschmitts.

My own politics seemed petty by comparison. My own ambitions pale. My recent crime, conversely, became to me more reprehensible, my culpability unmitigated by a purpose higher than the desire to please my father. But I didn't have much time to brood. My "campaign" ended on a Tuesday, May 28.

I was elected by a margin of sixty-seven votes.

I received the final count on the opposite side of the courthouse from Leroy and Bennett. When we passed in the hall, Bennett looked stunned. Leroy did not; waddling that considerable bulk ahead of his son, he called to me from across the corridor, "I'll not take your word again, Carter Buchanan! *Ever.*"

There was no victory celebration. Just a drink with the judge and sheriff in the former's study. It was the only time I can remember Blacksheer offering me anything from his ostentatious decanter.

"Congratulations, Carter." The judge poured me a shot in a dusty jigger. "I assume you know who won you this election."

"I'm sure I do."

"Very well!" The old crow smiled. "Now see if you can stay out of trouble till January."

There was no vacation forthcoming. Once free of the minimal obligations required to best Bennett Sessions, I became a serf in Dave Ogilvie's tobacco field.

Chapter twenty-one

Aletris lutea, ("Aletris" probably refers to a slave)

Against my father's hopes, Dave's crop had grown splendidly. No blue mold to ruin the beds, no flood, no drought. By the last week in May, Dave Ogilvie had one of the finest stands of tobacco ever seen in three counties and was only a week away from his first harvest.

First, though, he had to top and sucker each individual tobacco stalk. Suckers are simply growths along the nodes of the stalks that soak up water from the rest of the plant. It was necessary to break or cut the top off each tobacco stalk and also to cull every sucker from each plant.

I arrived at six on a Wednesday morning to begin work. Dave had put a crew in the field days earlier, but they were nowhere near finishing. The leaves had grown so thick and heavy that you couldn't get between the rows without being soaked from head to foot with the heavy dew.

"Here," Dave said, giving me a paring knife and a whetstone.

Wyatt had his own tools, I noticed. So did Ray Henderson's three whelps.

"Don't know what you're waitin' on, boys," Dave barked peremptorily, and we waded in to work.

I shivered with the first deluge of dew, freezing until the sun was well up. Frying afterward.

My arms, after the first half-mile row, felt as if they were falling from shoulder joints on fire.

Wyatt was delighted with my torture. "No big shots out here, are they, Carter?"

"Wasn't a big shot before, Wyatt," I responded neutrally.

Cackles of glee from the Henderson boys. We were two miles from the house. They could do what they wanted with me in that field, and they knew it.

They waited till noon. The sun had fully risen, a mere preview of the summer hell to come, but hot enough. The water jug was passed around, passed around. But not to me.

"'Bout sending that thing over here," I suggested casually.

"Why don't you come git it?" Wyatt snarled.

This was the moment I had been dreading all morning, the moment that had to come. Even a year earlier, I would have delayed that moment. Would have put it off. But I had learned something, at least, from my father.

I didn't say anything. I simply moved as if to return to my row of indenturement.

When Wyatt turned, so did I. I balled up the paring knife inside my fist and hit him as hard as I could in the kidneys.

It wasn't enough to kill him, not even enough to cripple him. But it bought me time to tear into his face and stomach with my paring knife before the Henderson boys dragged me off.

Wyatt had me now. There were a trio of Ray's bunch, and they weren't about to let me up.

Wyatt pulled out his own knife—"First, though—!" he said.

And kicked me in the privates.

When a man gets kicked in the balls, he goes down. The pain

is excruciating, but worse is the sense of absolute nausea and weakness that doubles you up like a rag doll.

That's what I was on that hot sand, a rag doll doubled over on my side, legs bicycling weakly. The Henderson boys didn't need to hold me now. Wyatt could do anything he wanted.

He wiped his knife on his pants—

"I see you boys workin'?"

Dave Ogilvie stood at the end of the row, a phantom arrived as if from thin air.

As miserable as I was, I saw the abject fear that checked Wyatt's knife in his hand.

"Just gettin' water."

"Get it, then. And nothing else. Or I'll be taking my strop to all of you."

He didn't offer a remark to note the kitchen-knife cuts on Wyatt's face and torso. Didn't even waste a look on me. Did nothing in fact to acknowledge me writhing there on the new-ground.

"Don't you cross me!" Wyatt hissed to me in the rows with his daddy well gone. "I don't give a shit what Pa does, I'll gut your ass!"

"Listen, you stupid son of a bitch," I replied. "Ya'll may make this crop, you may not. If you don't, I'm your daddy's insurance, so why don't you think about that before you go and get your ass whipped."

He would have kicked me again if I was down, but I was upright by now and armed, and the Henderson boys had no intention of enduring Dave's belt for Wyatt's pleasure.

"Leave him alone, goddamnit," the eldest said. "We got work to do."

The day ended with no further incident. I was washing my hands and arms with kerosene on Dave's back porch when the rear screen door banged flimsily open.

Wyatt looked up. I followed his eyes to find Julia standing there, still in her schoolmarm attire.

"Last day of classes," she said.

Which meant that soon Julia would be in the fields and barns. We would see each other. We could be together.

Wyatt slapped his hands angrily through a thick washrag.

"Just stay away from me," he told his sister.

Almost as soon as the field was topped and suckered we began the harvest. The tobacco raised in our region ripens gradually. Leaves nearest the ground ripen first; the last harvest comes from the top of the stalk. It took six and a half long weeks to crop Dave's field, sandlugs to tips, and it damn near killed all of us. We had croppers collapse from the heat. We had a boy snakebit. And most of us got caught by the bear.

A cropper who's "bear-caught" is afflicted with nicotine poisoning. The symptoms are universal. Extreme fatigue comes with sudden vertigo and then nausea. And then you hallucinate.

You're back in the field, in the suffocating heat. Every sensation is magnified—the sound of leaves popping off the stalk, the smell of tar and filth. You can hear the insects in that field of nicotine dreams. You can feel the sweat sting your eyes. But more than anything, you feel the absolute, rock-bottom depths of fatigue.

The bear's chasing you now, and you keep cropping that 'baccer, cropping that 'baccer. You want to stop, would give anything to stop! But you can't.

Then the nausea and vertigo prevail. You come out of the nightmare long enough to vomit—then start all over, hallucination alternating with vertigo until your system has shed enough toxins to allow a welcome stupor.

People who smoked, I noticed, did not get sick as often as those who didn't.

If it weren't for Julia, I don't believe I could have made the season. Just to be able to see her, to watch that ball of twine tumbling and to know what waited!

One day, four or five croppings into the harvest, we had finished for the day. Dave and Wyatt were firing up the barn. Julia and I were walking back to the house. It was late afternoon, hotter than four hundred hells melted twice each and then poured fresh into a tin thimble. A sweltering sun had baked the white sand around the tobacco field all day long; by now that ermine loam was damn near as hot as the inside of a curing barn.

Julia glanced over her shoulder to the barn. "Let's go swim."

"We get caught, Dave'll skin us," I replied.

"He'll skin us wet, then," she said and took off running.

It was over a half mile from the barns to the Suwannee. I wished for Spence's legs and lungs as I clambered after Julia. She led me to a spring that flowed bright and bone cold from the edge of Dave's property into the river's chocolate current.

We stripped and plunged into that water. GOD, what a restoration! The water cool and clear and boiling up from some subterranean freezer! Joints and tendons once stiff now gone in an instant slack as rubber! Water in your mouth, in your eyes! Water in your hair. All up on your sunburned back and reddened neck and pale-white legs!

We probably didn't stay in that water ten minutes, but it was worth it. When Dave saw us come to the house soaked, he knew what we'd been up to. He knew, but he didn't say a word.

He didn't say anything about our nights either, though he must have known that, too. I would meet Julia frequently on those sultry evenings. We made love in the Sand Pond, in the trees. We even made love, once, in the smokehouse.

We talked during those stolen hours about what we would do once the crop was in, once Dave had his land secure and our separate obligations were fulfilled.

"I want you to finish at Emory first," Julia said.

"I don't know ..." I only half protested.

"You first. Then me."

"All right."

"But first we've got to get married."

Married? Well. We had talked.

"What's the matter, Carter?"

"Nothing's the matter."

"We *have* planned on marrying, haven't we? Haven't you?"

"Just seems like a bad time, that's all. The worst time."

"What do you mean? The crop's good. Papa says he's sure now we can pay Leroy his interest. That means your daddy won't get the mortgage, isn't that right, Carter?"

"That's the contract, yes."

"So you'll be free. We'll be free!"

"Looks that way. I hope it's that way," I hastily added.

"We've talked about this, Carter." Fear put the edge of anger into Julia's voice.

"I know."

"I can't wait, don't you see? I've got to get *out!*"

She started crying then. I took her in my arms.

"All right, Julia, all right!"

"Don't be afraid, Carter!"

"No," I told her. "It'll work out. It'll work out fine."

This was by now past the middle of June. That night in my hotel I was thinking of Julia. What it would mean to be married to her. What it would mean to have Dave Ogilvie for a father-in-law.

Would I ever, ever really be my own man?

There was some excitement around the radio. My fellow boarders seemed agitated.

Hitler had taken Paris.

Chapter twenty-two

Sweet Everlasting, *Gnaphalium obtusifolium*

D ave got six croppings off his twenty-acre field that year. We were finished harvesting by the middle of July but were nowhere near finished with our labor, for now came the crucial phases related to curing the last of our barns and preparing our stockpiled tobacco for market.

With help from Julia, I had managed to endure the heat and harvest, but having reached the easier weeks of my ordeal, I was desperate for sleep. Unlike the other field hands, who worked only during the day, I was obligated with Dave, Wyatt, Julia, and Sarah to work at least some portion of virtually every night.

The barns kept us up. Barns were fired all night, and you had to keep an eye on them. I believe I've mentioned that not all varieties of tobacco are cured with artificial heat, but ours certainly were, which made for nerve-racking work.

Curing a kerosene-fired barn required constant inspection and constant adjustments of burner and vent. The curing leaves had to be kept moist enough to retain their grade and value but dry enough that once taken out of the barn they wouldn't mold or rot.

But the big danger was fire. You can take a cup of ordinary kitchen flour, pour it gently down a four-inch pipe to a candle beneath, and you'll get a fair-sized explosion. A barn of curing tobacco has a nuclear potential in comparison to that modest home experiment.

We'd watch the barns continuously, working shifts of two or three hours each, all the way through the night. The work was tedious but not without reward. Nothing in my experience smells more wonderful than a barn of tobacco curing, unless it's a fall of freshly washed hair. Julia frequently shared my shift. Sometimes Sarah would come with coffee and conversation. Those were moments of grace, sitting with Julia and her mother in that heavily scented atmosphere, looking through the arms of trees to the constellations above, those ancient patterns of destiny and doom.

Dave would drift in and out of that circle of company without pattern. He'd come at eight in the evening, ten after two in the morning, you could never tell. He would appear out of nowhere, just stroll up and enter a barn. Then up through the hanging sticks he'd climb blind, sometimes a hundred and seventy degrees inside those barns and still he'd climb, thrusting his hand into the leaves to judge the texture and order of the curing tobacco. Checking the burners and flues for any hint of danger.

Then he'd leave, to return, or not, at random. Made it hard to risk anything with Julia more intimate than a quick, urgent kiss.

Dave was in the best spirits I'd ever seen that July. He had accomplished something most farmers thought impossible, harvesting and curing twenty full acres of Harvest Gold Tobacco in what looked to be a golden harvest. Enough to pay off *two* years of interest at Leroy's bank. Maybe more!

His stock was rising. I often wondered how my own father was reacting to the prospect of Dave's success. Was he furious? bitter? implacable? Once the possibility of taking Dave's land was finished, would he reach back to claim me as his son?

I pondered those thoughts gloomily as I walked, the Sunday

after Dave's last cropping, to his church. I wanted to see Julia, of course, but on approaching I first saw her father. There was Dave receiving emissaries from constituents lately laggard in compliments and now, hearing of Dave's golden harvest, eager to once more court his favor.

Leroy Sessions was even at services that morning. Brought Bennett with him.

I skirted the yard to avoid them all.

Bennett followed me. "Carter, morning."

"Morning, Bennett."

"Looks like your daddy bet a losing horse."

"It's his business, Bennett. Not mine."

"Hell you say." There was no longer the veneer of a Sunday smile on Bennett's face. "I was in that office with you and your daddy. I know."

"Have yourself a fine Sunday, Bennett."

"I'm runnin' again!" he snarled to my back. "You won't beat me twice!"

"Have no intention," I replied wearily.

All that morning I saw Dave reaping the rewards of his labor. Once again the deacon had defied the odds, had thrown a bad pair of dice and was set to win. But Dave was not a man to count hens before they hatched. He wasn't letting up; there was still work aplenty to do before the leaves turned to real gold.

Once cured, tobacco had to be taken out of the barn, stick by stick. The leaves then had to be unstrung from their sticks, one hand at a time. First thing you did with the leaves once unstrung was grade them for value, it being important not to mix the more valuable leaves with an inferior grade.

Then the leaves would be stacked stems-out on a burlap sheet spread onto a packhouse floor. We'd get a girl, if we could, to walk the leaves. I loved watching Julia's calves and legs work as she toured round and round, higher and higher, pressing the tobacco into a golden cylinder.

Once you had a good-sized barrel packed down, the four

corners of the burlap would be pulled up from the floor, joined over the top, and tied. Only then would you have finally produced, ready for market, one finished sheet of tobacco.

The Live Oak market opened in two weeks. The first of August. Markets open nowadays before the crop's even in, keep banker's hours, and run on for twelve or fourteen weeks. In those days the warehouses stayed open around the clock, and closed around Labor Day. You had four weeks, five at most, to make your fortune or lose it.

Whole families flocked to the tobacco market. It was much more than a place to sell. It was a noisy, exuberant, twenty-four-hour affair, a carnival and come-on. It was the only purely secular gathering of entertainment I can recall, fiddle players and hillbilly singers replacing gospel and prayer.

Buyers from R. J. Reynolds and Philip Morris were the ruling panjandrums, chewing expensive cigars and sweating, as Taff used to say, like a French whore in church. Everyone was buying or selling something, hawkers moving cotton candy and soda water, boys running with flat boxes hung with string about their necks singing, "Peanuts! Getchu biled peanuts heah!" Competing ceaselessly for that small business.

The warehouses competed too, giving away wringer-washers and harrows to coax farmers onto their scales, competing in the space of weeks for the profit that would have to last a year. The city opened up its doors for this sudden deluge of cash. Local businesses offered food and hospitality. More prizes. More promotions.

Market was the only time a dirt farmer wasn't treated like dirt, Mac Morgan used to say. None of the farmers had any illusions about why this was so, but they welcomed the hospitality anyway as a welcome respite after a season of sweat.

The one paramount event in this three-ring circus, naturally, was the auction itself. The auctioneer was usually an out-of-towner, a ringmaster and celebrity in his own right, often rumored to drink whiskey shot with rattler's venom—the fastest-talking, fastest-thinking white man alive.

You had to think fast to do the job. It was the auctioneer's job to make the big boys pay the highest price possible for each sheet of tobacco, but he had only seconds, sometimes less, to effect a sale.

Imagine a warehouse lined with *thousands* of tagged sheets. Identification, weight, and grade scrawled onto each paper tag. The auctioneer watching his buyers, knowing intimately the import of that raised finger, that scratched ear. The slide of a palm across the damp hatband. Every buyer talking to the auctioneer in his secret code, the auctioneer singing a thousand words a minute the whole time ... seventeen centacentaELGHTteencentacenta pound ...! Sell and move, sell and move, sell and move. You couldn't make money standing still.

And so it went for each single bundle of tobacco up and down the arrow's shot of that warehouse floor, farmers trailing behind in a wedding train, straining in anticipation to see the final price awarded their precious crop, heart stopping to see the buyer thrust his hand into the heart of his bag—

WARM! The buyer scowls.

The buyers then tearing into that sheet; they find the snuff used to scent the rotten leaves inside. The auctioneer observes with equanimity, dismissing the token bundle like a bag of shit.

Who-gimmee who-gimmee FOURcenta, FOURcentapound?

You followed those buyers through piles of tobacco as if seeking water in a desert, wondering what caprice of buyer or seller would make your hard summer's work a boom or a bust.

Dave Ogilvie had followed in that train before. He knew, too well, the capriciousness of the auctioneer's song.

But it looked good. We were almost two weeks ahead of the market. The crop was in. All but the last two barns had been taken out. Through Herculean labor we had sheeted and stacked everything else. The biggest problem had been finding a place to put it all.

Dave had close to twenty thousand pounds of tobacco ready for market by the middle of July, but the market didn't open for another two weeks. In the interim the sheets had to be stacked dry and secure. The packhouse intended for that purpose was bulging to the rafters even before the harvest was completed. The rest of the tobacco, nearly a third of the entire crop, was stacked in a crib backed almost onto the packhouse itself.

This particular crib would not normally have been used to shelter tobacco. It was a crude, roughly sealed shelter used normally to store corn and fertilizer. Caleb kept his squirrel in that crib. Kept a bucket of pecans or corn handy for feeding. Kept the water changed and the cage clean. But the crib was high-roofed and mounted on stumps secure from the damp, and so, with nearly twenty thousand pounds of tobacco looking for a place to wait, Dave told his son to find another home for his pet.

Caleb did not remove the squirrel without complaint. The crib had been ideal. Caleb could open the cage and watch his Henry leap and chatter and run without fear that the animal would escape. Even after the crib was filled with tobacco, Caleb would sneak back inside, set Henry loose from his cage, and watch him cavort through sheets of Harvest Gold. Delighted and without envy, little Caleb laughed to see his squirrel run and jump in ways he could not. Even Dave allowed that innocent transgression.

But one afternoon Dave found Caleb chasing his pet atop the stacks of tobacco. In the haste of play, Caleb bruised the tops of a few precious sheets. Anyone else would have received a hiding for such an infraction. Caleb got away with a cuff on the ear and a disappointment.

"That's the last time you're bringing that squirrel in here, you understand me, boy? The last time!"

Caleb was crying. "But Papa! He loves to run!"

"NOT IN MY CRIB!" Dave bellowed, "NOT IN MY 'BACCER!"

⁊⹀

We were shutting down our last barn that evening, waiting for the tobacco to come to order. There was no reason to stay up. The burners were killed. No fume or spark to be found in the flues. No sign of weather either, not even a vapor of cloud to filter the moon's bright light.

It was the last day of the last barn. Sarah came back out with Caleb, surprising us all with a homemade cake.

We ate the cake. A small attempt at light talk aborted quickly. We finished up in silence, and everyone went inside. I made as if to go home but doubled back. Julia and I had planned to spend some time together, a late-night tryst. We were brazen. We had cached a couple of burlap sheets to make our rendezvous more pleasant, though I'm sure if pressed we'd have mated on a bed of nails.

A magnolia tree marked the spot, *M. grandiflora,* its blossoms heavy with perfume. We both fell asleep, lazy with lust, not a hundred yards away from Dave's barns. We were downwind, I know that. Otherwise I would not have smelled the smoke.

"What is it?" Julia stirred in a curl at my loins.

"Oh, Jesus!"

I scrambled into my trousers on the run to sprint barefoot and barebacked toward the unmistakable aroma of pine and tar and tobacco in combustion.

I thought it was the barn. The one last barn of the season. But as I came skidding to a stop beside that familiar tar-papered box, I could find no trace of either smoke or fire.

"Oh, God, Carter!" Julia was beside me now, gasping for air. "Oh, God, it's the packhouse!"

Julia and I ran all the way through the tobacco field. We raced down that soft road, through that druid's arbor to the cattlegap, and beyond the house to where Dave had packed his season of gold. A quarter mile away we could see clouds of blood-red sparks thrown like sparklers to a velvet heaven, each ember chasing another on vortexes of superheated air, the cooler constellations above now made invisible.

We got there to see Dave and Wyatt and Sarah standing numb before a steady howl of combustion. I had not expected that, the sound of the fire, and then to see the packhouse and crib alongside wavering in uncertain resolution like mirages in an awful desert, the heat bending light and sound in an awful moan of destruction. Everything going up in waves and waves of pitch-black smoke. A hoard of gold gone up in smoke and flame.

There was nothing to be done. Nothing would stop or even slow the annihilation that drove us back with its heat and black, black smoke. Nothing to recover that which was lost.

Wyatt seemed hysterical. Sarah appeared solid enough until her knees turned to water. I caught her as she sank to the warm sand.

"Mrs. Ogilvie?"

She did not answer. I could see the fire dancing in her eyes, two bright circles filled with flame. Julia crouched beside her mother, both women rocking now. Back and forth. Like infants.

"GODDAMNIT!" Wyatt screamed.

Dave did not offer a rebuke. He had managed to pull a pair of sheets out of that holocaust. Three hundred pounds saved of the twenty thousand now exploding—whoooooosh!—as dust and oxygen combined in a virtual explosion.

We fell back, smitten by some invisible hand. I remember thinking that we'd better retreat to the house lest the embers and sparks should set that structure too on fire.

I was thinking about that when Sarah's hand suddenly bit deeply into my arm.

"Oh dear Lord!"

"What is it? What is it, Sarah?"

She didn't answer. But Dave seemed to know, seemed to sense, at least, the concern his wife was too terrified to voice.

And then Julia knew—"Oh, Mama!" she said. "Where's Caleb?"

❧

It takes only an ember to set a house afire. How much less to strike in an obedient boy a spark of independence or rebellion?

It took almost two full days for the fire to abate enough so that an inspection could begin of the powdered remains. Sarah was not allowed near the smoking ruins, and that was good; the bones of her little boy were not found entire. He'd been cremated.

It was apparent that sometime during the night Caleb had

sneaked his pet into the crib—the squirrel and cage were missing from their place on the porch. Missing too was the porch's kerosene lantern, along with a box of kitchen matches. Perhaps while playing, the squirrel knocked the lamp over. Perhaps the boy did. There was no way to know.

Preacher O'Steen offered what comfort he could. Going on about God's purpose and such. I do not believe in offering to parents grieving the loss of a child such a rationale. Better to recognize the pain. To offer God as one intimately familiar with the loss of children. To offer His love as a balm for that uncomprehended hurt.

There had to be a burying. There was no need of a coffin, but Dave insisted on building one. Dave held himself responsible for his son's death. It was he who had forbidden the boy, after all. His command moved Caleb to rebel.

The coffin gave him something to do.

Caleb Richard Ogilvie was buried in a small cemetery behind Jimmy Broughton's place, a wonderfully secluded cedar grove that a black family used to keep raked and tended year-round. An iron fence surrounding the yard was crowded with sweet everlasting.

Folks gathered for various reasons, pity or curiosity or obligation. I was allowed to attend, though not as part of the family. Dave would not have that.

My father was there too. He did not join the congregation, not Tink. His was a distant observation. I spotted him by accident, the sun that July Sunday glinting off the reins of his mule. Tink watched, mounted, from some distance in the understory of the forest that tangled all around that cedar grove.

He seemed at first erect and familiar in his saddle. I wondered what was going through that stubborn mind and heart, seeing his enemy's innocent son buried. Seeing Caleb's death as the cost for Tink's sudden and unearned opportunity.

For make no mistake about it; if the crib and packhouse had not burned, Dave would have been able to pay Leroy Sessions every dime of interest owed on his mortgage with thousands left over. Leroy was certain, before the fire, to get his money. My father, before the fire, would have gained nothing.

I wondered what Dave was thinking about now, there beside his little boy's grave. Did he blame himself for Caleb's death? For the rebuke that drove the boy to rebel? Who could imagine the consequence of such a gentle revolution?

Or was Dave grieving the loss of his land, wondering even as the coffin lowered his son to rest why, with this loss, was his home and property also snatched away?

Child gone and land in one swift, sure stroke! Who could comprehend such a loss?

"The Lord giveth and the Lord taketh away." The preacher supplied that explanation too often.

Did God, then, intervene to right the scales of justice? Did he answer summer prayers for a golden harvest only to scourge it with fire so Tink might reclaim his father's land? Was the boy's death thrown in for good measure? Was God really so capricious or so cruel? Did the Almighty really involve himself in such affairs?

Dave might have sought after God's heart in the quest to answer such questions. I did. But I knew my father would not. Tink would not be giving God credit or blame for anything.

But something must have touched that obdurate heart, some sense of irony or loss to bring that sudden posture of despondence or grief that I saw distantly as my father watched Caleb's funeral from the woods. It would be natural for Tink to feel burdened, knowing the land he was about to gain came with the perpetual lien of a child's death.

Leroy Sessions bore no such burden. Leroy was a true vulture, the bank's chief officer now pressing Sarah's hand and Dave's, offering the most public of condolences. But I knew in September Leroy would take my father's forty thousand dollars without breaking wind. A contract was a contract, and there was after all, Leroy would posture, nothing in the business between him and my father that would bring Caleb back.

A child's funeral prompts the most awkward attempts at consolation. It was painful to see neighbors and extended family make the attempt. Dave refused all such efforts with a demeanor so granite and remote as to seem unnatural. Sarah was unfailingly gracious in her own despair. I saw only one token that appeared to briefly lift her spirits. It was the only sign of solace, in fact, that I saw that day.

It was an arrangement of wildflowers wreathed in vine. Summer blossoms, as I recall, very simple, blue curls and blue sage. The hues, a mix of purple and blue, royalty mixed with a boy's color. The stamens of the blue curl were very long. They were arranged in a wreath the size of a large dinner plate. The blossoms were woven into an intricate vine, the pattern reminiscent of something I'd seen before. Some other pattern.

Mac Morgan brought the handwoven laurel.

"From Martha," I heard Morgan whisper to Sarah. "Martha Buchanan."

"Oh, they're beautiful!" Sarah said, cradling that wind of summer life in her arms as if it were a baby.

She kept those flowers in her lap the whole day long. She did not part with them even when finally pressed to accept a bite of chicken and some iced tea.

After supper Julia and I found some privacy near the ruins of the crib. It was terrible to see that scar on the ground, that blackened polygon of ash and death.

What would it mean for us?

We talked in secret, ashamed to speak of anything regarding ourselves so soon after Caleb's death, afraid not to.

"How much money do you think Tink's made so far, Carter?"

"Enough to buy out ya'll's mortgage. More than enough."

"When is Leroy supposed to sign it over?"

"September sixteenth. Monday," I replied.

That gave us roughly a month and a half. A month and a half to find a middle ground between our warring fathers.

"Let's just leave," Julia said.

"It might not be smart." I dragged my heels.

"We need to get married."

"I don't know…"

"Carter, we've talked and *talked*—! I've got to get *out* of here, don't you see? No matter *what* it takes!"

"All right, all right!"

"No." She pushed away from me. "It's *not* all right! What am I to you, Carter? Just something to lay with? Something you can roll up and use when it's convenient?"

"You *know* that's not true?"

"How do I know? Show me! *Show me.*"

"How? What can I do?"

"Go in to Papa right now. Tell him the season's finished, and so are you. So are we. Tell him, Carter. Or don't come back here for me!"

I knew I had waited too long. I knew somewhere deep inside, someplace I did not care to visit, that Dave Ogilvie would not give me his daughter. That I would have to either take her or buy her with the coin of some awful realm.

But I resolved that moment to go to him, to tell him exactly what Julia proposed. We were going to marry and be free of his feudal hold. I went to tell him that.

Chapter twenty-three

False Moneywort, *Alysicarpus ovalifolus*

I found Dave alone, smoking Prince Albert in his large bedroom. There were flames licking the iron dogs in his fireplace even though it was the middle of summer. All the windows were open, and still it was unbearably hot in that room. Dave sat there soaked as if in a sauna.

"Come in, Carter."

I have no idea how he knew I was at the door.

"Yes, sir."

"I haven't heard from your daddy."

"Well, the contract doesn't take effect till September sixteenth," I said. "That gives you a month and a half."

"No," Dave said slowly and turned to face me, turned and took my eyes straight into his own. "No, Carter, it gives *you* a month and a half."

Sweat stung my eyes. I wiped my brow with a stiffly starched sleeve.

"Oh, I don't know."

"Make a stab."

"Four … five thousand dollars," I replied. That was a common reserve of cash.

"Well, there's your opportunity, Carter."

"Sir?"

"Say you find five thousand dollars in that safe. Three of that will bring me justice. As for the rest—don't you see? You can take it for yourself. Two thousand dollars, or three, or four! That's *your* money, Carter. That's money your daddy has taken out of your pocket, money that's rightfully yours. Say you just got two. Two thousand dollars'd take you back to Emory, wouldn't it? Why, you could go this week! Sure you could! Just resign from office and leave. It's been done before. Bennett Sessions'll be happy to get his job back, and you can go where you want to be. Where you never wanted to leave, *and*"—Dave's eyes spread wide—"you can take Julia along with you."

I just stood there. He backed away from me a moment. Inspected me closely and then, as if suddenly losing interest, turned back to his bed of coals.

"I was wrong. You don't have the gumption to do it. Not even for yourself. Not even for Julia!"

"I didn't say I wouldn't."

"I s'pose we'll see," he said, dismissing me with a wave. As if I were the most completely unimportant speck in the tapestry of his future.

"I said I'd do anything, and I will," I declared without conviction.

He was already back to the hearth, back to the fire.

"Go on, Carter."

I didn't do it right away. I saw Julia first. Took her to the Sand Pond. We didn't have to be nearly so careful about sneaking away now. I just went right up to the porch and told Sarah we'd be out riding. Dave didn't raise a finger to object.

I still had my campaign car. We drove as far as we could on Ogilvie property to a pasture near the Sand Pond. Then we got out and walked. One of the charms of landlocked northern Florida is that it doesn't cool a jot at night. By the time we penetrated the pond's heavy forest boundary and found a likely spot in the interior, we were both soaked in sweat.

Usually on these assignations we'd take a dip in the ponds, skinny dipping either before or after. Sometimes both. Usually, too, I would remark on the summer-blooming flora that made our bed-sheet. That pleasure seemed now an artifact, some passion come from an ancient and cast-off curiosity.

We walked without laughter or conversation to a patch of sand secluded by pine and fetterbush. On that spot, naked and anxious, I told Julia what was contemplated.

"You think I should do it?"

"Oh, Carter, I don't know!"

"It's wrong," I held her close. "It's wrong; I know it is."

"But your daddy's wrong," Julia whispered. "Mine too. We're *all* wrongheaded, *all* of us!"

I've often wondered who talked to that snake first. That night, at least, I know who brought the apple.

"It's the only way I can see us having any kind of freedom," I might as well have begged for her complicity. "We don't want to be stuck in this county forever."

We coupled again. But I recall that union as more desperate and urgent. When finished, we turned away from each other, lying back to back on our bed of moss.

꩜

The very next Saturday, sometime well after midnight, I left my hotel room, climbed into my borrowed car, and headed for Fort McKoon. I didn't carry a gun. I didn't want to handle any kind of weapon.

It was pitch dark beside the log pond, not a hint of activity in the yard, the mill, or the drying sheds beyond.

There was no electricity at Fort McKoon; work quit with the sun. I could hear the river rolling slowly over that long promontory.

And I could see the flint shelf glowing dull as a butter knife beneath a moon filtered through heavy clouds.

No breeze, but the air was redolent with the aroma of sawdust. Cypress and pine. An ever-present incense. The lanterns of the camp that housed my father's laborers winked like fireflies not too far away. I wasn't sure what to do on the off chance I ran into some hanger-on or drunk from the camp. Play drunk myself, probably. Just got a hair up my ass, I'd shuck and jive. Had to see the old mill. I even half hoped for such an encounter, anything that would give me an excuse to abandon my mission.

But there was not a soul at the mill. Last place you wanted to be on a Saturday night was where you busted your hump during the week.

I clung to the shadows of water oak just a spit from my metal office, ears craned for some sound that would signify a sentry. All I could hear was my own blood pounding with each heartbeat in my ears.

This was it. Time to fish or cut bait.

With my light in my left hand, I reached into my pocket with the right and rubbed my office key. It was only about twenty yards across open ground to my old tin shack. Best to look natural, I told myself. Don't run, for God's sake.

I hoofed quickly to the lee of that shed. I fumbled to fit the key into the rusted padlock that secured the door.

It wouldn't fit! Oh, Jesus, had Daddy changed the lock?

But then with a "snick" the padlock released. I snatched it free of the latch, shoved the door open, and was inside.

I closed the door. A flood of memories came back with the sight of my old desk. I checked to make sure the windows were latched shut before risking my flashlight, then crossed behind the desk to the safe.

It was a simple floor safe, an old Mosler double-walled against fire. I had opened that safe hundreds of times; even so, I held my breath, turning the dial through its combination, waiting for each old tumbler to fall. I took the handle firmly, turned, and pulled.

It opened without a squeak of protest.

I kept the flashlight low as I peered inside.

There was a bottle of whiskey. Some turpentine. And then there was money. Neatly folded by denomination, bound with rubber bands. More money than I had ever seen.

For a moment I saw spots in front of my eyes. My God, was I doing this! Another moment of indecision, of shame, and then a rush to finish and get out!

I took three thousand for Dave, pulling wads of hundreds from the safe, counting feverishly. The hoard looked nowhere close to half empty.

I was ready to leave when I realized I'd brought nothing to carry the money away in! Idiot! But it was only three rubber-banded wads of paper. I stuffed the bundles into my shirt, closed the safe, and was spinning the tumblers when the door exploded open like a shot.

The cash fell from beneath my shirt as I flattened back against the wall. I raised my hands to ward off the light in my eyes. I saw the shotgun.

"Don't shoot it's *me!*"

"Carter—?" the astounded voice was familiar. "Carter, whutchu doin' in here?"

It was Spence. I edged away from the safe. His flashlight speared the floor, pooling in yellow the wads of money lying there.

"Spence," I said. "Spence, it's not like you think."

"Hell it ain't; you done robbed our safe!"

"Partly mine," I said, my teeth chattering. "Only what's mine."

He stood there black and immobile and hard as anthracite.

"Spence, listen. I know this looks bad, but think what's going to happen if Daddy gets that mortgage. You know what it's going to cost, you more than anybody! Forty thousand dollars for a piece of property worth less than twenty! A fortune for revenge; does that seem right to you?"

"Don't make this right," Spence replied. "Got nothin' to do with this here."

"Yes, it does," I burst out. "Goddamnit, it's got *everything* to do!"

I stooped down like a child retrieving marbles to scoop up the stolen cash.

"Cain't let you do this, Carter!"

"Shoot me, then," I snarled. "Shoot me and then in the morning you can tell Daddy. I'm sure he'll be happy with your decision!"

"Cain't let you go!"

"You could wait. Tell Tink first thing in the morning. Hell, tell him tonight. For all you know he sent me here; tell him that! Tell him I was here taking out cash and I told you it was all right, that he sent me. He'd believe that. Hell, he'd believe anything *you* told him!"

Spence blocked that door black and hard and massive. As tall now as his father had been.

"I'm going now," I said, my voice shaking. "I'm going unless you kill me."

I walked to the door. I don't think Spence took that light or either barrel of that shotgun off me the whole time.

"Don' do this, Carter!"

"He'll ruin you too, Spence; he will. He'll waste everything you ever did or ever wanted to do, you and Polly and Little Saint. Even Eida Mae if he has to. And all over a piece of dirt. Let me stop it, Spence! Let me!"

He just stood there, shotgun and light leveled on me like a gator in a pond as I edged out that door. And still stood, weapon and light trained like a marksman, as I shuffled across that hated yard.

Each breath in my lungs I expected to shatter with buckshot, but it didn't happen. Spence MacGrue, my old boyhood friend, caught me red-handed and then watched me walk away.

I figured to be arrested or killed by morning, so I determined to deliver the cash to Dave that night.

I trembled like a leaf on the way over, my arms shaking so badly on the car's steering wheel I nearly lost the road. I rolled down the windows, the wind tearing water from my eyes. Dave was waiting, propped up in a rocker as if people often came to visit at four in the morning.

Did the man ever sleep?

"It's me, Mr. Ogilvie. Carter."

"Done your chore?"

"Yessir."

"I'll come take it, then."

That's what he did. Didn't even let me in the yard. Just stilled his dogs with a grunt, came out, and took the wadded paper I offered.

"How much?"

"Three thousand."

"That's altogether?"

"Yes."

God, how I hated this man. He was already turning his back to me. No thank-you. No much-obliged. But why should he? I was just a thief.

"Julia and I are getting married," I said to his back. "Soon as you pay off Leroy."

"Hell, boy," he said without even bothering to turn around, "who was stopping you?"

Chapter twenty-four

Poison Ivy,
Toxicodendron radicans

I didn't go back to my hotel. I knew when I robbed Tink's safe that I had also taken away the single best chance he would ever have to reclaim the land lost hard by his father. But it wasn't just his money I took away, and it wasn't just the land. It was hope and dream and labor and fury and much more. I had broken faith again and again. Tink would come to wreak a familiar vengeance, I was sure of it.

I needed a place to hide. Live Oak was thirty miles to the east. Fifteen dollars bought a month's rent at a fleabag boarding house where I waited for my inquisitor like some character in a Russian novel, dreading each moment to hear that knock on my rented door.

A night passed. A week.

Julia and I had arranged to correspond clandestinely through her school's address. Her letters kept me informed and sane. I was amazed to learn that Tink was not, at least publicly, seeking justice against *anyone*. In fact, Julia wrote, "there is a kind of silence that is positively unnatural! No one seems to have heard *anything* from your father, and there is, so far, no public knowledge that a robbery of any kind has occurred at the Fort McKoon Mill.

⁊

It was early in September that I decided to risk a phone call to Judge Blacksheer, just to see if *he* had heard anything. I placed that call in the morning. It was late that evening when my landlady called me over to the hotel's one phone.

"From a Judge Blacksheer." She extended the receiver.

I took it. "Yes, sir?"

"Carter. I suppose you've by now heard."

"Heard what, sir?"

My heart hammering.

"Why, it's all over town, son. Dave Ogilvie hit the market."

"The market? Dave?"

"That old deacon," the judge chuckled. "Squirreled away enough for one last throw of the dice, I reckon. Commodities, Leroy said it was."

"Leroy Sessions?"

"Carter, are you ill?"

"I don't understand where you're headed, Judge Blacksheer."

"Headed? Headed nowhere now. No need. Dave Ogilvie's got the money to pay off the interest on his mortgage, can you imagine that? Money came out of nowhere, seems like. Just when we all thought the old bastard had a stake in his heart!"

I hung up. It was apparent Tink had not reported the robbery. More puzzling, he also wasn't making a visible effort to find the thief. But why not? Even if Spence had lied to protect *me*, Tink would know the money was stolen by *somebody* and would be hellbent to recover his three thousand dollars. It was, as Julia said, unnatural. It didn't make sense.

Then came a letter that, explaining nothing, ended my exile. I thought at first it was Julia's correspondence; I knew she had addressed the envelope, the handwriting was Julia's. And so was the dab of lilac

244

water which scented the envelope. But when I tore inside, I found a ruder hand waiting:

> Deerst Carter,
> No need to hide. Tink is not after you. Its saif.
>   Love, Mother

So she *knew*? Did *he* know? All Julia could tell me was that Martha had hand-delivered the note to her at school with the firm admonition that I was not to attempt further communication. My expulsion from the Big House was still fully in effect.

I drove back to Laureate and my familiar digs across from the courthouse. Even with Martha's reassurance, I sat out the month like Damocles on his throne, waiting with a trepidation long settled in my bowels for the thread that held the sword above my head to break.

It never did.

🌿

On September 16 Dave Ogilvie drove into town and parked conspicuously in front of Leroy's bank. Dave stepped out of his freshly washed Packard, shoes polished brightly, suit immaculately ironed and creased. He paused at the bank's bronze-handled door for the pretence of reconciling his gold-plated Hamilton with the courthouse clock. Holding on to his little drama for every second it was worth. Then, slipping the watch into his vest pocket, Dave pushed inside.

In less than a half hour, everyone in town knew that Dave Ogilvie had made his mortgage. The deacon's miraculous salvation was the talk of the town. Not many folks paid much attention to the other news: on the same day that Dave settled with Leroy, the Congress of the United States passed the Selective Training and Service Act. For the first time in our nation's history, a government at peace granted itself the power to conscript men for war.

For most of the world the war was already raging. As auctioneers hawked sheets of tobacco in Live Oak, young Brits in Hurricanes and Spitfires dogfought German pilots over the English Channel in the Battle of Britain. "HITLER HURLED BACK!" Fox MovieTone trailers extolled the grit of our cousins overseas, providing canned shots of young aviators in their flying machines or on the ground beside jerry-rigged squash courts, all smiles and crumpets and tea. Lowell Thomas provided commentary.

I began to imagine with a kind of perverse romanticism, born probably of boredom and unemployment, that my many sins could be redeemed by sacrifice to this larger and noble cause. All too soon my draft board received instructions that threatened to give me that opportunity.

Our local board's meeting place had a special aura of secrecy, convening as it did in the Masonic Lodge above Doc's drugstore. Edward Land and Mac Morgan served on the board with Leroy Sessions and Doc West. The board pulled numbers from an ordinary shoe box to meet quotas passed down from Washington. Of course, wealthy whites found ways to exempt themselves from the draft. Black people in Lafayette County, on the other hand, were not considered for induction at all. A black man could in theory pursue his right to enlist. But most blacks were trapped in local servitude by debts, dues, or outright intimidation.

Spence wanted badly to join the army. He was set to enlist, but Tink stymied him with a letter to the Department of Defense. Before Spence could even take a physical, he found himself exempted by reason of occupation. That high-handed intervention caused a real rift between Spence and Daddy.

I remember telling Julia I didn't know why Spence should be so eager to get his ass shot, never questioning my own freedom in that regard.

The prospect of the draft presented me with an interesting dilemma. It was by now the autumn of 1940. I had planned to resign as tax assessor and return with Julia to Atlanta, where I'd finally finish my education. But, in the first place, the fall quarter at Emory had already begun. More important, if I resigned from my elected office I'd be eligible for the draft.

Julia's opinion was persuasive in this regard; she thought I'd be crazy to give up an exemption from military service. "It's a death lottery," Julia told me, convinced that war was imminent. "Four years with the county, you'll be safe. We can marry knowing that if there *is* a war, you can wait it out. What good would it do to give up your exemption, start school in January, and then be pulled away to boot camp?"

I acted in accordance with the many descendants of Deserters' Island and decided to become a married man serving my county as its tax assessor.

Julia and I finally made a public commitment to our private union. We married October 3. An odd date, middle of the week, as I recall. But we did not want a large affair.

We exchanged vows in Laureate's First Baptist Church. Dave gave Julia away. I had Judge Blacksheer stand as my family. Mac Morgan was best man. Sarah was there, of course. Wyatt should have been there, but only the week before he'd sneaked off to Camp Blanding and joined the army. Dave maintained the pharisaism that he had encouraged his son's independence.

Tink didn't attend the wedding, maintaining a perfect absence from the Lord's house. Mother, even had she been allowed, would not come without my father. I understood that.

Martha did send a wedding gift, though, a handwoven quilt, not an Appalachian pattern but a comforter differently conceived, with long diagonals and bold swaths of color. "An Indian blanket!" Julia pronounced delightedly when she unwrapped it.

"Yes," I said. "I s'pose it is."

It made for an awkward ceremony, my mother and father absent, Julia desperate to cut off any tie with *her* father. Poor Sarah caught in the middle. We both worried for Sarah, with Caleb and Wyatt gone, isolated in the Big House with Dave.

Somebody kidding said that for the first time in his life Dave would have to make his tobacco with hired labor. Nobody much laughed.

We didn't go on a honeymoon—Julia was teaching. But we didn't mind. We had our own house, a white rental on Main Street wrapped with a big porch and hedged with azaleas and crepe myrtle. It took only a couple of suitcases to take everything we owned inside. Our first full night together was probably more an occasion of relief than joy, though Julia did surprise me the next morning, waking me early.

We went downtown for our honeymoon feast. There was only one cafe, Clarence Simms's, Clarence's mother cooked; his sister waited tables. The handful of regulars who showed up in the morning treated Julia and me with gentle humor and genuine goodwill, making us feel like newlyweds. They heaped our plates with sausage and grits and filled our chipped mugs with coffee hot enough to scald. Julia's color was high that morning. I was proud as a peacock.

❧

I had not seen or heard a thing of Tink since Caleb's funeral. I wondered what he was thinking, what he was doing. What plans he had for me.

I was sure Mother knew. I couldn't put a firm date on the last time I'd seen Martha—it was tempting to just drive out to the house. But the severe admonition relayed through Julia made it plain that a visit was not possible. I was not even sure Mother would accept a letter but decided it was worth a try.

I wrote a short note and recruited Taff to deliver it, enjoining him to place my envelope directly in Martha's hands. It was more than a week before I got her reply.

> Deerst Carter,
>
> Thank you so much for riteing. I am glad you and Julia too like the quilt. Ive been working on that thing seems like forever. It should last you.
>
> About your daddy. All I can tell you now is he is not here much. He is gone most days & stays in the woods like he use to with his survay equipmint and mule. I dont know most times where he is.

248

> Hes not himself I know that. Not even when
> he's home…

I stopped reading, alarmed. This retreat or exile, whatever it was, was not like my father. I felt more ashamed of what I had done than ever before. I took up mother's letter again. I received another cryptic surprise:

> Tink isn't rite inside, son, but you got to know
> and please beleve—It is *not you did it.*

She actually underlined those words, scored them with a heavy dark pencil. They didn't make sense. Of course I had done it! Who else had injured my father?

But the lines beneath my mother's words were stark and unambiguous. There was no hint of metaphor here. Mother meant for me to take her literally: "…it is *not you.…*"

What a relief, what a weight removed! But any diminution of responsibility I might be tempted to embrace was confused right away.

> You have to take my word for now. Please don't
> come see me I hate to think what mite happen if Tink
> found you here. I will rite when I can you were smart
> to send this by Taff.
>
> Your daddys not well I dont think but there is
> nothing you can do nor me to help him.
>
> Pray for your daddy, Carter. Pray that he finds
> some peece for himself somewhere in those woods. I
> think thats about the only thing that can help.
>
> I love you. He does too.
>
> Best to Julia.
>
> > Your mother always and always…

I must have read that letter a dozen times, each time searching for some hint or nuance that would allow its decryption. It was clear that since July my father had not been the same. My mother's letter freshly reminded me of that gaunt figure I had seen mounted and spying on Caleb's funeral.

I had to know. Cane grinding gave me the chance to find out.

Chapter twenty-five

Red Chokeberry,
Pyrus arbutifolia

I t was December and bitter cold when Julia and I were invited to the Hendersons' for their grinding. A cane grinding was not a thing so fervid as a sing or so grand as tobacco market, but it was doings enough. Old people and young worked side by side, taking plenty of time to admire the kiln's bright fire or the bees above the juice-barrel or to laugh at the children and grandchildren who invariably rode the mule hitched in perpetual orbit to the grinder.

The mule powered the grinder by turning a log geared to massive steel rollers that squeezed the juice from the sugarcane's tough stalk. That sweet, thick juice was transferred from a catch-barrel to an enormous cast-iron kettle mounted atop a brick kiln. You'd take turns firing the kiln, the heat searing your face, some ancient woman monitoring the froth and fluid that boiled in the kettle above—double, double, toil and trouble.

Julia and I loved the heavy, sweet aroma of a cane kettle cooking. We loved the sweet polecat that deposited like candy on the kettle's iron lip. I scooped up a sample on a scrap of stalk. We shared it like a lollipop.

It was a Monday. The kiln's heat melted the frost that had fallen hard and white on the tin roof over our heads. It was an animated gathering beneath, everyone laughing and gossiping, waiting for that magic moment when just enough water was evaporated from the raw cane juice so that it could be poured boiling into whiskey bottles as clean as any druggist's beaker. The old crone would make that decision, she who had tended a thousand kettles.

"Ah-hah, it's ready."

Once filled the bottles would be stacked to cool. Cane syrup once cooled shines like pure amber. The work was done in a day— the cane cut, squeezed, boiled, skimmed, and poured into the bottles, which our dry county supplied in ample plenty. Compared to what we had done all summer, this winter task was no work at all.

Half the people there were related to each other. Ray's wife, Erma, happily established their kinship to Julia and me in a genealogy more complicated than Jacob's. This was a common yeast of conversation, the endless construction and deconstruction of blood and marriage and relations.

It was a pleasant span of moments, Julia pretending to follow Erma's conjugation of bloodlines in great detail while working a hand into the small of my back. Ed Land's Rachel seeing that covert flirtation, laughing red-faced, winking. I can keep a secret, she was saying, even though we both knew she couldn't.

This is the way it could be, I was telling myself. This is the way it *can* be for me and for Julia. Forever! I think I might even have begun to believe it too, that the threatening thread had snapped, that whatever sword there was had long fallen and missed the throne entirely. I had begun at least to have that hope when into that carnival of delights rode my mother, nearly naked and brutalized.

❧

She rode up on my father's mule. She slumped stripped and blue-cold over the beast's bare back, her long legs cut to ribbons and dragging the ground, her breasts scourged too and sagging over the mule's stubborn neck. Only her hair and a scrap of undergarment to cover that tall, tall frame.

"My God...!" I heard someone say and turned around and saw.

"Mother?" I was jarred to an awkward run.

Two men reached her ahead of me. Erma whipped a blanket off the wash line for a wrap.

"Get her by the fire," Erma commanded.

She was nearly in shock from exposure.

"Martha, drink this." Rachel brought some heated juice.

She took it slowly, then a swallow, and then, eyes suddenly wide open, she gulped from the tumbler.

"Mother, what is it?"

"He ... burnt the house." She swallowed painfully.

Tink?!

Martha saw my misinterpretation. "No, Carter, your... daddy's in the woods.... I hid.... Hid Polly, Little Saint... back in the Sand Pond. But I was ... too late—!" Her almond eyes brimmed. "Too late for Eida Mae!"

"My God." Ray seemed late to comprehend what Mother was trying to say.

"Who was it, Martha?" Erma asked gently.

"Stanton Lee." For the first time a sob broke from my mother. "He came lookin' for Tink, I reckon, but Tink weren't home! I was by the lake. Gatherin' wood for the wash. I saw the fire first. The house? And I came runnin'. . . .

"Then I saw that black hat, that long coat draggin', and I knew."

Mother turned to me. "He didn't rape me, Carter. I didn't let him."

"My God, my God!" Ray kept saying over and over.

"Mother—Mother?"

I thought she was going to die.

"It's nice here by the kettle." She seemed to realize where she was. "Cold in that water, I can tell you."

"The water?" This from Rachel.

"Stanton Lee came for me." Martha nodded. "I surprised him, but then he saw me, and he came in those boots. But I can run!" She smiled. "I may be near to fifty, but I can outrun a fat white man, and I ran, Carter, I ran like the wind straight back to the lake!"

My God, my God.

"Straight to the water." Martha stretched a hand cold as ice to take my own. "He shot at me twice. Shotgun. Pellets all over, but I cursed him, Carter, I said—'Come on in here with me, Stanton Lee! We'll swim! I know where the *gators* are, do *you?*' Him cussin'. Breaking open that shotgun for to load. I shucked my clothes and I dived down, deep as Jonah's whale, then I swam till my lungs 'bout broke! Then I came up and dived down and swam away again. Out to the middle of that lake. I watched the house burn from there. Prayin' that Polly and Little Saint wouldn't see the smoke. Prayin' they'd stay in the Sand Pond.

"Thank Jesus, they did. Stanton Lee didn't stay long. Couldn't! That smoke going straight up he couldn't risk a neighbor seein'. Comin' over to help. So he left. Wasted a few pellets first."

"Mother, be quiet, now. That's enough."

"NO." She crushed my hand with a grip nearly as strong as my father's.

"I waited till he left, and I swam round the other side. Ran through the brambles to Spence's cabin. Nothing burnt. No smoke nor anything. But then I saw Eida Mae.

"He hung her, Carter. Hung her from the porch with the end of a bullwhip. He did some other things too. Terrible things. You got to get her down before Spence sees. Or your daddy."

My God, my God.

"What about Polly, Martha? And Little Saint?"

"I ran from the cabin straight to the Sand Pond. Found Little Saint with his mama. I just told Polly the Big House was burnt, for them to stay in the mayhaws while I went for help. I didn't tell 'em about Stanton Lee or Eida Mae, just told 'em to *stay*. Then I went and got old Hoover and rode on over here."

"My God, Martha!" Ray said, amazed.

"Get Eida Mae down, Carter," Mother told me. "Then get Polly and the boy. Then you better—"

"Mother? Mother?"

She roused briefly.

"Then you best send for Tink," she said and fainted beside the fire.

Always before I had had Mother or Daddy to do the hard things. To start them anyway. To make those first quick, crucial decisions. But now everyone was looking for me to take the lead. This was my mother.

"Ray can you go yourself or send a man to Fort McKoon?" I asked.

"I'll go," Taff volunteered.

"Thank you, Taff. Just tell Spence Daddy needs him home. Don't tell him about the house or anything else."

"How you gonna get holt of Tink? He could be anywhere."

"Ray, your place have a phone?"

"We do."

"Call Putnam Lumber Company. Ask for M. L. Fleishel. Tell him we need every man he's got in the woods looking for Tink. Just tell M. L. the house is burnt. And tell him Mother's all right; I'd rather have Tink come in thinkin' it's just the house."

"Awright. How about the sheriff?"

"You can tell him too. I doubt it'll do much good."

Erma and Sarah moved mother into the Hendersons' house. Mac Morgan went with me into the Sand Pond to find Polly and Little Saint.

❧

They were both blue with the cold and scared half to death. Huddled there behind the thorny mayhaws. Polly came out first. Came out as decoy, actually, not familiar in her fright with these white men stomping up through the woods.

"Polly, it's Carter!" I called out to stop her. "Mother sent me!"

"What happen yo' mama?" Polly asked as soon as she settled down.

"It's bad, Polly. Got your boy?"

"Ah'm right cheer." That small voice brave even in fright. I saw a rifle's slender barrel.

"You won't need that. Just ask your mama."

Only after Polly herself reassured him did Little Saint leave his cover.

"We're taking ya'll to Mr. Henderson's," I said. "Martha's there. She's gonna be fine."

"What 'bout Eida Mae?" Polly clutched her son like a jewel with her copper hands.

"Tell you on the way over."

⁂

I took Spence's wife and boy to the Hendersons', then drove with Mac and Ray and Jimmy Broughton to my old home.

It was the first time I'd been to the Big House since spring. The house was a charred mess of timber. The stumps remained, smoking piers beneath beams burned in two. The rest of the house was a blackened skeleton tottering over that smoking foundation.

"Whole thing'd shove over with a feather," Mac remarked.

"Let's see to Eida Mae," I said.

Spence's mother was hanging by the neck. A good hanging breaks the neck in an instant. That was not how Eida Mae had died. You could see scratches on her throat all around and blood on her fingernails where she had tried to work the noose free. A horrible thing to imagine, those hands old and frantic, trying to pry a space inside that cruel kerchief while Stanton Lee was doing that other.

That rocking-chair hand was finally at peace. We took her down and wrapped her in a bed sheet. Then we decided it would be best to wait for Daddy by the ruins of the Big House. Wasn't too long before I saw our truck bouncing up the lane. Spence was driving. He pulled up to the scorched yard. Got out of the truck.

Tink was with him.

Daddy looked a hundred years old. He was gaunt to the point of emaciation. His hair had not been cut, and if he'd shaved at all, it must have been with his Barlow.

"Mother's fine," I told him as I approached.

"What I heard," he replied. "She said it was Stanton Lee," Tink went on, as if providing me this information.

"Yes, sir," I replied.

"Polly awright? An' my boy?" Spence asked innocently, and I realized Tink must not have told him everything.

"Polly's just fine, Spence. So's Little Saint…"

I hesitated.

"Where's my mama?" Spence demanded, an alarm lit instantly behind those wide-set eyes.

"I'll take you to her," Ray interjected.

"No." Tink shook his head. "I'll do it. You men wait here."

I didn't know what to do. Whether to go with my father or stay.

Tink placed his hand on my shoulder as he passed.

"How you been, son?"

I couldn't speak.

Daddy patted me on the back. Just once and gentle like when I was little. Without another word he walked quickly with Spence to the Little House. We could hear Spence's lamentation that quarter of a mile away.

❧

I don't know how long I waited, five minutes, ten, before I decided I'd better check up on them both. I met Tink halfway coming back. Spence wasn't with him.

I had expected to see a rage in my father that would eclipse any I had seen before. But when I met Tink on that middle ground, he seemed in a state of perfect equanimity. He came to me composed. Calm. He appeared perfectly at peace.

"Daddy. Are you all right?"

"You stay here with Spence." He ignored my question. "Is Mother at Ray's?"

"Polly too," I acknowledged. "And Little Saint."

"Good." He nodded. "You did good here, son. Good as this goddamned mess allows."

"What are you going to do?"

"Going to find Stanton Lee," he replied matter-of-factly. "Then I'm goin' to kill him."

"Let me go with you," I said, alarmed. My father, once invincible, seemed now a vulnerable, even ridiculous champion. Especially against Stanton Lee Sullivan.

I wanted to go. Daddy wouldn't hear of it.

"No." He shook his head. "I took you once before. I shouldn't've done that."

I heard regret where I expected to hear recrimination. I heard compassion where I expected bitterness and anger.

"You can't go alone!" I protested.

"Carter, you didn't break this wagon." He smiled at me. "It ain't your job to fix it."

"Can't we talk, Daddy?"

"Some things you just have to do."

He turned me around by the arm back toward the house.

"I put you in a bad fix, son. Had it to do over, I hope I wouldn't. But I don't know."

"I want to go with you, Daddy!"

"I know you do."

He squeezed my arm in a nut-cracking hand.

"And I 'preciate it."

That was the end of our conversation. The rest was a matter of logistics. Tink charged Mac and Taff to keep an eye on Spence.

"I don't want to see that boy in town," Tink said sternly. "You keep him here. Shoot him in the foot if you have to; I don't want Spence to ruin hisself over this. If he goes after Stanton Lee, that's exactly what will happen."

"The hell d'you think's gonna happen to you?" Taff demanded.

"I'll be fine," Tink assured him. Then to me—"Tell your mother I'm sorry," he said.

"For what?" I asked.

"She knows," was his reply.

Then Tink climbed into his battered truck, cranked it up. He leaned out the window as he pulled around. Smiled broadly— "How's married life?"

"Good!" I said, not expecting that question. "Real good!"

He smiled the broader. "Know what's fine about a tall woman, Carter?"

"No, sir," I replied, uncertain of his intent.

"When yer nose to nose, your toes is in." He stuck his head out of the cab as he pulled away.

"And when yer toes to *toes*"—pulling away, now, shouting out the window—"when yer toes to toes, your *nose* is in!"

I laughed in spite of myself, my father's parting and vulgar and unoriginal humor having the effect of a benediction. Or absolution.

I watched Tink drive down our dogwood-bordered lane toward town and God knows what, laughing through my tears.

Chapter twenty-six

Bloodroot, *Lachnanthes caroliniana*

The next morning I was at Ray Henderson's. Tending Mother. Offering what little comfort I could to Spence and his family. Everything I can tell you about what happened in town late that morning I've collected secondhand from Doc, or third- and fourth-hand from the many others who, claiming in later years to have been there, were almost certainly not there at all.

Memory plays tricks on us. It gives us dots on a space of thoroughly blank paper and asks our minds over the years to make connections. It gives us clouds in an uncertain sky and asks of that ethereal stuff for castles and dragons and faces to be made.

But some things I can certainly record. The red glow of Doc's potbelly stove. The advertisements cut from catalogs and magazines and stuck with pins around the counter. The tin-thin drone of the radio. The pills and elixirs bright and clear as cane syrup taking the light from Doc's windows and casting it in a kaleidoscope onto his polished pine floor.

All those things I see.

And I can see Stanton Lee, that son of a bitch, slouching toward his reckoning over a cherry Coke, his long coat wet with lake water and gray with ash dragging the floor about his stool. Bloodstained, most likely. Listening to the radio, cussing the war and Roosevelt.

The stench of the man. Customers, if there were any, sliding to either side in wide berth. Stanton Lee sitting there enjoying the effect, still nervous from his recent occupation, still feral with his recent kill and secure or arrogant enough to believe he had time enough, more than enough! to indulge his sweet tooth. Figuring that no one in town yet knew what had happened, or, knowing, would be in no position to do anything about it. He hadn't counted on Daddy coming in early and without warning from the woods.

Doc said the minute he saw Tink, he knew there was going to be trouble. The buzz of conversation that had permeated the store ceased the moment Daddy stepped through the door.

He was dressed for work, the familiar short-handled axe hanging from a leather loop at his belt, the saddle rifle cradled in one arm, the Smith & Wesson stuck in his pants as casually as a comb. The brass knuckles plainly draped over a fist.

"Got that checkerboard, Doc?"

"Don't be careful, you'll be a regular," Doc replied warily.

Only then did Tink direct his attention to the counter. "Stanton Lee."

Stanton Lee stiffened slightly, according to reports. Just a little change in posture. But then he returned to his Coke just as if he'd heard nothing at all.

Tink took a line to a stool two down from Sullivan. Placed the carbine on a side distant from his adversary. Loosed the loop at his belt.

"What's going on here, Tink?" Doc had actually begun to place the checkers on his board.

"Had a house burnt," Tink answered just as if he were describing spilt milk.

"I had a brother kilt," Stanton Lee snarled.

"Had some cuttin' done as well," Tink went on as though Stanton Lee hadn't said a thing. "Some hangin' too. A woman."

About that time the patrons made a beeline for the door.

"Sounds to me like you oughta be talkin' to the sheriff, Tink." Stanton Lee displayed his rotten teeth in a kind of rictus.

"I just might." Tink nodded as if in sincere appreciation of the larger man's suggestion. "Then again, maybe I'll just settle it right here."

That's when *Doc* thought about heading for the door.

Stanton Lee swiveled on his stool to face Daddy. He had his bowie knife and revolver.

"How's yer shoulder, Tink?"

"Fair to middlin'. Where's your bullwhip?"

Stanton Lee pushed away his soda.

"You got something on me, Tink Buchanan? Then go to the law. If you *don't*—go to hell!"

"So you don't have a thing to tell me."

"She's your nigger," Stanton Lee shrugged.

Tink smiled. Seemed almost relaxed, according to people who may have been there or no.

"Now, that's a fact, Stanton Lee. But all I said was a house got burnt. And a woman got cut. I didn't say whether she was mine nor what color she was."

"I'm goin' for the sheriff!" Doc tried to intervene.

"Won't help." Tink shook his head. "Will it, Stanton Lee? Frank'd never make it stick."

"You're doin' the talkin', Tink."

"No." Daddy shook his head with that response. And then— "I'm done with talk."

Stanton Lee was only half off his stool when he met Tink's axe coming down. That's how you win a fight, Daddy always told me. Get in that first lick.

But Stanton Lee gets an arm underneath the arc of Daddy's axe, and next thing you know Tink's flying like a rag doll onto shelves stocked with pills and syrups and ointments. Bottles crashing down, spilling fluids slick as owl shit onto the floor.

Stanton Lee charging in with his bowie knife. He hits that slick and those square-toed boots fly out from under Stanton Lee just about the time Tink finds his feet. Tink going then for his pistol. Sullivan kicking it loose. Tink closing with the bigger man, hammering his knife hand with that awful brass-armored fist. Going then for face, nose, eyes.

Two men down on that oil-slick floor together. Fists and feet and elbows. Neither man able to get an advantage. But then things turn when Daddy gouges Stanton Lee in the eye. Stanton Lee jerks up screaming to a crouch, Tink sliding away now to retrieve his pistol.

Tink finds his .38. But the revolver is slick, the butt lathered with castor oil and cough syrups. Tink fumbling to keep that bone grip secure, to pull back the hammer to single-action, to make that one sure shot!

He's done all that, got the handgun, got it cocked and ready. Now turning to find Stanton Lee.

"TINK, LOOKOUT!"

Daddy turning then to see Stanton Lee straddling him like a pig ready to slaughter. Straddling my daddy with Tink's own axe coming down, coming down, coming down—!

That sharp steel wedge plunging past Daddy's bad arm all the way through the cage of his ribs and into his chest.

Tink's trigger hand jerks with the impact. Something like a cannon explodes in the small space of that store; the slug's recoil jerks the .38 from his hand.

Daddy lying there now with a steel wedge in his chest. Legs twitching like a spider's. Stanton Lee bends over, down to a knee.

Doc sees the red rose blossoming somewhere in his gut or chest or side. Stanton Lee clamps his filthy fist over the wound, cries out once with a sharp pain. But then Stanton Lee takes a deep breath. He gets his feet beneath that slack gut. He hauls himself erect.

He's on his feet now, swaying like a timber about to fall. And then, grinning through his pain, he spits on the man lying on the floor.

"Think you're…King Shit…now, Tink?"

He slips once on the way to the door, bringing another shelf of valuables to ruin. But Stanton Lee makes it to the street, everyone agrees on that. He's seen crossing toward the courthouse, shaken but clearly under his own steam, and he's seen sliding into a Chevrolet sedan. A few people even see the Chevrolet weaving away from town. But that's all they see.

And as for Tink? He has the shaft of his own axe gripped in those two Neanderthal hands. Gripping that short lath of hickory and fighting to pull its sharpened head free from his heart. He struggles there, the axe's handle shaking in his hands like a sheet in the wind. Struggling to pull it out, to rip it out! A curdle of blood bubbling at his mouth.

His cabled chest heaves with the effort. But then the hands fall from their task, arms and legs relax, and Doc hears a long sigh escape past the hemorrhage of bloodless lips, a long exhalation as if from a balloon slowly spent.

Doc rushed out from around the counter for form's sake. But he knew even before he reached him that Tink was dead.

Jack-in-the-Pulpit,
Arisaema triphyllum

Eida Mae and Tink were buried on separate sides of the only thing that could be described as high ground on our property. Daddy's site was, I thought, peculiar, but Mother insisted on it. From the rough knoll of earth beneath which Tink was laid to rest you could see straight through to the Ogilvies' family plot, or at least to the wreath of trees that framed the cemetery. I realized that it was on this spot that Tink had sat astride his mule, observing Caleb Ogilvie's interment. And here he lay now, a sentinel over that innocent grave until resurrection.

I don't remember much about Tink's funeral. There were few mourners, unlike Eida Mae's wake, where black people converged by the score. Once again I remained outside the fence, warded off by years of distance and by the bleach bottles. Those amber, broken necks kept all unsettled spirits at bay—including my own.

I could accept Tink's death. But that his death had come to Tink at the hands of Stanton Lee Sullivan was something I could not stomach. I didn't even know if that evil man was alive. Nobody did. Stanton Lee had disappeared. Sheriff Folsom found the Chevrolet smashed up at the edge of the flatwoods, but there was no trace of Tink's killer. Folsom was content to believe that Stanton Lee was a goner. "He left town shot and bleeding," the sheriff pointed out. "Must have wrecked the car, stumbled into the woods, and bled to death." But Frank couldn't find a body. Neither could a kennel of dogs.

I wanted to make sure.

I had a month to look. The county would not require my presence until January. Hunting season gave me an excuse to roam the woods. I was, after all, my father's son.

Spence helped me saddle up. I told him I just needed some time off. That I'd be hunting deer in the flatwoods. I took Daddy's rifle and revolver. I didn't take the knuckles; I had no intention of making this a fair fight.

I had a notion of how to track Stanton Lee. If alive, he was somewhere west of Laureate, somewhere in that huge region between the drugstore and the Gulf of Mexico. Licking his wounds. A gunshot man in that situation couldn't make it on his own. Stanton Lee would be forced to depend on other people for food and water. Probably also for whiskey and the rest.

I decided to try the turpentine camps. A man wanting to mend away from the law could do worse. There was usually a sawbones in the camps who could cut out a slug or staunch a bleeding wound. And no sheriff in his right mind went looking for trouble with turpentiners. They were a rough crowd to treat. But I had something the sheriff didn't.

I had money.

Two days after Daddy was buried I headed out. It took me a week to find out Stanton Lee was alive. That cost me ten dollars and a fifth of whiskey. Next camp, I found out Stanton Lee had himself some broken ribs—that told me he wasn't so badly wounded as advertised. With another week and less than thirty dollars, I tracked that slouch of a beast to Deserters' Island. While there, Stanton Lee had lost at cards and cut a man. He had picked up a whore afterward.

Told her he'd pay her five dollars to come with him. He was headed to Dead Man's Bay, a place I believe I've mentioned before.

Dead Man's Bay backs up from the Gulf like a half moon of shallow brine to beach on sawgrass and pine trees. There's no sandy strand along this coast. Nothing but snakes and cypress knees for company. There is good game to be had, and plenty of fish. The problem is—there isn't a lot of freshwater.

The land just behind the bay dips below sea level to make a kind of marsh. The few people who tried to settle in that morass had to give it up—their wells pulled up nothing but brine. Hunters rarely came this deep into the flatwoods for the same reason. When Tink's surveys brought him to Dead Man's Bay, he had to pack his own drinking water. But there was a spring that lay not more than a quarter mile off the bay, an artesian spring that threw water from a boil not much larger than a kitchen pot from some protected underground aquifer.

There wasn't a turpentine camp at that solitary source of water, but there was a loose bivouac of fishermen. It was not a bad place to heal up some ribs. Not a bad place to lay low from the law. It was, considering the season, a good place to hunt.

I came onto that patchwork of lean-tos and tents after dark. From my vantage I could see fifteen or twenty campfires. I saw planks set up for cleaning fish. I could smell a smokehouse. And I could make out the dim, uncertain shadows of men as they flitted in front of their fires like moths before a distant flickering light. But that was about it.

I decided to wait for morning. Most of these men were fishermen; they'd be out early. The camp would be as empty then as I'd ever find it. There was a trickle of a stream that spilled from the site's artesian well. I pulled back a ways along that cool, clear creek and let Hoover drink his fill. Then I topped off my canteens.

I made a cold camp in the cover of palmettoes, distant from the smell of fish and foul men. The mosquitoes were murderous that long night; I sweated inside a poncho fully dressed rather than be eaten alive.

The next morning I rose ill rested and stiff. A rising sun burned through clouds made of cotton. There was a heavy haze settled to the west. You couldn't tell by looking at the horizon where the water ended and the sky began. I drank half a canteen of water. I ate a biscuit and some sausage. I then cleaned the carbine and handgun, saddled Hoover, and followed the stream back to the fishermen's camp.

The camp was, as I'd hoped, largely deserted. Only a few men were about, most of them barely awake. I was wondering which of these shacks or tents I ought to be inspecting when I saw the smoke-house—

It wasn't much more than a cypress shack. A leather thong was supposed to secure the door, but it had come loose. Hickory smoke filtered through the open door; that would have been pleasant enough. But there were rows of mullet hanging inside, and their stench, especially with the morning's humidity, overpowered all other influences. I nudged Hoover to get upwind of that aroma when I saw him—

There was Stanton Lee.

He was kicked back against the smokehouse wall in a deerhide chair. The chair's front legs rose and settled with the bellows of his lungs. He was dozing. I could see the sorry excuse for dressing tied tightly around his ribs. The rags were soaked brown, no fresh blood. And I saw no obvious sign of fever or infection.

I tied Hoover securely to a sapling and unstrapped Daddy's 30-30. A fisherman eyed me over his cutting table.

"You need somethin'?"

"Got him, thank you," I answered and chambered a shell.

Stanton Lee came down from his deerskin chair slowly. His hands strayed, as if still asleep, for the bowie knife in his belt.

"No." I leveled the Winchester. "You don't want to do that."

The fisherman cursed under his breath and hip-hopped away.

Stanton Lee squinted into the sun.

"Who the hell are you?"

"Carter Buchanan," I tossed my hat to the ground so he could see me clearly. "You butchered Eida Mae MacGrue. And then you killed my father."

"I'll be goddamned," Stanton Lee snorted.

"Yes, you will," I replied, and I shot him through the heart.

The slug shattered those ocher linens and kicked Stanton Lee off his chair. I walked over, and as his fingers clawed the ground, I shot him again, right along the spine. I might even have swapped over to use the revolver a time or two, I don't remember.

I do remember the man who came rushing up with a shotgun.

"He killed my daddy," I challenged the newcomer, making sure both my weapons were trained on his belly.

A long interval passed before that scattergun wavered just a tad. I took that cue to back up to Hoover.

I freed the reins and mounted with my hands still filled. I didn't rush. One other man sprawled out of his tent cussing, but when he saw my tools he backed off. I rode off without having to waste another round.

I never told anyone, not even Julia. To this day, people in Lafayette County debate whether Stanton Lee Sullivan survived his fight with Tink Buchanan or bled to death in the woods.

❧

January came and went. But I never returned to Emory. My best-laid plans hit the shitter when the Japanese bombed Pearl Harbor. County officials were not so insulated as I imagined; I was drafted.

I wound up following "Old Blood and Guts" Patton through North Africa and Italy. His guts, the familiar humor went, our blood. Any notions of expiation for past sins quickly disappeared in the constant rounds of fatigue, diarrhea, and disease that punctuated the occasional relief of killing.

Most veterans of World War II don't feel easy recollecting much less chronicling their wartime experiences; I'm no exception. Suffice it to say that I went to war hoping that my previous killings might somehow steel me for this larger, more righteous slaughter and that somehow I would find or earn atonement.

I found none.

Spence didn't wait for the draft. With Daddy gone, he enlisted and was sent to Camp Blanding. He eventually wound up in the Army Air Corps and became a fighter pilot in an all-black squadron. They were called the Tuskegee Airmen. Spence distinguished himself in combat, then came home to find that it didn't matter.

Wyatt Ogilvie didn't come home at all. He drowned in the surf off Utah Beach before firing a shot.

I was discharged after twenty-three months of duty. Strep throat was my salvation. I collapsed in a fever following the tracks of a tank, wound up in triage in bad shape. Penicillin saved my life. I was discharged when an attending nurse alerted a doctor to the odd murmur in my heart.

ॐ

I was sent home to take over a business that had already failed. The tidewater cypress and longleaf yellow pine once common in the flatwoods had been cut to the point of extinction. Putnam Lumber Company had been liquidated in 1941. Soon there would be nothing but palmetto and the arteries of railroad tracks to show that the thriving town of Shamrock had ever existed. And without Putnam's sponsorship, our government contracts dropped to a trickle. Faced with these circumstances, Mother wisely divested or sold most of our turpentine and tung-oil interests, allowing the various leases to lapse without renewal. She got rid of all our pepperbox mills, keeping only the sawmill at Fort McKoon. By the time I got home even that yard was in virtual mothballs.

Dave Ogilvie was doing fine financially, but Sarah left him after Wyatt's death. She moved in with Julia at our Main Street home. I dropped my duffel bag on the porch to find Sarah waiting, tending the house while Julia was at school teaching. My own mother, set up with Tink's forty thousand dollars and a new house, lived independently in what we were already calling the New House.

But what would *I* do? I had now the means and opportunity to return to my first ambition, to finish Emory's course of study, maybe even pursue graduate work in botany. But I was not in good health, certainly not well enough to contemplate serious labor in Atlanta. And there was something else, something that had been building for a long time.

I can't blame it on the war. It's fashionable to do that, to point to any past trauma as an excuse for present malaise. The war affected me, no doubt about it, though that is another story. But the war did not forge in me anything that was new. It probably gave final mold to a project well under way.

I saw no flowers when I came back from Italy. I saw no colors. Not even black and white. Everything I saw or thought or tasted or felt seemed filtered through a gauze of gray. Modern therapists, including my perfectly valved young doctor, tell me that I must have been in the midst of a clinical depression. I prefer to think of it as a blight on the heart. Or soul.

I had ready excuses to delay an immediate return to Emory. Beyond recovering my health I had responsibilities to Julia and Sarah, to Mother. I even flirted with the idea of returning to Fort McKoon, thinking I might once again bring the mill to profit. But besides the fact that all the cheap labor had been drafted I had, quite literally, no heart to take on so onerous a task.

Martha saw it right away.

"Just leave it, Carter. Do something close to hand. The war will end sooner or later. We can think about the mill then."

That's when I began to teach school. There was a shortage of teachers, especially educators with scientific training, so I was quickly hired. I walked with Julia every morning to Laureate's high school to teach five classes a day on the far end of a Roman column from her own. Every time I saw a cloakroom, I thought of our first meeting in that concrete place.

I thought I'd just teach for a year. Maybe two, or just until the war was over. Truman ended the war when he authorized his generals to use the Bomb. That was 1945. Julia and I would teach for another twenty years, holding hands in the cafeteria like teenagers.

Spence came home in January of '46. I picked him up in Live Oak. What a figure he cut, an officer in the Army Air Corps. Those wings prominent on his chest.

"Good to have you home, Spence."

He didn't reply. Just ran a finger along the polished brim of his wheel cap.

"Polly's fine. So's Little Saint," I tried again.

"They've been writing." His reply let me know small talk was neither necessary nor desired.

His diction had changed, as had his manner. I began to see however dimly that my boyhood friend had grown into a man with whom I was not familiar.

"I'm sorry, Spence."

I don't know where that came from. It just boiled up.

He turned to me then and in an apparent non sequitur said— "How 'bout I drive?"

"Sure," I surrendered.

That's how we came into town. Spence the tall, handsome pilot. I hanging sickly in the right hand seat. He should have come home a hero, should Spence. But that was not the way it was going to be. I knew that. So did he. There would be no rush to give this black aviator a decent opportunity. So I sold him the business, our mill and holdings at Fort McKoon. I tried to give it to him initially. Just tried to give it away.

"No." Spence dismissed me like a corporal. "I don't want a favor."

"It's no favor." I tried to pander the paternal lie.

That's when Spence turned to me. "A man's got to have something he can call *his.*"

So we agreed on a price, which is to say Spence *set* a price, too high, I thought, and we agreed on a percentage of profit to be paid me for the time necessary to pay for the mill and forty riverside acres. Within fifteen years Spence owned Fort McKoon lock, stock, and two-by-fours. He was the only black man with a business of such size in three counties. One of the most successful men of any color in northern Florida.

I can't tell you we became bosom buddies. There was a divide between us. But over the years we would cross paths. And one day, one Sunday, Spence came driving up after church. "Come with me."

He didn't say to where. I just got in the car. It was a brand-new '56 Ford. Two-tone, red and white. Real nice. We drove out to the New House. Spence didn't live on our land anymore. He'd built himself a nice place on his own property just up the river from Fort McKoon. First residence faced in brick, I believe, in our county. I thought he was taking me to Mother's house, but we stopped on the back side of the pasture. He got out.

"Well, come on, Carter."

"Where we going?"

"See your daddy."

He meant Daddy's grave, of course. It was not uncommon in those years, of an afternoon or early evening, to visit some kin resting beneath a headstone or marker.

He opened the gate that led to that rise of ground too modest to be called a hill.

"Watch your step."

A cattlegap had been installed. The land so treasured by my father now fed Ray Henderson's bovines on a yearly lease. Spence lent me his arm. We reached Tink's grave without incident. It was a modest slab of marble wreathed in everlasting. The year of his death was clearly inscribed; we didn't know the precise year of Daddy's birth. Mother decided to leave that space of marble unmarked. "That way people won't know whether he was twenty when he left, or a hundred and twenty," she said. "Tink'd like that."

It was a peaceful place, if barren, catching whatever breeze was offered, shaded on two sides by scrub oak and hickory. And yet it seemed to me my boyhood companion was restive.

"Why we here, Spence?"

"Something you need to know," he answered directly. "Something I want you to know."

He turned so as to face me squarely.

"You recollect the night you took the money from your daddy's safe?"

"Yes."

"Well, I told him, Carter. I told Tink the very next day. I was terrified, having to tell your daddy such a thing."

Terrified, yes. I could imagine.

"What did Tink say?"

"Said it didn't matter."

I was dumbfounded. For years I had tried to bury the guilt of betrayal, of murder, of slaughter. And just about the time I thought I had succeeded, here came Spence, a man I no longer knew, to reopen the wound.

"I wish you hadn't told me," I declared bitterly.

"You got to know, Carter." Spence then reached out. I was startled to feel his broad hand on my shoulder.

"It's eatin' you up," Spence told me.

I marveled that he could see it. Or care.

"So it didn't matter." The ground seemed closer to my feet than it ought. "What do I do with that?"

"Talk to your mama." Spence crushed my arm in his black hand. "Talk to Martha, Carter. She *knows*."

So I did. Spence took me up to Mother's New House and waited outside in the car as I went in.

The home we had built to replace the Big House wasn't quite as large as the original structure, but it was roomy, high-ceilinged and substantial.

I found Mother sitting in a rocker in the living room. She didn't seem surprised when I walked in.

"Son. Good to see you. Whatchu been up to?"

"Walking with Spence," I said. I hesitated. "We stopped at Daddy's grave."

"Is it lookin' good?"

"Real good, yes, ma'am."

She was not yet sixty-five years old, though that head and carriage, so tall! had begun to stoop.

But this morning her eyes were bright, her hair was well kept and streaked with silver, and her head was high. She was wearing that hat, that floppy straw hat, the one Tink had given her so long ago. The brim kept up off her bright face with a clothespin. The ribbon, once scarlet, faded over the years to a pink as pale as the flesh beneath your fingernails.

"Spence said you knew something, Mother. Something about Tink. About that time I took the money. He said you'd know what I meant."

She nodded. "I should have told you before."

The air seemed suddenly too thin. My heart hammered in my chest.

"It didn't matter that you took that money," Martha began without preamble, "because Tink had already decided he wasn't goin' to have Dave's place. Wasn't gonna take it for any reason."

"Wasn't going—?"

"No." She shook her head. "He wouldn't've. He couldn't."

"Mother, that doesn't make any sense."

But with her next words I saw in an instant how it all made sense.

"Caleb didn't die in that crib by accident, Carter."

It took only an instant.

"Oh, Good Lord."

Martha nodded sadly. "Tink knew if Dave sold that tobaccer he'd make more than enough money so that Leroy was goin' to keep the note. Tink knew then if he didn't do something quick he'd *never* get that note.

"So Tink got on the mule and struck out toward the Sand Pond. I do remember thinking that was odd. It was late at night, and besides, why wouldn't he take the road?

"He rode off with a can of kerosene and a lamp. He asked me before he left if I had some old washrags I could part with. I got him some."

Mother paused, then, a moment.

"He didn't know Sarah's little boy was inside. Poor little Caleb!"

"Oh, Jesus God!" I said that over and over. Mother waited for me to settle.

"Tink saw you at the funeral, Carter. Saw you seeing him. Looking out from the gravesite through the trees? He thought you knew what he did."

"I didn't!" I cried.

She nodded. "He thought you did. He thought you'd know—that's why he didn't report the stole money, why he didn't come and take it out on you with his fists or his gun. What else would hold him back, Carter? Why else would he be somebody besides Tink Buchanan?"

"HE SHOULD HAVE TOLD ME!"

"Poor baby!" Mother dipped her fingers into my iced tea and pressed them cooled onto my forehead. "Yes. Tink should of told you, son. He should. So should I."

"When did he tell you?"

"He never did. But I suspected right away. And then when he went to the funeral and started roaming, and then when Spence told him you'd robbed his safe there at the mill and all Tink said was, 'It don't matter; it don't matter. It don't make a tinker's damn,' why, I knew for certain. He didn't have to tell me. I knew."

That was 1956. I remember because of Spence's car.

❧

I never intended to become a preacher. I do not claim to know how salvation is received, nor grace. I cannot even say, as some insist I should, that my way is the only way. I began preaching as did Paul, peering through a dark and murky glass to a world stripped of color.

My calling came when a little church outside town lost their elderly minister. One of the deacons at Scrub Creek asked me if I'd fill in. Just some words for the congregation. A Sunday or two. Just until they could find themselves a preacher.

So I went. Julia accompanied me. I never intended it to last. There was no road to Damascus, and Lord knows I was never one to testify to much except the weather. My salvation was gradual. A land of sediment accumulated layer upon layer. There were no miracles in those years. But there were moments of peace. Of deep and abiding contentment. Grace comes most often this way, I believe, in small moments, measured. Always unexpected. A whisper long ignored finally heard and later still, however dimly, understood.

Julia and I never had children. The school and church were our family. Boys and girls I'd see in biology class I'd see again in Sunday school. I didn't quit the high school, you see. Just kept school and church running together. Side by side. Did that for a long time. We'd organize picnics and I'd show the little ones the wildflowers and explain this making of sunlight into food and how new flowers came to be and other living things. What a miracle! All the wonders of God's garden I tried to tell the children who were not my children.

Sarah died after one of those picnics. Julia stood with me, away from Dave, at that funeral. Preacher O'Steen asked me to say a prayer. How could I pray for the mother who never knew that her boy died in a fire my father set? How could I hope to pray any kind of prayer, stained as I was with my sins, and Tink's?

"Our Father," I began, "who art in Heaven …"

Teach us, Lord, how we might pray.

Everybody joined in. Dave stumbled by afterward, when it was finished.

"Thanks for the words," was all he could say.

I should have had some instant reply of condolence or confession or absolution ready at hand. I didn't. But at least I could finally and without hatred look the man in the eye and tell him he was welcome, that we would keep Sarah in our hearts.

Dave didn't live long after that. He did, however, live to see his land at last taken away. Not by me, certainly. Oh, no. Not for all the tea in China! Dave couldn't work the place by himself. And then Leroy sold the bank to a larger institution out of Baltimore. Next thing Dave knew, he'd been foreclosed; the new bank took everything he had except a homestead, that mercy courtesy of the Roosevelt administration. But the rest, the entire one thousand acres, was carved up, sold and resold. Probably a dozen people own patches of that property now, including Bennett Sessions's grandson.

But no Ogilvie holds title to an inch of that dirt. No Buchanans either. And as for the land that my father by his own sweat acquired, the land my mother at his death inherited—it will go to Spence MacGrue.

I never wanted the land to begin with. I can't deed it over to Spence while alive; my experience with the mill taught me that. But there won't be much he can do about it once I'm dead. It's in my will, the lake, the New House, and the lands about, and of course the Sand Pond—all of it will go to Spencer Saint MacGrue.

I get no small satisfaction thinking of Spence's children, three of them, plus Little Saint, running on the unsullied sand that will one day belong to their father.

May they run forever.

※

As for Julia and me, we remained in our small white frame house for twenty years until one evening she said she had a headache. She went to lie down. Next morning she didn't get up.

That's her headstone, right out the window there. The ground is fairly open about her stone, just a sentinel or two of pine and cedar. And of course there's the dog fennel (was that *compositifolium?* or *capilifolium?* Odd, I was so certain before. It seemed before, the *name,* so important).

But perhaps it would be better for you to imagine our high-stalked fennel as a kind of daisy or aster forming about Julia's headstone a border of lace. A fringe of living lace around my lady's resting place. A pale skirt for a sweetheart.

With Julia gone I alternate my doings, weekdays teaching at school, weekends ministering to my congregation. Doesn't leave a lot of time for socializing, but that's probably just as well. Idle hands are the devil's workshop.

⁊⅊

As for Spence, I used to see him every Sunday. I had become accustomed, in fact, to having Cap'n MacGrue come by after church in his cherry automobile to drive me wherever it was I needed, or wanted, to go. Sometimes to Mama's. Sometimes to a friend of the family or someone from church. A sickbed. Spence would wait in the car. I am not good to drive myself. The heart flutters its alarm. The eyes dim. Spence, by contrast, can to this day shoot pecans from a tree with a .22 single and remains, as had his daddy, strong as a horse.

He met me one Sunday morning in military bearing, a handsome man in a pressed suit, his tie knotted in that double-Windsor required of officers and gentlemen.

"Where we going?" I offered that familiar greeting, as I always did. As if it were Spence coming to me asking for transportation.

"Wherever you like," was Spence's usual reply. Or sometimes, in pilot's parlance, "You got the stick," after which exchange I would direct a destination.

But this morning Spence did not follow his scripted response.

"Where we going?" I asked brightly, and Spence remained silent. He stood for a long moment, not rushed, not hurried. He paused as the last stragglers left the church, some stopping to nod to me or swap pleasantries. "Brother Carter" this, "Brother Carter" that. They neither nodded nor spoke to Spence; he was as invisible to them as any chauffeur, or valet.

It was hot, even shy of Easter, and I was eager to be about my business.

"Say something quick, Spence," I prodded, "or I'm gonna have to find me some shade."

Then it came.

"I'm calling the ride this morning."

A calm voice. Evenly cadenced. But I wasn't sure I had heard him correctly.

"Say again?"

"The Sand Pond." He seemed to have reached a decision. "We'll go there. Get in the car, Carter."

I was obeying the command in his voice before I could even register the enormity of the rebellion.

"I had some things needed tending," I protested weakly.

"We won't be long," Spence said and shut the car's two-toned door behind me.

With the new county road we were there in a quarter of an hour. We rolled past the New House, the porch where Tink once peeled his pears now rebuilt on a slab foundation. "I don't see Mama." I offered this in solicitation, of course. To give Spence the opportunity to reply, to inquire after my mother's health or occupation.

"We'll just get out near the fence." Spence ignored that convention, turning onto the sandy ruts that tracked across the pasture, out back behind the house and toward the Sand Pond. We parked along the same strand of barbed wire that, in our youth, had been Hadrian's Wall, or Pickett's fence.

"This'll do."

Spence got out of the car, and I realized I was expected to follow.

"Take off your shoes," he directed, and without demur I did.

There is a boundary you always penetrate when entering the Sand Pond, a passing from the smell of grass to moss, from warm air to cool. I had almost forgotten the experience of piercing that integument. We walked unshod as men where once as boys we ran. There was no confessional. No summing up. I don't even recall if we had anything like a conversation on our pilgrimage into that musty interior, but as I passed with Spence through the ponds' mysterious boundary of oak and entered its quiet sanctuary, and as the unblemished sand again worked its way between my toes, I began for the first time in years to see the colors.

I saw sycamore leaves as green as jade. I saw the pink blossoms of redbud trees. The blooms of dogwood glowed like pearls, and the sky was baby blue.

Every sensation seemed reborn, attentive, acute. I smelled the pungent aroma of moss, that druid's beard that hung on the gray, stretching limbs of trees. My mouth watered with the sight of blackberries hanging from their vines, and persimmons. I could hear the gossip of squirrels and blue jays. I could feel when we passed beneath the oaks the marble of acorns that that winter would bring a feast for coots and mallards.

"Over here." Spence swerved with purpose toward the Hendersons' fence line, and there, well maintained and waiting, was the cast-iron pump that had so often slaked our boyhood thirst. A tin cup dangled by a length of wire from the handle.

Within seconds Spence had it primed and pumping water. Cool and clear as crystal.

He filled the cup and without deferring raised it for himself. A long draft. Once done he pressed the sleeve of his coat to his mouth.

"I won't be picking you up Sundays anymore, Carter."

It was as though I had been slapped.

"… Well, certainly," I caught up. "I mean, if you have business, Spence."

"No, Carter." He shook his head sadly. "Business or no. You need to find another ride."

"Well, if I had known …" I began, but he stopped me with another shake of his great head.

"No, no. Nothing needs saying. It's just time is all. Just time."

I felt a flutter in my heart. The maze of vine and limb and moss dissolved into a kind of collage. If Spence noticed, he did not inquire. I stood there a while. Until the vertigo subsided.

"Here."

Spence rinsed the cup before refilling it for me. He folded my hands around that receptacle carefully, almost tenderly.

"Still the sweetest water in the county," he said finally, for my benefit.

"Sweetest still," I affirmed. Nothing more.

I brought the offered chalice to my lips. The water was icy cold, as cold as I remembered, but it was not the same. It could not be the same, I realized. Ever again.

A lump hardened in my throat.

"You all right?"

"Certainly," I replied, and smiled. "Just fine."

I followed him back to the shiny car in silence.

"Drop you off?" he offered pleasantly as I was installed.

"In town, if you don't mind. The house."

Fifteen minutes later he let me out. It was the last time I ever rode in that car.

※

I've thought about it since, how it was that a black boy and a white one, unfettered in the simple shade of oaks, feet burned equally in hot white sand, could go from dog-fennel forts and blackberry dreams to this new, cold civility.

I thought about Tink and Dave. My Julia. I thought about wars, small and global. About Stanton Lee and burning crosses and an old woman hanging from her porch. There was Spence, right through it all, dragged like a comet through the violent ellipses of our enmity. Touched by it, scourged, scarred. I wonder, if he told that story, how it would be revealed differently than mine? What dots would he connect, and what picture would come from them?

I keep thinking there must be one picture we could both see, something we could both embrace and say—"Yes! This is it. That's the way it was." And sometimes I think I have it, sometimes a picture comes clear and I can almost hold it in my hands. Touch it, almost.

In that instant I imagine myself again with Spence, men this time, not boys, full grown, striding side by side, unleashed through the Sand Pond. A conversation running all the while. Punctuated, of course, by Spence's concern for my welfare.

"Sing, Carter!"

"Why?"

"Keeps yo' lungs in line with yo' heart."

But then our darkened orbits collide in the world of day-to-day, at the feedstore, outside the grocery or courthouse. Spence will nod to me and I to him, and I know we are strangers. A hurt lances my bowels, and I recall with shame the thousand indignities I perpetrated to ensure that estrangement, the affronts to dignity, large and small, to Spence and his family. The things I hid behind to keep him, and all men like him, at arm's length, separate and forever subordinate in our society.

I am angry on occasion and purge these thoughts. Let bygones be bygones, I rage. But there is nothing gone by of the separateness that divides Spence and me. The thought chills me. But the truth is, even while we were running together, I took Spence for granted. My best friend, the truest friend I would ever have, that any man will ever have.

And now my memory revises, rectifies, deceives. That crystal-clear picture turns to pewter. It fades untouched, and I cannot think how to make the water sweet again.

Acknowledgments

I owe thanks, first, to Mr. Robert Redford and the ladies and gentlemen of the Sundance Institute for their early encouragement of this story in its dramatic form. I am privileged to thank Steve Yount, a fine author himself, for editing the book's first draft. Next to thank are Matthew Miller and all the ladies and gentleman of The Toby Press, along with my agent Marcy Posner. Closer to home, I am glad to recognize my father, Ed Wimberley, and Mr. J. Ellis Crosby, Jr., both of whom walked the now-extinct timberlands of northern Florida. My comrade-in-arms Mike Fagan was an invaluable source of information regarding the lumberjack's daily life. Abner and Wanda Wimberley patiently answered my questions regarding the ancient cultivation of tobacco. Edward and Virginia Henderson were similarly generous in their instruction and wisely directed me to Pleas Strickland, Florida Department of Agriculture, who provided a wealth of detail. I owe a special debt to Dr. Homer Sharp, retired professor from Emory-at-Oxford, whose knowledge of botany, the university, and human nature greatly enriched this work of make-believe.

Thanks, finally, to my wife, Doris, daughter, Morgan, and son, Jack, as unselfish, untiring, and enthusiastic a trio of champions as can be imagined.

About the Author

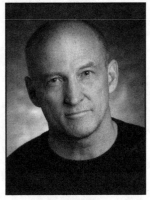

Darryl Wimberley

Darryl Wimberley is an author and screenwriter who resides with his family in Austin, Texas.

The fonts used in this book are from the Garamond family

Other works by Darryl Wimberley
available from *The* Toby Press

The King of Colored Town

The Toby Press publishes fine writing,
available at leading bookstores everywhere. For more
information, please visit www.tobypress.com